DORSEY ADAMS

EVERNIGHT PUBLISHING ®

www.evernightpublishing.com

Copyright© 2025

Dorsey Adams

ISBN: 978-0-3695-1224-6

Cover Artist: Jay Aheer

Editor: Jan Suzukawa

DORSEY ADAMS

DEDICATION

For my three daughters. Your support means everything.

DORSEY ADAMS

Dorsey Adams

Copyright © 2025

Chapter One

Rio Lang was bad. Not bad in an unhealthy, or ill behaved, or even in an evil way. He was bad in the way of the soulless. He just didn't give a damn.

To him, people were not individuals. They were numbers. His job was to protect, or save, or shield whomever he'd been assigned to, and the hell with everyone else. People called him cold. He wasn't cold. He was indifferent.

Black Eagle, the deeply secret organization that employed him, was a shadowy cell operating inside the CIA, but definitely outside its official parameters. Most Americans were blissfully unaware of the need for men with his particular ex-Special Forces skills. Black Eagle kept a tight leash on his missions, and on him.

Or so they thought.

Women were attracted to Rio's six-foot-three, movie star good looks—his blond hair, his bold blue eyes, and his musculature. By any judgment, his physique was toned and in top condition. So he took the women who offered, took them without emotion, without promises. He just didn't think about it. Why should he?

Rio was bad, with no conscience to speak of, with no family to care about except Big Jim, his adoptive father, and Sarah, his little sister. Back home on the sprawling Montana cattle ranch, his family was safe, and few knew about their connection. Although this meant he only saw Big Jim and Sarah infrequently, it was without question for the best.

It made sense to remain a lone wolf. People who became associated with Rio, the ones he *wasn't* protecting, tended to get dead.

Now, crouched in the dark of night outside a hole-in-the-wall Mexican cantina's bathroom, he kept hidden and well below the window. How the hell he'd ended up so deep in the country, in the middle of dangerous Chihuahua State at this out-of-the-way dump, he wasn't quite sure.

The one thing he was completely certain of was the importance of this job to his future. His last contract had ended in a colossal screw-up, and he'd been running the show.

One more mistake and he'd be out of work. That was unacceptable, because the job was his life. Given his isolation from family, from most others, he lived for it.

Tonight, nothing dared go wrong.

The unholy stench in the underbrush reflected the overall cleanliness of the establishment. Had he given in to olfactory assaults, he would have been repulsed by odors of human waste, fetid vegetation, and spoiled food. He ignored them. On equally dangerous missions overseas, back when he'd served in the military, he'd smelled far worse.

In Nigeria, he'd tangled with Boko Haram. In

Iraq, he'd fought the Taliban. In Yemen, he'd saved a British journalist from a certain beheading by drug-crazed ISIS fighters. Across his stomach he still bore the scar, courtesy of the madman's long knife.

During his military service as team leader to get his men to safety, he'd crawled over rotting corpses. Oh, he'd smelled far worse than this worn-down cantina.

Inside the restroom, the woman was taking so long that he nearly gave up, leaped through the window and made off with her. This was to be a one-woman hostage grab, and he'd been patient, more patient than he'd been in a long time. After all the following, anticipating, and stalking he'd done across Mexico, the right moment to wrest her from her captor's grasp was at hand.

The criminals had finally made a mistake by allowing her to go unescorted into the saloon's bathroom. They weren't completely stupid, and for their short stop, they'd set roving patrols. The last team of armed banditos had just sauntered by him, never seeing him in the darkness. Special Ops guys were trained to become invisible. Rio was especially good at this game. He was good at a lot of things.

Just three days ago, the criminal cartel had forcibly snatched their target, an American heiress, from the United States ambassador's Mexican mansion. The ambassador's summer residence was located in Matamoros, near the Texas border. His official home was in Mexico City, but nobody wanted to go there. Too much industry, traffic, noise. In contrast, the compound in Matamoros was lovely, with an enormous home, tropical plantings, and a huge rock pool.

Rebecca De Monte had been visiting her former college roommate, the ambassador's daughter. The thugs' obvious intention was ransom. While still young at twenty-eight, Rebecca De Monte had a rich daddy—a thriving Texas businessman—and one day she would inherit a small fortune. The bandits stood to make at least a million bucks off of Rebecca's panicked father.

Normally, the FBI, Homeland Security, and a host of other alphabet organizations would lead a mission like this. However, Rebecca's father was reputed to have important political ties. An international incident involving kidnapping could blow up in the press like an IED exploding beneath a Humvee. Rio had been there, suffered that, and it wasn't fun. Such an outcome was unacceptable.

Thus, he'd gotten the job. Keep it quiet and get her back. Simple.

He grimaced at the knotting of his thigh muscles. He'd been hunkered down in the rotted underbrush beneath the window for so long his quadriceps protested.

At last he heard the bathroom stall door creak open.

Making a quick search around and finding the patrol gone, Rio shoved up the old casement window, hoisted himself onto the frame and hopped smoothly into the small bathroom.

At the sink drying her hands, the woman gasped.

Before she could take a second breath, he was on her. As she whirled to run, he wrapped his arms around her from behind and slammed a hand over her mouth.

His lips touching her ear, he whispered, "Shhh, Becca. I'm Rio and I'm here to save you."

Instead of sagging against him in relief, the damn female struggled like a she-devil. She made urgent noises against his hand. He kept it tightly bound to her lips, and then dragged her over to the wall.

She tried to kick backward at his knees, but he easily out-maneuvered her. Struggling in his arms, she clawed at him, attempted to bite him, thrust her head back in an effort at a backward head butt.

She was no match. Taller by a good twelve inches, heavier by nearly a hundred pounds, he squeezed tighter in warning, nearly crushed her until she couldn't breathe. It was necessary.

For a small thing, she had generous breasts. He could feel them heaving against his folded arms. Right now, that didn't matter.

"Shut up," he commanded in a harsh whisper. "I'm here to rescue you. Got that? Now, start cooperating or those assholes that grabbed you from the ambassador's house will hear. You'll get us both killed."

At that moment a loud and insistent knock sounded on the door. "*Señorita, estes bien?* Are you well? Come out now."

Becca froze.

Whispering urgently, Rio said, "The Michoacán Cartel who kidnapped you? They're disorganized. Sloppy. Half their captives are killed before ransom is paid. Think your chances are better with them? Or with me?"

The knock and imperious demand came again. "Señorita? Open the door." The doorknob rattled.

Because she could barely move, he wrapped his fist around her long, dark braid and yanked her head back. A pleasant, sweet scent came off her hair, and put him in mind of little yellow flowers.

However, because she was of no more importance to him than a sack of potatoes, a sack he was nonetheless tasked to protect, he didn't care. It mattered little to him whether she smelled like mildewed potatoes or fresh spring flowers. She meant one thing to him: money. Her scent was simply something he noticed. A man in his profession must remain observant.

She was forced to crane her neck and look up into his eyes. Unblinking, he met her gaze. She needed to make her decision within seconds. If she screamed, he was prepared to throw her out the window and as he followed, draw his Glock.

In that event, his chances for mission success would suffer.

He knew she was wealthy, spoiled, and probably petulant. Coddled types like her usually were. Over the years he'd dealt with plenty of her breed. At thirty-five, he'd been doing this for a while.

Yet she did have an excellent degree from a snooty university. Hopefully an education like that also translated into at least average intelligence. Maybe she was capable of making the right choice. It would definitely simplify his life.

Her eyes were large and a deep, snapping brown. He knew the color by studying her file, now confirmed in the low bathroom lamplight. The hue was the same, but the photos hadn't revealed the fire burning within their depths. As she glowered, sparks shot at him like lasers. An angry line appeared between her brows.

A feisty one, he realized. Warring in her eyes with fear was also fury. This one would fight.

Despite her anger, he felt her entire body trembling.

The man on the other side of the door pounded on the wood. "Señorita!"

"*Decide.*" Rio squeezed her again.

Against his hand, Becca nodded once.

With great care, he slowly lifted his palm.

Still holding his gaze, she cleared her throat and called out, "*Un momento.* Just a minute. I'm coming out."

Good. She had at least half a brain. That would be helpful.

"Salir, ahora. Come out now!" came the impatient demand.

Quickly, Rio pushed her to the open window and unceremoniously shoved her through.

She fell the five-foot drop and to her credit, when she landed on her side, made only a small squeak.

Rio dropped beside her, already clamping his fingers under her upper arm to drag her forward. With his other hand, he drew his pistol.

Behind them, he again heard the man outside the bathroom shout for Becca to come out. He pounded harder on the door. In seconds, Rio knew he'd break inside.

They rushed to the corner of the dilapidated wooden building and he peered around. The two sentries were headed for them. The men didn't appear in a hurry and apparently had not yet heard the commotion starting in the bathroom. In the next heartbeat, they would.

Damn.

Rio reversed course and moved the other way. They hurried back beneath the window and to the opposite corner of the saloon. Because he'd thoroughly staked out the landscape before approaching the building, he'd learned that just beyond the dirt parking lot was a concealing clump of low trees and shrubbery. In the snarl of vegetation was his prize.

"See those bushes, those trees?" He pointed.

She nodded.

"We've got to make it. Run fast. Go!"

Together they sprinted for the bushes.

Sweeping flashlights swung by them, hit their backs. An outcry rang out.

Shots were fired.

They plunged into the vegetation.

Shit! He wasn't getting paid enough to eat a

bullet. And if Rebecca De Monte were killed, he wouldn't get paid at all. Add to that, his career would go the way of the Dodo bird. That was a non-starter.

Rio flung himself into the clump and pulled out a small, two-wheeled motor vehicle with a long seat. "Get on."

He swung his leg over and fired up the engine.

In disbelief, Becca hesitated. "A scooter? This is your getaway car? A little Vespa?"

Shouting voices neared them. A bullet whined overhead. They both ducked.

"It's either the Vespa or a donkey, Buttercup. Figured you'd prefer this. Now, get on."

"Buttercup," she sputtered, but threw herself onto the seat behind him.

Before she was settled, he hit the gas. As she was flung backward on her seat, he shouted, *"Hang on."*

At full throttle, they burst from the bushes. A hail of gunfire stitched the ground, pelted the leaves overhead. To slow their fire more than hit anyone, Rio raised his Glock, pointed it backwards, and unloaded a barrage of spray-and-pray rounds. They needed only a few seconds to get away.

Keeping Rebecca De Monte alive and in one piece represented his entire future, as well as a hefty paycheck.

And Rio meant to collect.

Chapter Two

The man who'd whisked Rebecca De Monte away from her Mexican captors, who'd said his name was Nino, Nero, Reno, she wasn't quite sure, kept their motorized getaway vehicle rolling at breakneck speeds for what seemed like hours. They passed ramshackle homes and soon were on bleak and uninhabited country roads.

Within minutes, she was cold, and within half an hour, chilled to the bone. Wearing only a cotton blouse and the slacks and loafers in which she'd been kidnapped, and with the night air blowing past her at sixty degrees, it was no wonder she was freezing.

Her teeth chattering, Becca had little choice but to wrap her arms around the man, not only to stay aboard during his swerving, speeding driving, but also to steal his body heat.

The only thing warm on her entire body was a burning sensation on her lower calf, and it was on fire.

Furthermore, she really had no idea whether she'd traded in her Mexican abductors for someone even worse. Was she possibly in more danger? Who was this guy?

He wore only a white T-shirt, with a zippered oilskin bag hung across his shoulder to his opposite side. No coat at all.

She imagined her father, who must be sick with worry, sending in an Army brigade to free her. She imagined heavy-duty firepower wielded with overwhelming force. Cannons and rockets and dozens of soldiers.

Not a lone man.

Had he even been sent by her father? Or was he

operating on his own in some far more nefarious plot?

If so, she'd better begin figuring out an escape plan.

At last he slowed. She could tell he'd avoided any thoroughfares or well-traveled streets, and had chosen back roads, sometimes bumpy and winding, and they seemed to be climbing in altitude. Higher and higher they went, uphill, upward, always upward. In the darkness, they saw no other vehicles or people.

He seemed to know where he was going, and they appeared to be heading to a higher elevation, going even farther uphill. The air took on a new biting chill.

Finally, he left any semblance of a road and wended his way between the tall trees of a forest. He bumped them up a wet creek bed so that water splashed her slacks, making her, impossibly, even colder. He avoided boulders and even bigger trees, drove deeper into the wilderness until at last, *oh God, thank you, thank you, Lord*, he stopped and cut the engine.

"Get off," he said.

Wanting off the scooter more than anything in the world, yet so stiff from the cold she could barely move, Becca tried to swing her leg over the bike and instead fell to the ground in a frozen heap. Miserable, she lay in the fetal position. Her entire body wracked with shudders.

So far, her escape plan wasn't working out real well.

The man leaned the scooter into the shadowed lee of a wild oak tree, lifted a gas can hidden in the brush, and refilled the tank. Then, he pulled a tarp from a branch. He threw it over the Vespa and took what looked like netting and completely covered the vehicle with that, too.

"Follow me," he said, and strode off into the forest heavy with towering oaks.

By the time the jerk managed to figure out she was unable to go after him, she'd gotten up on one elbow. It took all her strength to do even that, and she grimaced in pain. She glanced down, but in the moonless dark couldn't see anything. Her leg really hurt.

The man came back to her and put his hand under her elbow to draw her upright. He pulled her to her knees before she collapsed back on her bad leg.

"Ow," she said. "Oh, oh, ow."

"What's your problem?" He glanced around the forest. "We've got to get inside."

"My l-l-leg hurts." Her teeth clattered like falling dominoes.

"For fuck's sake," he muttered, bent down, and easily swung her into his arms. He carried her beneath close-growing trees before coming to a small shack. With one booted foot he kicked open the door and shut it behind them, still using his foot.

Becca's alarm skyrocketed. It appeared more and more like she'd made a terrible decision—to go with him instead of staying with her Mexican captors.

Was this guy going to rape her? Kill her? Leave her for dead in this remote place?

A battery-operated lamp set on a table cast a weak glow. The shack couldn't have been bigger than a ten-by-ten foot square. Pushed up against the wall sat a quilt-covered bed. A large cooler and a canvas bag were set in the corner.

He placed her on the bed, not roughly, but not gently, either. Taking his bag off his shoulder, he dropped it near the door. "Let's see the leg," he ordered.

"Do you have a co—a co—" she stammered, unable to force her lips around the proper words. The cabin was only marginally warmer than the outside air.

"What?" he said impatiently.

She licked her dry mouth. "A coat? I'm fr-freezing."

As though she were a nuisance he'd rather do without, he stood over her frowning. Picking up the canvas bag, he rummaged around until he found a few garments. Pulling her into a sitting position, he yanked a thick fleece sweatshirt over her head.

"Hey!" she protested, disliking being manhandled.

As though she hadn't reacted at all, he jammed a knit cap onto her hair. Grabbing a blanket, he wrapped it around her shoulders and propped her into a sitting position against the wall. "Better?"

Still shivering, Becca briefly closed her eyes. At least he hadn't killed her yet. And he wasn't bent on rape … yet. "I'll l-let you know in a minute."

He went to collect the lamp and held it over her lower extremities. "Take off your shoes and pants."

Everything left in Becca that wasn't already cold rocketed straight to frigid. Her eyes snapped open. "Wh-what?"

"Your pants are wet. Take 'em off."

As cold as she was, removing her slacks in this tiny room with a big, strange man didn't seem like a good idea. She shook her head. "Not gonna happen."

He shrugged. "Your choice." Sitting beside her on the bed, he eased up her pants leg.

A dark slash oozing blood covered her entire calf. Becca gasped.

He studied it, then swore softly. "They winged you. Huh. Wonder why they took such a chance." His eyes, which she could now see were a vivid blue, caught hers. They were as cold and hard as chipped glass. "Understandable they'd want to kill me, but you're worth at least a million. That was a stupid risk."

She blinked at him, feeling stupid herself. "I-I've been *shot*?" The chill had slowed her thinking process to the consistency of mud. She had a hard time placing one thought after another.

"Why'd they do it, Becca?" He stared at her, accusation darkening his brow.

"Why'd they d-do what?" She huddled into her sweatshirt and blanket.

"Take chances with their valuable captive. Why'd they shoot at you? Well? Tell me. *Now*."

"Look, Nemo, I d-don't know what—"

"What'd you call me?"

"It isn't Nemo? What is it?"

"I'm Rio."

She blinked at him. "L-like the Brazilian city?"

"Just like that."

Exotic. The fleeting thought trailed through her mind on a wisp. But he didn't look Brazilian or South American. With his height and bulk and coloring, he appeared closer to a Norse god. Like Odin, father of Thor. All he was missing was a long golden beard, chest plate, and fearsome iron hammer.

Goodness. Her would-be savior was *hot.*

With effort, she focused her mind. "Okay, Rio, look, I-I don't know anything. I don't know why those men took me unless it was for—"

"Ransom." He bit out the word.

"Right." She felt her chin trembling. It was the only logical conclusion. "How much are they demanding?"

"They haven't made any demands yet." He got up to rummage again in his bag.

Her eyes widened. "But it's b-been at least a couple of days!"

"The cartel snatched you almost four days ago."

Her mind reeled. That long? She'd thought only perhaps forty-eight hours had passed. The past days and nights had run together. It felt like forever since the violent assault on the ambassador's Matamoros mansion, where a dozen men wearing drab green had overwhelmed the small security force and burst inside. Shouting and waving guns, they'd forcibly taken her, only her, into their waiting transport truck. Left behind were the ambassador and Maria, his daughter. Screaming and crying, Maria had been tied up, together with her father.

The men had kept on the go, traveling around the clock. They hadn't hurt Becca, but neither had they pampered her. She'd been fed twice a day, yet she'd been so frightened she could barely eat. They'd given her a pallet and blankets in the locked back of the truck on which to sleep. As if she could. Beyond that, they refused to answer her questions, even though she entreated them for answers in near-perfect Spanish. The ordeal sapped her strength, exhausted her.

She simply didn't know what was happening beyond guessing that they planned to exchange her for money. Her father was quite wealthy. Ergo, steal his daughter away while she was in another country and hold her for cash. It made sense. Holding her for days without any sort of communication did not. She wanted to ask if Rio was going to make a demand of his own. She had to fight him, to somehow get away, get free.

Rio pulled a small package from his bag. "I've got a first aid kit, but it's basic. A bullet creased your leg. No stiches, but it needs cleaning." He met her gaze steadily. "Your pants and shoes and socks are soaking. You'll never warm up until they come off."

He stood, holding the first aid pack, and waited for her answer. She got the idea that he didn't really care which way she decided. He merely offered her a choice and let her decide.

Despite her strong misgivings, she knew he was right. Her slacks hung on her limbs in a sodden, muddy mess. If she removed them, she could slide beneath the heavy quilt and hopefully continue to get warm. She didn't want to do it. Everything in her screamed *no*! Yet, she knew she'd be better off.

"Okay," she said reluctantly. Peeling off her wet shoes and socks, she said, "Turn your back." Her hand went to her waistband.

He didn't turn, just gave her his dispassionate perusal. "Listen here, Buttercup, you're on my turf. I'll give the orders, not you. I don't turn my back on anyone."

It was a Mexican standoff, Becca thought wildly. Her mind a jumbled mess, she knew her nerves were stretched to ragged ribbons. After being an unwilling captive, shot at, and actually struck in the leg, she was now expected to disrobe in front of this man she didn't know.

Both from cold and from fright, her fingers shook uncontrollably. Some part of her whispered that if this Rio character wanted to rape her, given his size and bulk and their isolation from the rest of the world, she'd never be able to stop him, slacks or no. Her screams would go unheard, her cries for help unanswered.

She was still very cold. Cloaking her legs beneath the mountain of quilts beneath her sounded better and better. This guy seemed like a real asshole. However, frozen as she was, she wasn't going anywhere right then. The logical thing would be to first get warm.

With great reluctance, she unbuttoned her waistband and slid down the zipper. Easing the pants off her hips and over her legs, she kicked them to the foot of the bed, and then hurried to lift the bedcovers. At least her modesty was still protected by her cotton panties.

"Not yet." Rio stayed her movements with a hand on her bare thigh.

Becca stiffened.

He sat again on the edge of the bed and laid out his supplies: a thick stack of gauze, a tube of antiseptic, and a roll of white tape.

With his fingers curled over the skin of her thigh, Becca could hardly breathe. Shrieking alarms screamed throughout her system, shouted at her to leap up, to run, to get away. A new chill chased up her spine and the fight or flight response burst to life. "Move your hand," she demanded. "Don't touch me."

"Easy, now," Rio said in low, rumbling tones.

His fingers did not creep up her thigh, as she feared, nor did it caress her skin. His touch seemed … somehow … rather clinical.

He lifted his hand to open the gauze package. Carefully, he placed a clean towel beneath her calf, opened a bottle of rubbing alcohol, and held it over the wound. "This'll sting," was all the warning she got.

The pain flashed into a new, sudden burning. Becca jumped.

Quickly, he dabbed away blood and fluid, spread antiseptic cream over the graze, covered the area with new gauze, and taped it into place. Taking up his canvas bag, he withdrew thick woolen socks and impersonally pulled them onto her feet. "You can get under the covers now," he said, capping the alcohol bottle.

Lifting her bottom, she slid her legs beneath the covers. Under the sheets, it was cool, but she knew it should warm within moments. Already she was feeling better. Exhausted, terrified, but better. She didn't know if she should thank him or castigate him.

Getting up, he moved to the corner and came back

with a thermos. "It won't be hot anymore, but it'll do."

Hesitating, she accepted the offering and raised the thermos to her mouth. Warm black coffee slid down her throat and she groaned in pleasure. All her adult life she'd been a coffee lover. A coffee fiend. An addict. The blacker, the hotter, the better.

In the past harrowing days she'd had exactly none. Now, to have this manna from heaven seemed like pure bliss. She made no pretense at manners: she gulped.

Again he watched without emotion.

"Hungry?" he asked. A muffin materialized in his hands. A blueberry muffin: her favorite.

Even as she reached for the treat, suddenly ravenous, she wondered at the coincidence of how he'd magically produced her favorite snack, coffee and a blueberry muffin. Weird.

While he took her wet slacks and slung them over a rafter to dry, Becca drank her coffee. With care, he set her shoes side by side onto the floor and laid out her wet socks beside them. She took a large bite of the muffin, chewed it gratefully, and swallowed. As she watched him, he re-rolled the remainder of the gauze and put everything back in its original package. Again he went to the corner, to a large cooler, and when he opened it, he took out a water bottle.

He wore only a white t-shirt, brown cargo pants, and boots. Except for a hunk which refused to stay back and instead fell over his forehead, his full head of blond hair grew longish and heavy to his nape. As he worked, the muscles of his arms tightened and eased smoothly beneath his skin, and she wondered at his past. His chest was broad, his belly flat. Had he been some sort of body builder? Maybe he was ex-law enforcement. Maybe he'd been a Marine.

Perhaps her first guess was correct and a new

villain had taken her from her original captors to muscle in on the money. A mercenary.

At last, warmth begun to creep through her veins. Her shaking subsided. She wanted to demand the truth. Instead, she decided to start with a safe question. "Weren't you cold?" she asked him. "Out there on the scooter?"

Unrolling a sleeping bag, he unzipped it until it was completely open. He shrugged. "Naw. I tend to run hot." Shaking out the sleeping bag, he folded it in half and half again, forming a large square. This he settled onto the end of the bed, and sat down.

"Are you going to sleep in that?" Feeling her eyelids begin to droop, Becca didn't want to lose consciousness. She needed to remain vigilant. She needed her wits about her.

However, she'd barely slept in four days, and then only in quick snatches. The pull of slumber dragged at her. She figured the ordeal had finally gotten to her. After this interminable week, her body needed rest.

"Sleep in the bag?" As though in surprise, he pointed at the bag at the foot of the bed. "No. I'm sleeping with you."

Unsettled, Becca glanced over the bed. It was no larger than double, not near enough room for her to share with a stranger. She put her foot down. "No," she told him in a determined tone. "You are not. I will sleep here, alone. Is that understood?" She gave him her most fearsome glare.

If she hadn't been observing him so closely, she might have missed his sudden change in manner. He literally froze. His gaze shot to the wooden rafters. His entire body stilled.

"*Shit!*" he muttered, and suddenly sprang into action.

Leaping to his feet, he caught up the sleeping bag and snapped it open. Jumping onto the bed beside her, he spread the bag over them both, over their entire bodies and their heads. "Quiet," he commanded. "Do not move."

Startled into compliance, it was only instants later when she heard it: the sound of helicopter rotors beating overhead.

DORSEY ADAMS

Chapter Three

Rio thrust the sleeping bag up with one fist at each corner, his arms locked straight out. He held it as high as possible, tent-like, over their bodies. Becca didn't question him, didn't move. Her heart pounding, she froze into stillness.

The helicopter's engines whined overhead. Louder. It sounded like the chopper sailed directly over their tiny cabin. The beating rotors thundered, shook the small shack. Time stalled.

Somehow Becca knew that Rio had gritted his teeth. In their dark cocoon, she couldn't see him, she just knew. As though his concern leached unease into the very air, Becca experienced a new dread flowing through her. Jammed beside his big body, she pressed herself to him. With her fingers, she clutched his shirt, and could feel the warmth of his skin. She heard the thudding of his heart. He smelled of the wind, blowing through a mountain forest. Her face in his neck, his beard stubble rasped against her cheek. She was afraid to move a muscle.

One part of her wondered how covering them with a cheap sleeping bag could be effective. How did hiding from the boogeyman like frightened children beneath bed covers help them?

At last, the helicopter's noise grew faint and disappeared. Rio let out a breath and flung off the sleeping bag. He got to his feet. "I don't know if the cartel's helos are outfitted with FLIR capability. The roof and overhanging trees will mask some of our heat signatures, but I wanted to make sure."

"FLIR?"

"It means Forward Looking Infrared. It's thermal imaging. The sleeping bag will mask our heat, but only for a couple of minutes. Once our body heat transferred to the fabric, we'd be visible to them."

She felt her mouth form into an *O*. "That's why you held it up off our bodies."

He nodded. "Like I said it only works for a minute or two. If they hovered over us for long, and if they were looking in the right place, we'd be sitting ducks."

Now it made sense. She felt a little foolish. "What is this place?"

"Just a hidey hole. I've used several of them across Mexico. I was here this morning. Left that light on." He gestured at the battery lamp. "Lucky for us the cantina where I grabbed you is fewer than fifty miles off. The next cabin's two hundred miles farther south. We'd have had a lot longer ride."

She tried not to gape. What sort of person maintained *hidey holes* across a foreign country? Bewildered, she shook her head to clear it. "Where are we?"

"Chihuahua State, partway up the Sierra Madre Occidental mountain range." He refolded the sleeping bag and placed it back at the end of the bed.

So far away, she thought in dismay, from the ambassador's house, up north by the U.S. border in Matamoros. Again, she imagined forming an escape plan, of somehow getting away, getting to safety. No sense in letting him know that. Attempting to sound innocent, she asked, "How long should we stay here?"

"Depends on how close those bastards are, how bad they want you. We may leave at dawn. We may stay put. I'll decide tomorrow."

She blinked at him. "Who *are* you? Did my father send you?" It could certainly be possible.

"In a roundabout way," he answered.

A small measure of relief crept through her, instantly followed by a new suspicion. "So, my dad *didn't* actually hire you?" Quickly she sifted through possibilities. "The government got involved."

He gave her a pained look. "Of course. The US of A can't tolerate having American citizens kidnapped from a foreign dignitary's residence. Especially from an ambassador's house."

"And it puts a black eye on the Mexican government." She thought about this. "I work for my father's San Antonio business, a hubcap distributorship. With my dad's close ties in government, he's politically connected."

His glance was considering this. He picked up a water bottle and brought it to the small table next to the bed. Beside that, he positioned his handgun.

She watched him. "So ... you'll be making money off me."

He met her gaze squarely. "A lot of money."

"From who? Who's paying you?"

"How about you answer my questions. What else do you know? Why you? Why'd the cartel grab you, Becca?"

Her energy reserves waning, Becca wished she had all her mental faculties to continue demanding answers from him. But the exhaustion overtaking her was too strong. Her mind felt like sludge. "I don't know anything else," she said. "I wish I did." Again, she felt her eyelids droop.

"We'll talk in the morning. Move over." Rio pointed to the opposite side of the bed.

Momentarily, she revived. "I told you, you're not sleeping here—"

"Move or I'll move you." He waited, once again with a strangely dispassionate demeanor, as though it didn't matter to him what she did. She knew that if she didn't make room for him, he would physically set her aside. He was getting into the bed with her no matter what.

Grudgingly, she scooted toward the wall, where the bed and wall met. Rolling tensely onto her side, she faced away from him. As he lay down on his back beside her, she felt rather than saw him place his forearm over his forehead.

Outside, in the black darkness of the forest, she felt certain that those men—*the cartel*, Rio had called them—were relentlessly hunting her. Naturally they'd be eager to recapture her. The idea of returning to the imprisonment of that awful truck, to possible death, horrified her. She wanted nothing more than to go home to her condo in San Antonio, Texas, to her nice, quiet life, to her ordered existence, to her family and friends. If only this harrowing interlude would end.

As her eyes drifted shut, she drew her knees up to her stomach. Her leg throbbed. Exhausted, she tried concocting an escape plan. She didn't know whether she could trust this Rio guy. So far, she'd been unable to stop any of these events from happening, all of them crashing down on her. With everything out of her control, she felt off-kilter and unbalanced. Normally in charge of her own destiny, she abhorred the feeling. "Rio?" she asked.

"What?"

"You're supposed to get me back home?" She whispered the question.

"Correct."

Maybe, she thought. And maybe he was just pretending in order to keep her compliant. After a long moment, she asked, "Who are you really?"

"I'm Rio," he said. "And I'm here to save you. That's all you need to know."

"You'll save me?" she whispered again, this time softer. She didn't want it to be a dream, a fairy tale. She wanted it to be real.

"I swear it," he said. "It's my job."

****

When Becca awoke, she was alone in the bed. Her eyes popped open and she experienced a moment of disorientation. In the next instant, her predicament came back with a terrible rush.

Sitting up, clutching the covers to her throat, she glanced around the cabin. The gun Rio had carefully placed on the small table was gone. Where was he? Had he abandoned her, out here in this wilderness? Would he come back?

Her thoughts frantic, she tried to figure out what to do.

Should she take the opportunity to run, to get away from him, find people—some sort of country home—and implore the residents to help her? She spoke excellent Spanish. She hoped she could come across nice people who were not in cahoots with the cartel.

That seemed the best plan. Her pants still hung on the rafters and she imagined they'd be close to dry by now. Perhaps her socks and shoes were as well. With no idea how far she'd have to run or how long it would take her to find someone, she figured she'd need food and water. No doubt there would be supplies in the cooler. The sweatshirt Rio had given her would serve her during the day, but if she were stuck out at night, it would not be enough. She glanced down. Lugging along several of the quilts wouldn't be easy, but she had no choice. She had to get away.

Beneath the bed covers, she shifted her legs and was instantly reminded of her injury. Her leg still hurt. A lot.

Abruptly the door swung open and Rio filled the doorway. A frigid blast of air flowed inside. His head covered in a knit cap like the one he'd given her and wearing a sheepskin-lined coat, he appeared huge. Last night, Becca hadn't fully realized how tall, how burly he was. The man was *big*.

He slammed the door and stamped his feet. White material flew off his shoulders and boots onto the floorboards. "Snowing out," he said. "And I saw some good sized tracks nearby. Mountain lion."

Becca's hopes sank. Now that he was back, she didn't suppose she'd be able to get away. Maybe it was a poor idea anyway. With the change in weather, she wouldn't make it even a mile. If it were snowing, no bundle of quilts would keep her warm.

She'd need the scooter.

Before he'd closed the door she'd spotted the telltale outline of its shape, covered in tarp and netting under the wild oak. And she remembered now that he'd gassed it up. As a teen, she'd had her own scooter, and knew how to operate one, no problem.

She'd wait, and watch. Maybe she'd get a chance. Becca huddled into her covers, pulled the cap down over her ears. She sniffed. Her nose felt a little runny. In the opposite corner of the room, she spotted a tiny fireplace with a tiny mantle. "Can we have a fire?"

Taking off his coat, Rio cast her an incredulous glance. "Smoke can be seen for miles. We're trying to hide, not send out a beacon." He hung his coat on a hook beside the door.

"Where did you go? Is the cartel nearby?"

"Spotted them twenty miles south. They're sending out patrols, canvassing the countryside in a search grid. Right now, they aren't close, but they're on the move." He set down a pack she hadn't seen before.

"They aren't close?" she breathed.

"No, but it won't be safe to move today. Here." He withdrew a thermos from his pack. "I rode in the other direction, stayed out of sight, went to see some people I know." He handed her the thermos.

Uncapping it to the aroma of freshly brewed hot coffee, she sighed in pleasure. Sipping the delicious drink, she said, "You must speak Spanish."

"Yeah. And Arabic."

She peered at him. *Arabic?* The two languages didn't seem particularly alike. Strange.

It was time she got some answers. "How much are you being paid to deliver me back to my father?"

"A bundle."

"How much?"

"You don't need to know, Buttercup."

"Why do you keep calling me that?"

"Cause your hair smells like little yellow flowers."

"Don't," she said, frowning. It sounded far too intimate and she didn't like it. "Don't."

"Don't, what?"

"Don't go smelling my hair … or my … anything."

"Sorry," he said, not sounding sorry at all. "In this place, we're sorta up close and personal. Can't really help it. Hungry?" Once again, he held out a blueberry muffin. While it looked tempting, she had a more immediate need.

"Actually, I, uh, need to answer nature's call."

"Gotta pee?"

She frowned. "Yes." Did the man have any social graces at all?

"Put on your pants and shoes. I'll take you outside. You'll go in the trees."

She sighed. Indoor plumbing, it seemed, was only a dream, a luxury. "Great." Just what she wanted to do, *go in the trees*.

The air outside was even colder than she'd imagined. Drifting snowflakes landed on her sweatshirt, on her nose. The ground was more than lightly dusted. A good four inches crunched under her loafers. Her toes already felt like ice cubes. The shivering began instantly.

In the light of day, she noticed the shack had been built in the middle of a dense copse of trees, making it unrecognizable from only yards away. If one didn't know where it was, the hut would be nearly impossible to find. At least that was comforting.

Rio led her some thirty yards away, pointed at a thatch of underbrush, and strode off. As quickly as possible, Becca did her business and hurried back to him. All she wanted now was to climb into bed again and warm up. From the activity, the wound on her leg ached. She limped the last few steps through the snow.

Back inside, and behind her, Rio barred the door. As Becca resumed her place on the bed, the sound of the heavy wooden latch swinging down held the bang of finality. She clutched her coffee. In a very real sense, she was trapped in the middle of a frozen forest, inside this small room with an unknown entity. She eyed him nervously.

Before facing her, he shrugged out of his coat again and placed the gun back on the table. His fingers went to the hem of his t-shirt and he pulled it over his head.

Becca gasped. Now half naked, he was even more intimidating. His shoulders, pectorals, and abdominal muscles were developed and sculpted. A thin line snaked over his belly, a scar. Heat and power emanated off him in waves.

He returned her gaze. His expression held no humor, no emotion. His blue eyes pinned her. "Scared?"

DORSEY ADAMS

Chapter Four

"Of course I'm scared," Becca snapped at Rio. Her brown eyes blazed. "I don't know you, who you are, what you'll do. I'm trapped here. Any sane woman would be frightened out of her wits."

Suddenly Rio felt his temper rise. "If you're frightened of me, you've got your villains mixed up." He pointed to the door. "It's those assholes out there you'd better worry about. Think I was kidding when I told you at least half of their kidnap victims are killed before the money is paid? If they feel like making a point, or getting revenge for some wrong imagined, they'll gut you. They'll cut your head off and hang your mutilated body from a highway overpass. It's a warning to others—don't mess with the cartel." With angry movements, he rummaged in his canvas bag until he found a new t-shirt and pulled it over his head.

Most of the time the people Rio was tasked to protect were terrified, but they could at least think somewhat rationally. They knew their best chance would be to cooperate with him, not figure *he* was the enemy. He cast Becca a dark glance.

Lord save him from shallow, illogical females.

With any luck he'd be able to load her up on his Vespa tomorrow, sneak out of Chihuahua State, and deliver her into the hands of the proper authorities. He wasn't really going to take her straight to her father, as he'd implied. She didn't need to know that. He would simply pass her on to Black Eagle operatives, the organization that employed him. That was how he liked it. A simple hand-off, a contract fulfilled, pay me now, thanks.

Next!

Right then, he needed the job to go smoothly, with zero fuck-ups. For anything less than a perfect result, this time his employer, Harrison, would can him.

When he'd left a sleeping Becca this morning, he'd had to travel miles away from the mountains to get proper cell phone service and communicate with his Black Eagle boss. He knew how to avoid major roadways, stay out of sight. On the outskirts of a small village he'd gotten two bars on his cell and pulled the Vespa off road to make the call.

Harrison was pleased to learn he'd grabbed the girl. "Bring her back healthy," Harrison warned. "A lot's riding on this. Her father's an important man."

"She's healthy," Rio told him. "No worries. Just got a little graze on her leg during the getaway."

"A graze?" Harrison missed nothing. His voice hardened. "What sort? Don't tell me by a bullet. Do *not* tell me that."

"Er, it's shallow," Rio prevaricated. "Nothing serious."

Harrison swore softly. "I don't need to remind you that there can be no repeats of the last contract. Screw up again, you're done."

"No worries," Rio said. "I'll have her to your men by morning." He gave Harrison a delivery time at a predetermined location, a small valley several miles away. Harrison had no idea where his mountain cabin was, and he'd keep it that way.

It couldn't be soon enough. While Rebecca De Monte was more than pleasant to look at, with long, thick mahogany hair, a slim figure and an impressive bust line, he didn't need to spend any more time with her than strictly necessary. Shame, though. Her breasts were amazing.

However, it was always best to remain detached.

Glancing over at her now, he saw that her eyes were rimmed with fluid.

"Are you crying?" he asked, frowning. That was all he needed. She hadn't said anything after his rant.

"No." She rubbed at her eyes, dug her fingers into their sockets. "My eyes are just watering. I woke up with the sniffles. Maybe I'm catching a cold."

He noticed for the first time that her nose was pink. Shadowy circles ringed her eyes. She really didn't look all that well. Digging in his pack, he found a few clean cloths and handed them over.

"Thanks," she said, and looked at him. She pressed the fabric to her nose. "I really don't want those men to cut my head off."

He grunted. If she were at least smart enough to do as he said and not give him any trouble, she'd survive just fine.

As the morning wore on, Becca looked worse. Her nose began to pour in earnest and Rio was forced to rip a towel into pieces so she could staunch the dripping. Her eyes drooped tiredly and she didn't move from the bed, didn't eat the muffin or sandwich he offered, and didn't want more coffee.

For a caffeine addict, that was strange. He knew about her love for the drink. He knew other things about her, too. It was part of his job to research his subjects thoroughly and know going in what he was dealing with.

Rebecca De Monte lived alone in a nice San Antonio, Texas, condominium. In high school, she'd excelled on the swim team. She'd graduated from University of Texas at Austin with a business degree. She had no current boyfriend, a wide circle of friends, and a robust social life. Her clothing was always stylish, yet she stuck mostly to stark black and white. She was close to her two brothers and they all worked for their father. She kept an aquarium of frogs. She loved dark chocolate. And muffins.

In another life, in different circumstances, he might have tried to date her. Not in a committed sort of way, that wasn't him. Rather, in a consensual, sleeping-together-when-it-suited-him way. There was absolutely no doubt in his mind he'd enjoy bringing her to multiple orgasms. Studying her, he recalled the luscious, silky feel of her flesh when he'd placed his hand on her thigh. He wondered what she'd be like in the sack. Soft, kittenish and shy? Or a wild, raging tiger on the attack?

The sensual speculation made him instantly hot and hard.

However, in their current circumstance, he would remain hands off. This was business. He couldn't touch her that way.

He wouldn't. Never.

During the next several hours while Rio cleaned his gun, Becca dozed. By late afternoon she was running a temperature, the fever coloring her cheeks a splotchy pink, heating her skin, and making her shiver.

"I'm so c-c-cold," she told him, huddling into herself. Still in the cap and sweatshirt he'd given her, and buried beneath the quilts, she looked miserable. Her body shook.

It occurred to him that her wound might have become infected.

He stood up. "I need to see your leg."

"No," she said firmly. "It's fine. I want to stay under the covers."

Despite her vehement protests, he lifted the quilts and firmly took her calf into his hands. "Just take a second."

For a moment she fought him, clung to the quilts, but he won and she fell back, weak as a child.

Carefully unwrapping the tape and gauze, he inspected the wound. While it still oozed fluid, it looked clean, without any puckered and red angry edges to indicate infection. Re-wrapping the leg, he knew the gunshot she'd endured wasn't the problem. While in the captivity of her Mexican kidnappers, she'd contracted some sort of virus, or maybe a bacterial infection.

He let her slide back under the covers.

Well, *shit*. This sure threw a crowbar into the workings. If in the morning the bad guys hunting them weren't too close, he was planning to pack her up and escape down a track of off-road mountain paths he knew about. But with Becca sick, she'd be too weak to hang on the scooter.

Briefly, he considered some way of strapping her to him, then discarded the idea as unworkable. The paths would be bumpy, and they'd get knocked around. He couldn't risk having her fly off the Vespa into rocks and trees.

He let his glance dart around the cabin. In the cooler he had plenty of provisions to last days, no worries there. He always planned ahead for such eventualities. As long as they laid low, he knew the shack was well camouflaged in the forest, and unlikely to be found.

This was a setback, but not a failure. So it took one more day? No big. His employer wouldn't be happy, but too bad. Harrison might not like the delay, but it couldn't be helped.

"Rio," Becca said softly. "*Rio.*"

He leaned over the bed. "What?"

"I'm so co-cold. I'm dying."

"No. Your leg isn't infected. You picked up a nasty bug. In a day or so you'll be better."

"Why can't I get w-warm? I just want to warm up."

Rubbing his jaw's day-old growth of beard, Rio blew out a breath. Quickly, he shook out two ibuprofen tablets from the first aid kit and got them down her. Glancing around the spare room, he didn't see any additional way to change her circumstances.

The warmest thing in the room was him. He'd told her he normally ran hot. He guessed he should utilize himself as a resource.

"Take off your sweatshirt," he told her.

She frowned at him over her shoulder. "Are you insane? I want to put *on* another s-sweatshirt, not take anything off."

With one knee on the bed, he drew back the quilts and pulled Becca up. She fought like a cat, tried to punch him, scratch his face.

Naturally he prevailed, and pulled the fleece sweatshirt over her head. "For this to work I've got to get close to you. You can keep your shirt and the hat on," he said, and then slid under all the covers with her.

Wracked in head-to-toe shivering, she glowered at him.

As she flopped on her side facing away from him, he spooned up against her, and pressed his chest to her back. His legs tangled in hers, and he fit his crotch snug up against her bottom—her white-cotton, granny-panty covered bottom. Oh, he'd noticed.

"*What are you doing?*" she screeched.

"Shh," he said. "I'll get you warm, that's all." He held her in a tight grip until she stopped struggling. All her thrashing caused friction between their bodies and Rio felt himself go on high heat. He had to hold her across her breasts. As she wriggled, her bottom slid back and forth over his pants front. *Damn.*

With effort, he forced his mind away from thoughts of Becca's sweet rear end and things he'd like to do to her.

Placing his left arm under a pillow, he kept his free arm closed around her.

Finally, she stopped fighting. In his arms, Becca felt small, vulnerable. She was sick and defenseless. Those jerks who'd stolen her away from her friend's family home should be shot. As she shook, he held her tighter.

His body heat already enveloping her, he knew it was working when her shivers subsided and she sighed.

"Little warmer now?" he asked.

She nodded, her hair escaping the knit cap on the pillow, tickling his lips.

"I was right," he said.

"About what?" Her voice was resentful and petulant.

"Your hair. It does smell like little yellow flowers."

****

From freezing cold to a raging fever, Becca spent a miserable night. When she grew hot, Rio lifted the covers off her body, fanned her, gave her water. When she chilled down again, he pulled the quilts over them both and held her close. She wouldn't admit it, but she was grateful for his big warm body. It kept the frigid air at bay.

He did it all impersonally, with a calm manner of one assigned a task which simply must be done.

At dawn her fever broke for good, and she was left listless, but better. She had to use the restroom, but so loathe to leave her cozy nest, she waited until she was near bursting before she told him.

In the end, she struggled to put on her pants and shoes, and by the time she had them on, she was completely winded. Rio had to carry her through the snow to the underbrush, and return when she was finished to lift her into his arms and carry her back.

When she was settled, he offered her peanut butter spread on hard crackers and canned peaches, more water, and a few grapes. Hungry at last, she ate it all and lay back again. "You said we might leave today. So I can go home."

Considering her, he shrugged. "You're too weak to hang onto the scooter. It'll be rough terrain. For miles. Maybe tomorrow." He zipped into his heavy coat and jammed a cap on his head. Over his neck he looped a pair of field glasses. "I'll hike up the mountain, have a look around."

"You're going?" Instantly she felt anxious. She didn't want to be left alone—here in this wilderness.

"There's food and water in the cooler, if you get hungry."

"How long will you be gone?"

He lifted a careless shoulder. "Few hours." He turned to go.

"Rio?"

"Yeah?"

"How much are you being paid? How much money?" For some reason she really wanted to know.

"A lot," he said. "A small fortune, but not as much as the cartel would get for your ransom, that's for sure."

Becca firmed her lips. How tired she was of being a pawn in someone else's high-stakes game. How bitter it made her! "I'm just dollar bills to both you and the cartel," she said. "Just cold hard cash."

"Correct." From a hook on the wall, he collected a pair of heavy gloves.

"Gee, thanks."

He hesitated. "If I was smart, I'd contact the cartel

boys and cut a deal. Probably I'd get a lot more money. The way I'm doing it now, I'm leaving a lot of cash on the table." Clicking his tongue in regret, he left, slamming the door behind him.

Becca blinked at the now closed door. Alarm shrieked up her spine and adrenalin shot through her veins. With both fists, she gripped the quilts.

Before Rio changed his mind, decided that the cartel would pay him more than whoever it was that hired him, she had to get out here.

She must escape.

DORSEY ADAMS

Chapter Five

Rio said he'd be gone a few hours. He said he was going to hike up the mountainside. That meant he wouldn't be taking the scooter.

Becca's chance was now.

She didn't like the way he'd manhandled her. She didn't appreciate his laconic, close-lipped demeanor. He wouldn't tell her hardly anything, and despite his caring for her during the night, she still had no idea who he was working for and even if he truly would deliver her back into her father's loving arms.

She could not take a chance.

What she represented to him was the almighty dollar bill, and she had no confidence that he wasn't, even at this moment, contacting the cartel who'd originally kidnapped her. The chilling possibility had infected her mind: maybe that's why he wanted to climb the mountain—-to find cell phone service and make that call.

As he'd told her, he'd get a lot more money for her—from them.

With no time left to consider her predicament, Becca was galvanized into action. She slid out of bed and hunted for her shoes. Despite her determination, she was tired, and weak, so weak she felt as though she could sleep for a month. By the time she got her shoes on, she had to sit on the bed and rest. The damn flu was exhausting her. She wiped her drippy nose.

With her plan to take the scooter, she had no need of the food or water from Rio's cooler. Standing up, she moved to the door. It would be cold outside, and she had nothing more to wear than the sweatshirt and cap. They would have to do until she could find a nice rural family kind enough to take her in. In her experience, the Mexican people were by and large lovely and generous. Her proficiency in Spanish would aid her. She'd promise a hefty and grateful gift if they would give her safe haven.

Meanwhile, there was food here, and water. Rio wouldn't perish without the scooter.

Hand on the door, she lifted her chin. She must do this. Rio hadn't mistreated her. He'd been heavy-handed, but everything he'd done had been to aid her. Becca felt a twinge of guilt, leaving him alone in this wilderness.

It quickly passed.

She didn't trust him. With both hands, she shoved open the door.

Like a baseball bat to the face, the cold morning air slammed into her. She gasped. Ice hung on tree branches and a blanket of snow covered the ground. She shuddered, wrapped her arms around her waist and hurried through the snow to find the tarp-covered Vespa. Her hands already chilled and stiff, she pulled away the netting and yanked on the tarp. In moments she had the vehicle uncovered. The effort tired her, but grimly she pushed on. There was nobody around to help her, so she would rescue *herself*. Within a minute, she'd be gone.

A movement in the trees caught her eye.

Something tawny-colored and furry moved slowly toward her. She peered at it. A mountain lion.

Becca gasped. Had Rio mentioned something about seeing a big cat's tracks?

With unblinking concentration, slanted yellow eyes watched her. It sat, tail twitching, inspecting her.

Becca froze. She held her breath, didn't move.

Using great care, the big cat placed one paw slowly in front of the other. Head lowered, gaze fixed, it slunk in her direction with all the determination of a housecat hunting a mouse. It was thin and looked ravenous. Revealing sharp fangs, it opened its mouth to let out a terrifying hiss.

Every hair on Becca's body stood on end.

Wildly, she cast a glance toward the shack, but it was too far away. The scooter was her only chance.

Yanking it upright, she turned the key to unlock the steering wheel, then switched it to the on position. With one hand, she held down the brake lever. With the other, she pushed the start button.

The cat advanced.

Near panic, Becca bit down on her lip. Throwing herself across the scooter seat to keep it upright, she placed her feet on either side.

Straight at her, the lion burst into a dead run.

From up the mountain came a great roaring sound. The trees shook. Both she and the mountain lion jerked upward to the noise. Down the incline of trees and snow, Rio half ran, half slid toward them, waving his arms and shouting. Ice skidded beneath his boots.

The great cat's ears flattened. It broke its stride.

Becca gave the engine gas, and the combined noises of Rio's shouting and the roar of the engine frightened the animal. In great bounds, it ran off into the forest.

Now, Becca had only one predator to escape. Leaning over the handlebars, she gunned the engine. The scooter leaped forward. Her feet found the floorboards. In the snow, it fishtailed and she had trouble straightening out the front wheel. Finally, she got it going.

Along a ledge above her, Rio was still running.

She had mere seconds to escape.

DORSEY ADAMS

Chapter Six

Hunched low over the handlebars, Becca aimed the scooter at the only path that led out from the heavy thicket of trees.

Unfortunately, it also aimed her toward the ledge where Rio was moving fast above her. She had to make it past the choke point where the trees closed off one side and Rio's ledge bracketed the other. After that, the forest opened to flat dirt. She had to get by him, past the point where he might stop her. She knew one thing: if she failed at this escape attempt, he'd never give her another. She could do it. She must.

If he caught her, who knew what he might do?

Desperately, Becca gave the engine all the gas she could while still keeping the handlebars straight. The ground was uneven, rife with gopher holes, tree branches, underbrush, and snow. She bounced on the seat.

Above her, Rio ran a parallel course along the ice-covered ledge.

At last the ground evened out, and nearly to the choke point, she sped up.

That was the moment Rio flung himself off the ledge.

Like an NFL tackle, his big body slammed into both her and the Vespa. Man, machine, and Becca flew yards across the ground. Like a spinning top, she skittered over snow, dirt, branches, and rocks. She crashed to a hard stop wedged against the trunk of a gnarled oak. The wind was knocked from her lungs. She lay stunned.

Drawing her knees to her chest, she wheezed, and at last drew in air. Pain lanced through her wounded leg, and shrieked from a dozen bruises. Covered in mud, leaves, and snow, she felt a new cold leach into her very bones.

Rio recovered before she did. He got up, dusted off snow, and righted the Vespa. He thrust it into some deep undergrowth. Then he turned to her.

Still on her side, she couldn't help it. She cringed.

He said nothing. His face grim, he merely walked to her, pulled her up, and slung her over his shoulder like a sack of stones.

Becca groaned. She kicked her legs, got one free and tried to drive her foot into his groin. He captured her legs and held them to his body. On his back, she pounded her fists to no avail. His thick coat protected him.

Back at the cabin, he took her inside, bolted the door, and threw her on the bed without regard. She bounced on her hands and butt. Dread flowed through her. What would he do now? She only knew that no matter how futile, she would fight him.

With sharp movements, he took off his coat, pulled off his gloves, hung up his field glasses. His features appeared carved from the mountainside. Facing her, he set his hands on his hips. "Got a death wish?"

"What?"

"Do you want to die?" He wasn't shouting, but the intensity in his voice sounded like it.

"Of course not. I just want to get away from you."

His lips firmed and went flat. "You're safer here with me. Out there, you're like red meat to that big cat stalking you." He shook out his snow-dampened hair, and glowered at her. "Worse, to the cartel, you're a million bucks sitting on a scooter."

"How do I know I'm safer with you?" Despite her fear, she flared at him. Still on the mattress, she got up onto hands and knees. She shook with cold and adrenalin. "I don't know you. You won't tell me anything. You said you'd make more money off me from those men than whoever's paying you."

He opened his mouth, then closed it. Frowning, he said, "I would, but I'm not going to do that."

"Why not?"

"I've got some integrity. It's not my style."

"How do I know that?"

"I'll show you." On a low growl, Rio hunted around the small room until his glance fell on the cold fireplace. On the small mantle, which held an old tin coffee percolator and two chipped ceramic mugs, he pushed aside a box of matches and a rusted screwdriver to find a piece of soapstone. Dropping to the wooden floorboards on one knee, in angry movements he quickly sketched out the mountain, their cabin, the nearby roads. "See this? Here is where we are." He tapped the cabin.

"So?"

He made the mark of an "X" to the south of their position. Then, he drew another to the north, then more surrounding them. "These are the squads of cartel men, looking for you. Right now. Saw them with the field glasses. Out there, you wouldn't have lasted ten minutes. You were about to drive right into them."

Her mouth fell open. Her gaze dropped.

"Yeah," he said, sounding disgusted. "I just hope they didn't hear the Vespa's engine." He looked pained.

"Well, how could I know they were so close?"

"I told you," he said through gritted teeth, "that they were out there. I said I'd protect you." He grimaced as though she were a complete idiot. "God, lady, you never listen."

"Well ... how do I know you'll protect me?" Her voice fell to a whisper.

In exasperation, he flung the soapstone aside, got to his feet and gave her his back. He turned his head to the side, and she saw only his profile. His hands hung loose at his sides. Beneath his shirt, the muscles in his back shifted. "Have I hurt you?"

"Well ... no."

"Did I get you away from men, to whom, despite the ransom, it might not matter whether you live or die?"

"I—I suppose."

"Have I fed you, brought you your precious coffee, warmed you up?"

"You ... you did."

He swung around, his chest rising. "Then why did you run?"

She didn't know what to say. All at once her reasons didn't sound as logical as they once seemed. She felt small. "I—I just want to live, to go home. Back to my normal life." The ordeal had thoroughly tired her out. Between the cold, her sickness, and all her new bruises, she only wanted to get warm again, to lie down.

He was right. He'd treated her well, kept her safe.

"You have to trust me," Rio insisted. "This is what I do. It's all I do." He looked away.

That one small movement roused her, sharpened her attention. "All you do? What does that mean?"

His expression made no change. "Means I don't have hobbies."

She eyed him narrowly. "Not a big social life?"

As though finished with the subject, he shrugged. Moving to the cooler, he knelt down and busied himself rummaging around inside.

Becca got the sense he was uncomfortable. It was the first sign of unease she'd seen in him, a crack in his carefully constructed, detached persona. She sat back on her haunches. So, Mr. Cool wasn't the robot he wanted her to believe. She guessed it was worse than that. He had a dearth of human contacts, little family, few friends.

Thinking of her own busy life, her deep friendships, her family, her social agenda, she wondered at his isolation.

"You're not married, are you?" she asked, already sure of the answer.

Over his shoulder, he glanced back at her. Hesitating, something in him seemed to change, to lighten. The tension eased. "Naw. No time. Besides, no woman would put up with me. I'm an adrenalin junky. I live for excitement. Wherever the action is, I've gotta be there." Shocking her, his mouth turned up in a half smile, revealing straight white teeth and, surprisingly, a dimple.

Becca caught her breath.

Suddenly, she realized that with his attractive face and strong body he could have easily become a high fashion male model. Or an actor. The camera would love this man.

Despite all she'd been through, she could no longer deny one compelling fact: he was extremely attractive. Becca wasn't sure if she even liked him. So far, he hadn't been all that charming.

None of that changed one element; he was damned good-looking.

And at least he wasn't going to kill her.

DORSEY ADAMS

Chapter Seven

Rio wasn't really mad at Becca for her escape attempt. If he were honest with himself, and he was scrupulously so, he knew that in her position, first violently kidnapped by one entity, and then stolen from them by another unknown, he'd have done the same thing.

He'd have run, too.

Seeing the mountain lion stalking Becca had frozen his very veins. In winter, food for such an animal, possibly nursing babies, was scarce. While normally it might keep shy of humans, the cat could be near starving and driven to hunt creatures it usually wouldn't.

It had been a big cat, running fast and right at her. He shuddered, and pushed aside thoughts of what would have happened if the beast had caught her. No sense in dwelling on that.

Soon after they hashed things out, she fell asleep and he spent time sitting quietly, just watching her. Over her full breasts the quilts rose and fell softly. Her lashes lay like dark butterflies on her cheeks. Studying her face, he found he enjoyed looking at her. She was pretty.

She didn't know him, and women were funny about the trust issue. If they didn't feel sure of a man, they could be damnably uncooperative. But once they felt they could rely on him, often they were loyal to the end.

He needed to get her to a place where she could be comfortable with him, would follow him, would do as he said. Any more attempts to flee him could end in disaster, for both her and him. Most importantly, for the mission. He sorted through options.

He could get her conversing, encourage her to share her feelings with him, get her to carry on about her life, her interests. It usually wasn't difficult to start a woman talking. The female of the species needed to do a lot of that, and in their conversations, he often noticed, they let down their guard.

He could spend time drawing her out, making her believe he was truly interested in every aspect of her life, every thought in her pretty head. He could do all of that.

Or he could just seduce her.

It wasn't against the rules. In hostage rescue, there were no rules. His self-imposed edict to remain hands-off might not serve his purposes. Not this time. His long-standing policy should, possibly, be reconsidered.

****

Harrison kept his voice low and urgent. The phone pressed to his ear. "I'm telling you, fucking get the girl to me now."

On the other end of the line, Harrison heard wind soughing through high mountain trees. His man, Rio Lang, said, "Can't right now. Unless you want to send me a couple of Marine Seahawks loaded down with armament—say hellfire missiles and door gunners with belt-fed machine guns, and maybe a platoon of SEALs. Yeah, get some of my old teammates up here. Then, sure, you can have her now." He paused. "Other than that, we're trapped."

"No, no," Harrison said impatiently. "I've told you more than once this must be handled delicately. We can't involve the Mexican government. An assault like that from American forces would draw unwelcome attention and make international trouble."

The ambassador and his daughter had been roughed up a little, but released. At least they weren't killed. However, they'd been instructed to keep their mouths shut about the incident and allow the proper officials to do their job.

From his anonymous penthouse office in an equally anonymous American city, Harrison sat forward in his leather chair, and cast his gaze over the view of the downtown city lights. Few knew where he worked, and he kept personal control of Black Eagle. All his contracts were awarded by phone or through the Internet, and the payments made by cash transfers to anonymous drop locations. Between his superiors, himself, and the men who worked under him, were many layers of secrecy. In his line of work, Harrison had a lot of leeway to make decisions.

"For now, we're pretty much surrounded," Rio said. "But hidden. If we lay low for at least another day, I can get Becca out of here, no sweat. Those assholes will never find me."

Aggravation gnawed at Harrison's stomach. He flipped open a medicine bottle of antacid and chewed up three tablets. He was getting too old for this crap. It was nearing time for him to forge a new path. Dealing with rogue characters like Rio Lang, guys who'd served in Special Forces, highly trained but supremely arrogant, was proving too big a headache. They always wanted to do things their way and were nearly impossible to control.

"I'm warning you, Lang, no mistakes this time or you're done. Got that?" The last job he'd given Rio had been a doozy. Matters went sour when the man he'd been protecting was shot. He wasn't killed, but the wound was serious. It hadn't been Rio's fault, but Harrison deliberately allowed him to believe it was: men were easier to manage if they were worried about job security.

For Harrison, keeping Rio Lang off balance had become a fine art.

At the same time, he knew Lang was one of Black Eagle's best men, perhaps the very best. For his efficient work over the years in covert ops, then for Black Eagle, and earlier than that, for the United States government, Harrison knew that the government was far more in Rio's debt than Rio would ever guess.

And Harrison vowed to keep it that way.

Rio grunted. "Gotta go." And he cut the line.

With satisfaction, Harrison leaned back in his luxury chair. Rio had gotten the message. Of one thing Harrison was certain: Rio would do his job.

****

Becca spent a second night with Rio snug against her backside. While she was still weak from her illness, she was no longer feverish or sick. He'd left the battery-operated lamp on all night and it was still going strong. It was plenty cold enough in the cabin to justify the snuggling.

Because she'd been so ill the night before, Becca had barely noticed.

But now she was well enough to recognize his hard-on, pressed to her backside. With her pants still damp and muddy, she'd been forced to remove them again and wore only her white cotton panties and his wool socks.

At midnight, she stirred, waking up.

"I'm not gonna apologize," he whispered into her hair.

She shifted away and understood exactly what he meant.

"Won't deny it either," he said. "You're an attractive woman, Becca. Damn hot. Obviously I want you." He waited, apparently hoping she'd respond favorably.

"Not gonna happen," she said, inching farther away. "I don't even know you."

Relaxing his hold, he allowed her to move. "Your

choice," he said. "Either way."

She rolled onto her back and slanted him a glance. "When it suits you, you keep giving me choices as though you don't care. But you're not the robot you pretend to be, are you, Rio?"

"Never said I was a robot." He flicked his eyes downward toward his lower body. "Clearly I'm a man. And you do know me. I'm Rio. We've spent two days together. And now a second night. What's the problem?"

She got up on one elbow, her long hair framing her face and hanging down to the bed. Grudgingly, she admitted to herself that she found him physically appealing. He was like a golden, Viking demi-god. His physique. His face. Both were magnificent.

Yet that was only how he looked, his appearance, his outer shell. But what about his character? As she'd told him several times, she didn't know him, didn't fully trust him. Whether she was attracted to his fabulous outer layer or not, that didn't mean she was going to toss aside her normal reserve.

While she knew herself to be a sexual being who enjoyed lovemaking, who even felt occasional urges toward exhibitionism, she'd never indulged those urges. She'd long fantasized about driving past men and ripping off her top, just to see their faces. It was a secret fantasy. Maybe one day she'd be able to do it.

That day had not yet arrived.

She'd never had sex with a stranger, or even a man with whom she didn't already have a strong dating relationship. Certainly she wouldn't change now.

Instead, she told Rio, "You're not getting paid to bed me."

"No need to pay me. I'll provide the service for free." He gave her a small smile.

She glared. "I said no. If you try to take me, I'll

claw out your eyes. And it will be rape."

His smile faded. "I don't do rape. If a woman I want is amenable, I have sex. Period."

"This woman is not amenable." She tapped her chest and beneath her shirt, felt her breasts sway.

His gaze dropped to her chest. "Sadly, you've made that clear."

****

At dawn Becca came to a woozy consciousness, her body warm, her private parts even warmer. In fact, her vulva throbbed with sexual heat. Her breasts tingled and her nipples grew hard.

A big male body was flush against hers and his thick penis was rock hard and pushed up against her butt cheeks. If she hadn't been wearing her underwear, he would have been inside her.

Still groggy and without thinking, she pushed back, made slight grinding movements against his hard-on. God, it felt good. It had been a while since she'd had sex. Her body let her know the time was now. She was a sensual woman, one who enjoyed intimate sexual expression, was often eager for it. She loved the closeness, the warmth, the earth-shattering orgasms.

Sighing in deep arousal, she took a short breath and sighed again, and gave a little hum. Sliding her hand down her body, she wormed her fingers beneath the waistband of her panties.

"If you touch yourself I'm gonna explode." A male voice rumbled in her ear.

Becca's eyes flew open.

Rio.

She froze and withdrew her hand. She was in bed. In the mountain cabin. With a man paid to take her home.

In the morning light, stark reality crashed back into her consciousness. A little fantasizing was one thing.

Actually acting upon those fantasies was another.

He placed his hand on her hip, caressed it. "Say yes, Becca, and I'll do the work for you. My fingers are magic. You won't be sorry, I promise. Say yes." He kissed her ear, gave her a tiny pelvic thrust, rubbed the hard length of his penis against her.

Pushing his hand away, she rolled to her belly and got up onto her elbows. "Sorry, I was still asleep," she said, aware that at least some of this was her fault. "The answer is still no."

"A shame." He sounded disappointed, but not greatly so. And so impersonal. At least she knew that Mr. Cool got raging hard-ons. He wasn't so cool down below.

Seeing the impassivity in his expression made her glad she hadn't succumbed to him. He wasn't Mr. Cool. But he wasn't all warm and fuzzy, either. "Can you get me out of here today? I need to find out about Maria, my college roommate, and her dad, the ambassador—see if they're okay. I'm not sick any more. Can we leave?"

He groaned and rolled up off the bed. Thrusting his hands through his hair, he said, "I need to scout the area." Methodically he pulled on outer clothing, and when he was dressed for the outdoors, he hesitated. "I'll need to climb the mountain. Keep watch for a while. Are you gonna run again?"

Becca licked her lips. "No. You've kept your word to me. I'll stick with you."

He gave only a curt nod, and left.

When the door slammed, leaving a gust of frigid air to swirl into the cabin, Becca felt alone. Her body wished she'd had a bout of good, clean, mindless sex.

And her vulva still throbbed.

DORSEY ADAMS

Chapter Eight

On the long trek upward to a lookout where he could see for miles around, Rio dug his boots into the mountainside. Carefully he kept tight to the tree line, out of sight of anyone possibly watching. His binoculars swung on his neck and the cold tried to creep through his clothing.

He was glad of the low temperature because it helped douse the raging desire he'd felt for Becca. Getting cooped up for two days in that shack with the young, sexy spitfire had tested his restraint. This morning, when she'd shimmied her ass against his dick and began to slide her fingers down her pants to pleasure herself, he'd nearly lost it.

He didn't think he'd ever been as hard as he'd been at that moment. All he could think about was plunging deep inside her, bringing her to the orgasm of her life, and then doing it again. And again. He wanted to suck on those luscious breasts, lick his way down her neck, her belly, to her sweet nether regions. He'd make her come like a landslide crashing down the mountain.

But she'd said no.

At last he reached the stand of concealing boulders and crept through them to lie on his stomach. He lifted the field glasses. From his perch on high, he was careful not to silhouette himself against the sky. Miles to the south, he saw only the normal vistas of hillsides and small ranchitas. Plumes of smoke rose from several chimneys, warming the small and modest homes.

To the east he saw no unusual activity. The roads were quiet and not well traveled. To the west were only more mountains. The cartel had moved on.

For a moment Rio considered not telling Becca.

He felt certain that if they stayed one more night, he could work his wiles and convince her that sex with him would be wonderful. He'd never had any trouble bedding women. The two of them could enjoy a long day and night of lovemaking under the quilts. He couldn't imagine a more exhilarating interlude. Those hours would be plenty of time to slake his thirst for her and then deliver her to Harrison's men. After that, he could be on his way.

She wouldn't go unrewarded. He'd give her all the orgasms she wanted and more. For several moments he allowed the notion of giving her those memories to hover pleasantly in his thoughts.

Rio rubbed his neck and came back to reality. The men hunting her were no longer in the area and that meant it was time to leave. He disliked making the decision, but he was paid to do a job.

He'd do it.

Taking out his cell phone, high on the mountainside, he was able to get one bar of connectivity and called Harrison. Quickly he made arrangements to rendezvous with a Black Eagle team Harrison would send some forty miles to the north. He and Becca would leave at nightfall, quit the area under the cover of darkness.

Halfway down the mountain, Rio stopped beside a stand of trees, opened his pants and took himself in hand. Thinking of Becca's rounded ass rubbing against him, he jerked off into the snow. If he was going to survive more hours with her in that cabin, it was necessary. He'd told her he didn't force women, and he didn't. However, a man had his limits. Jerking off was the only way to get through spending more time alone with the alluring Rebecca De Monte.

Returning to the shack, he yanked open the door and stepped inside. Before he could slam the door, his breath strangled in his throat.

She was nude from the waist up.

Becca sat on the bed washing her face and arms with a piece of towel dampened from a water bottle. Her back was to him, but startled by his entry, she turned and gasped. Her breasts bounced.

"I thought you'd be gone longer," she said, breathless.

He gaped, stared, almost swallowed his tongue.

Full, rounded, and with light pink areolas, they were the most perfect tits he'd ever seen. He went instantly hard. A droplet of water clung to one sweet nipple and his mouth went dry. Both her nipples were puckered, as though hoping for a man to suckle them. Hoping for *him*. He'd pay a king's ransom to sip from that breast. He'd give all he owned for a single taste.

She whirled away, and snatched up a garment from the bed to cover her chest. Yet she'd turned too late and he'd gotten a clear view of her glorious breasts.

All the furious beating off into the snow he could ever do would not douse even the tiniest spark of desire he had for Rebecca De Monte. He knew that now.

She hurried to pull a garment over her head, and he saw that it was one of his old white t-shirts. She must have gotten it from his bag. While not snug, the fabric was worn and thin. It lay over her chest with only the barest of covering. The outlines of her breasts were obvious. Her nipples thrust against the cotton and he stared at them. He was wholly unable to blink.

"Sorry," she said, eyes downcast. "I—I've been wearing my shirt and bra for over a week and I stink." She gestured at a small pile of clothing she'd thrown onto the floor. "Couldn't stand it anymore." She gave a weak laugh. "Like I said, I thought you'd be gone longer."

"Don't apologize," he said hoarsely. Turning

away from her, he took off his coat and cap and squeezed his eyes closed.

Mercy!

For something to do, he knelt at the cooler and took out a red apple, two granola bars and two bottles of water. With a folding knife from his pocket, he closed the cooler, sat on top and peeled the apple. He tried to still his shaking hands.

When she said nothing further, his brain slowly began to clear. What a coincidence that was, him coming in and finding her damn near nude. Yeah, sure.

Men in his line of work didn't like coincidences, didn't believe in them. They were to be distrusted, disbelieved.

Had Becca *wanted* him to see her?

Rio stopped in mid-peel. He glanced up at her and found her staring at her fingernails. As though she thought the thin t-shirt maintained her modesty, she made no move to cover herself further. Staring at her nipples, he felt his mouth water. A simmering satisfaction started low in his gut and rose into his chest. If she even wanted him a little, he now knew what to do. Hadn't she been the one to rub her butt cheeks against his cock?

****

"It wasn't really a coincidence today, was it?" Rio asked Becca suddenly. The apple in his hand, he paused, mid-peel.

Becca jerked her head up and she wondered what was on his mind now. "What?"

"You know what I mean. Me coming in. You half naked."

She sputtered. "You think I *planned* that?"

He showed his teeth. "Didn't you?"

"No!" Still sitting on the bed, she faced away from him. "You're crazy."

Rio set down his apple. "You don't have to be afraid of me. If it happens—us two in the bed—it will be your choice. Hell, it'll be your idea. Okay?"

"You're damn right." As she climbed back beneath the quilts, Becca fumed. How dare he assume she'd been waiting for him with her breasts on full display? Why, the idea was ridiculous. He *was* crazy. She'd merely taken her time, thoroughly washing her arms, her chest, her face. Of course she knew he was coming back.

While he was gone, it was only natural to give her poor beleaguered thoughts some free rein. For almost a week she'd been terrified, knocked sideways, sick, out of control. Finally she'd been able to let some of her tension subside. Before then, she'd hadn't a moment to herself to relax, to do even the smallest thing. She wanted a wash. So what?

So what if during that time she'd indulged in a little sensual fantasizing? Particularly the fantasies she secretly desired … exhibitionism. Perhaps the big strong Viking-looking man might come back and catch her bathing? What difference would it make if she slowed her ablutions and let her mind take flight? He'd seemed intensely interested in her breasts. For her entire adult life, she'd always had ultra-sensitive nipples. In the past, she'd encouraged her few lovers to concentrate on lightly pinching them, rolling them in their fingers, suckling them. It made her lower extremities pulse in delicious throbbing heat. When attention had been paid to them during lovemaking, she always reached orgasm in a hurry.

She knew her face was attractive, even pretty. However, she'd never tried to fool herself that she was beautiful. She kept herself fit and her hips were slim, her legs shapely. Yet there was no doubt that her breasts were her best feature. Was there anything wrong with a woman enjoying what providence had given her?

What could be the harm in allowing an appreciative man like Rio a glimpse?

She forced herself to consider his conclusion: had it been a coincidence, when he'd come in to gaze upon her nude flesh? She pondered the thought and felt a tiny smile come to her lips.

Well … maybe a little.

****

Rio had been right about his chances of seducing her, and now he knew it was possible. She wanted him, but like a skittish, wild doe, she needed charming, wanted leading, would respond to tender coaxing.

He would provide that coaxing.

"Breakfast is ready," he said, setting the food on top of the cooler. "But first I'll need to see your wound. Gotta change the dressing." He moved to sit by her on the bed.

"Okay." She sat up and slid her leg outside the quilts.

With both hands, he glided the fabric of her pants up past her knee, making sure his warm hands slid along her skin. With care, he peeled away the bandage. The wound was healing. Deliberately he smiled gently into her eyes. "Looks good."

From the first aid kit, he pulled out fresh gauze and tape and took his time replacing the old dressing. It became necessary to hold her soft calf with one hand in order to cover the wound. "Does it hurt?"

"Only if I bang it into something or move too much," she answered. "The gauze is helping protect it." She eyed his face. "So, can we leave today? Are those kidnappers gone?"

He hesitated. "Maybe we can go tonight," he said,

"or maybe in the morning," knowing full well they would have to leave when dusk fell.

There was lots of time between then and now, many hours of pleasure possible during the interim.

He pulled her pants leg down over the dressing and scooted closer to her on the bed. Smoothing a strand of hair off her face, he said, "Becca, somehow we got off on the wrong foot. I like you. You didn't deserve to be stolen away. You deserve to be delivered home." He was surprised to find that he meant it. He caressed her slim shoulders. "Remember, I promised to get you back to your dad, and I will." He tried to project sincerity through his gaze.

As she returned his look, he saw the first hint of vulnerability in her eyes. "Thank you," she whispered.

It was all the opening he needed. Grateful women could at times be convinced to lie down.

"You're welcome," he said, easing her back into the pillows. Using his fingers, he tilted up her chin and smiled. Her brown eyes wide, she stared up at him, her lips parted. His gaze dropped to her mouth. Slowly, he lowered his head.

DORSEY ADAMS

Chapter Nine

"I have to go pee," Becca said.

"Ah." Becoming increasingly certain that she would allow him inside her sexy body, Rio decided a small delay wouldn't matter. He straightened. "Put on your sweatshirt and cap. I'll take you out."

With the mood broken, if only for a short time, Rio shrugged into his coat, and when she was ready, he took her hand.

She let him.

First, he insisted on scouting the area for the mountain lion. Only when he found no sign of it did he allow Becca outside.

In the snow, they walked together to the now familiar underbrush. "I'll get the scooter back over here and cover it with the tarp. Call me when you're ready."

"I can go back to the cabin myself," she said. "It's only right there." She pointed at it, not many yards away.

"Sure," he said. Maybe by the time he got back she'd be waiting for him in all her nude splendor. He touched her nose with his index finger and was rewarded by a shy smile.

With the scooter down in the tree line, it took him several moments to reach where he'd stashed it. Behind him, he heard the cabin door open and close. He smiled.

He dug the scooter out and walked it back to its original place by the shack, then hauled out the tarp. Getting ready to spread the heavy and concealing fabric over the Vespa, he hesitated.

A distant thumping sound quickly became loud.

A helo!

Diving under the tarp, Rio jammed himself up against the tree trunk. Had Becca heard the rotors?

He dared not check. If the men in the helicopter above were watching, any moving figure would be spotted.

He couldn't afford to be found. Not only would they kill him, but worse, they'd take Becca. With all the trouble she'd caused them by escaping their grasp, they might not be kind to her once she was back in their control.

No matter what, he did not want that to happen. As he'd told her, Becca deserved her freedom, deserved to be restored to her family. She'd done nothing wrong. He couldn't stand by and see her hurt.

And he must complete his mission.

When he judged the helicopter to have finished its pass, and listening while it continued on its straight line trajectory, he threw off the tarp and raced to the cabin. In the snow his boots gouged great chunks that flew yards in each direction. If they'd been spotted, the bird above would make a sharp banking turn.

While he listened hard, the helo kept going.

Yanking open the door, he slammed it behind him and found Becca huddled on the floor at the foot of the bed.

Under the sleeping bag.

Lifting the corner, he sank to the floorboards and climbed under with her. Pulling her into his arms, he held her close for a moment and shut his eyes. Not only was she beautiful, she was smart. She'd done the right thing. Becca wasn't just attractive, she had a brain in that pretty head.

"Are they c-coming back?" she asked, clinging to him.

"Not sure," he said. "Since they haven't found us, apparently they're going over the same ground again. It's what I'd do." But he *was* sure. They'd been flying arrow-straight. They wouldn't be back soon.

Beneath the sleeping bag, he again tilted her chin. "Remember. No matter what, I'll take care of you, Becca. I'll keep you safe."

She nodded.

This time he would not be denied. With a relief that surprised him, he let his mouth close over hers.

She accepted him as he'd suspected she would and her capitulation was sweet. Tenderly he thrust his tongue past her lips and explored the inside of her mouth. To cradle her, he placed his arm behind her neck and her head fell back. She moaned. Dragging his lips down her throat, he placed little kisses along her neck. With his free hand he cupped her cheek.

"Want me?" he asked, giving her a little nod. He needed her permission. He needed to know he'd been right about the *coincidence.*

With her tongue, she wet her lips. "I'm not sure. I'm overwhelmed. Scared. My leg does still hurt."

He clicked his tongue. "Excuses, excuses."

She searched his gaze. "Give me some time. I need to think about it."

Time? Within hours, he'd have to pack her up on the Vespa and leave. No way would he tell her that. If he pressed her now, and if she knew, she'd surely deny him. Let her think she had much more time in which to decide. Too bad that time was the one thing that had run out.

With a reluctance far greater than he could have imagined, he eased away. Why the *fuck* had he even asked her?

"Can we have the food now?" she asked.

"Sure."

Together they sat, companionably eating the apple and granola bars. Offering her a sip of water, he asked, "Are you thinking about it? You know … us? Over there?" He pointed at the bed.

She pursed her lips, appearing to hide a smile. "Yes, I'm thinking."

"Are you thinking … about me making you happy? Have you considered what I can do for you with these?" He held up his hands and waggled his fingers.

Her mouth twisting, she tried harder to suppress her smile.

"How about my mouth?" he asked. "Have you thought about that? Or my tongue?"

In a brief flash, her eyes glowed and he saw it, dammit. He saw the telltale spark of sensual interest. But then, they glinted in renewed humor.

"Or this?" Dropping his hand to his pants, he cupped his sex. "Come on, Becca. A woman doesn't come by opportunities like this often. I've got mad skills. Come and get it."

Becca burst out laughing.

Not the reaction he'd been hoping for, but not bad. He could be charming if the situation warranted. He shook his head in pretended regret. "Your loss."

To Rio's everlasting regret, Becca spent the entire day *thinking*.

When the shadows lengthened, he knew it was time to leave. He wasn't going to bed Rebecca De Monte after all. The idea soured his mood and he became curt with her.

"Get ready and put on your hat," he said gruffly.

She didn't seem to notice. "We're leaving? Now?"

He nodded once. "I'll get the scooter. We'll be at the rendezvous in about an hour."

"Great!" she said. "Do you want me to turn out the lamp?"

"Yeah." He banged out the door and stamped

towards the Vespa. Damn women! Once he made the delivery, he'd never see her again. He really hated lost sexual opportunities.

Maybe he'd even miss her a little.

DORSEY ADAMS

Chapter Ten

A full moon offered diffused light to the outside landscape. Its glow illuminated the hills and trees and emphasized shadows. The woods smelled like damp, leafy foliage. With a sure hand, Rio drove the scooter efficiently through the forest, and down mountain paths, and finally, onto paved roads.

Becca clung to his back, bounced on the seat and tried to hang on. Her time had come; she was going home.

Rio had made repeated promises to care for her, to get her back to her family. She believed him now, had no reason not to. He'd taken care of her, fed her, warmed her with his body. He'd even saved her life from certain mauling by the mountain lion. He hadn't forced her into sex when she hadn't given him the go-ahead. For all that, she appreciated what he'd done.

In another life, she now felt certain she might have wanted to date him.

She was just as sure she'd never see him again.

Clearly, Rio was a loner who moved from job to job, wherever it took him. He wasn't one to commit to anything or anyone except that. Deep down, she knew that he wasn't exactly the *dating* type.

In the deep freeze of night, she hugged his back and laid her cheek against his shoulder blade. Chilled once again, but with layers of fear removed, she relaxed. The cold didn't bother her as much as it had. It simply felt a part of her life now.

During the hour-long drive, Becca noticed that whenever they came to a fork in the road, or to an area which appeared occupied by a farm or rural house, Rio slowed their speed to a crawl, and lowered the Vespa's noise level. He took no chances of their being heard or spotted.

At last they approached the upper lip of a small valley. He pulled the scooter to a stop. "The team waiting for you is just over this rise," he whispered to her, and pointed ahead into the darkness. "But I want a look first. Hang on, we'll take the high ground."

Eager to discover if her father or brothers had come for her themselves, she nodded. He eased the Vespa into a stand of towering pines. She noticed the incline began to get steeper, and still they climbed through trees. Stopping beneath the overhang of a great tree, he switched off the engine and took her by the elbow.

"Come on," he whispered, "but don't speak at all. Out here, voices carry a long way."

She indicated that she heard him.

They climbed on foot another hundred yards. He helped her. By the time they got to a spot he deemed safe, she was thoroughly winded. Her leg throbbed.

He found a gathering of boulder-sized rocks and wended his way between them. She followed. At last their view opened up to the valley below.

He lay flat on the lower of the two boulders, so the top one loomed over them and cast them into shadows. She lay beside him. On the valley floor she could see flickering lights, an ancient wooden barn, with several trucks spread out, their headlamps on. Even from their height, she could hear men's voices, yet couldn't distinguish words.

A couple of the men seemed to be patrolling the lower edges of the valley.

From his coat, Rio withdrew binoculars. For several moments he watched. Beside him, she grew impatient, but knew better than to say anything. She just wanted to go down to the valley floor, find her family, and have the men return her home.

"I don't know," Rio whispered at last. "I just don't know."

"What?" In the moonlight, she searched his carved features.

"Something's off. Can't put my finger on it."

"What does that mean?"

"In the SEAL Teams, we're taught to trust our instincts, to ask questions, to question anything that doesn't look right."

Her mouth fell open. "You were a SEAL?" she whispered. "Like a Navy SEAL?"

"Left the service early. Wanted to do something else." He shrugged. "Miss the lads, though."

Wow, she thought. The Navy SEALs were legendary. They were supermen. She knew the acronym stood for Sea, Air and Land, which meant they were proficient in all those arenas. They could swim like dolphins, parachute like eagles, fight on land as lethal warriors.

She filed away the new knowledge for contemplating at another time. "Well, what down there doesn't look right to you?"

He put the glasses back to his face. "Not that many men. Why so few? And where's the extract helo?"

"The what?"

"Your helicopter. It looks like they want to put you in a truck and drive you away. Why? It's hundreds of miles to the border. Wouldn't a wealthy man like your father have you flown out?" He rubbed his chin.

"I guess so." She hadn't thought about that. Apparently her father and brothers weren't there. Disappointment settled over her.

"Their guns," he said. "I don't like 'em. Too many Kalashnikovs. They don't look like Black Eagle operatives or even FBI guys." He handed her the binoculars.

Five men, all dressed in drab camouflage, stood around talking. She wondered how *operatives* were supposed to look.

Below, they heard a shout. A man on the edge of the valley pointed upward into their direction.

"*Shit*," Rio muttered. "We're busted." In a hurry, he slid backward off their rock and landed on his feet. "Get down. We're outta here."

She slid off and he caught her. "Wait." She put her hands on his forearms. "Aren't those guys here to take me home? I need to go to those men, not away from them."

"We've been double-crossed," he said. "Those guys aren't friendlies. They'll kill me, grab you, and you're right back where you started. In trouble. Maybe worse trouble."

"But … how do you know that?" It seemed like she'd asked him that same question a dozen times.

"Experience. I've been in battle, in war. I've faced the enemies. I smell a rat."

She shook her head. None of this made sense. She should be going down into the valley, into those men's care. They'd been tasked to take her home. Oh, how she longed to go *home*. What was Rio talking about?

He watched her face. "Looks like you get to choose again, Becca."

"Choose?" she squeaked.

They heard voices moving closer.

"Choose me," he said. "Or them."

She gaped. The night spun around her and she went lightheaded. Confusion filled her mind. A team had been sent for her and Rio was saying the opposite? To her, nothing she'd seen about the men looked suspicious.

What had he noticed that she hadn't?

"Buttercup," he whispered the endearment, "I'll take care of you. I'll keep you safe. *Trust* me." He threw a glance over the boulder. "You have five seconds."

She needed one.

Together they ran, slid, and half-tumbled down the mountainside back to the scooter.

Abruptly, gunfire shattered the night.

DORSEY ADAMS

Chapter Eleven

Rio grabbed the Vespa. As one, both he and Becca leaped aboard. Just as they had when Rio first took her from the cantina bathroom, bullets whined overhead, and cut into the ground around them. Sounds of shouting voices and thudding boots came down from above them.

A bullet screamed by her head, embedded itself violently into the trunk of a nearby tree. Becca shrieked.

"Duck," Rio ordered. "Stay low." Clinging to him, Becca hung on for dear life.

Twisting and turning the scooter in a serpentine pattern, Rio kept them headed almost directly downhill. Becca had no idea how he could see, how he avoided the trees and rocks, but she was grateful he did. Before he got them out of sight of their pursuers and free of immediate gunfire, it was the longest twenty seconds of her life.

Rio kept off the road and roared through the forest. Gradually, those following fell behind.

Grimly, Rio drove through the night. He said nothing to Becca, and she didn't want to distract him. Onto dirt roads, some partly paved, and through wild animal tracks, he weaved across the Mexican forests and countryside for nearly two hours.

At last he drove them into a familiar stand of oaks, stopped the Vespa, and helped her off. Their little shack stood only yards away, dark and shielded by overhanging trees.

"We're okay for now," he told her, covering the scooter. "I took a long roundabout trip to get here, but we lost them at the beginning."

Becca nodded, stiff with cold.

Tucking her under his arm, Rio guided her to the cabin, turned on the battery light, and bolted the door.

Pushing her to sit on the bed, he removed her shoes and massaged her feet.

Her mind dull, and shivering violently, Becca merely watched him. They were both alive. That was all she knew.

He eyed her with concern. "We've got to get you warmed up again."

With effort, she dragged herself across the bed and climbed under the quilts. Where was her father? Her brothers? Who were those men and why did they shoot at her? In misery, she lay on her side facing the wall.

Rio piled quilts on top of her, took off his coat, and then climbed beneath the layers to take her into his arms.

"Why?" Becca asked him, teeth chattering. "Why did they shoot at us? Who were they?"

"I don't know," he told her. "Yet. And you're right. They weren't just aiming at me. It's clear they want to kill you, too. Doesn't make sense. Your dollar value is high. Can you think of anything? Any reason why someone wants you dead?"

"No." She moaned.

"Do you have some sort of valuable information? Any knowledge that someone might not want out?"

"No, no! I work at my dad's hubcap business, remember? In the purchase order and shipping department! After work, I go home, eat dinner, watch TV. On weekends I go to the movies or have a drink with friends. I don't do anything illegal."

With tender fingers, Rio smoothed the hair off Becca's forehead. His hand lingered, cupping her cheek. "Somebody thinks you have something, or knows something that would hurt them. That's twice now they've shot at us. The first time I didn't understand why they'd take a chance at hitting you. If they wanted you dead, why not kill you when they first found you? But they didn't. Not until it looked like you were gonna get away."

Becca shifted to her back and met his gaze. In the lamplight, his eyes held hers. "Rio," she said, then something caught in her throat. "Rio, I'm not a bad person."

"Of course not." He ran his hand down to her shoulder, caressed her through her shirt.

"Th … There's nothing I'm hiding, I swear." It seemed vitally important he believe her.

"I know that."

"Why," she whispered, through a suddenly tight throat. "Why is this happening to me?" A tear squeezed from the corner of her eye.

Rio kissed it away. "We'll find out," he vowed, nuzzling her. "We'll get to the bottom of it. I don't like being double-crossed. I'll talk to my employer. His explanation better be good."

"I—I," Becca stammered. "I don't want to die."

"Not on my watch," he promised, and he dusted a kiss across her lips.

She believed him.

Reaching for his face, she drew him closer. The warmth of his body began to warm her, too. After coming so near to death's door, she needed his life-affirming touch. Purposefully deepening the kiss, she eased her body closer to his. She knew the unspoken message she was sending.

It was time to let go.

DORSEY ADAMS

Chapter Twelve

Rio had assumed that when and if the time came that Becca capitulated to him, the sex would be hot, furious, and fast. He didn't anticipate long, slow, luxurious lovemaking.

Yet he found he wanted to take his time, enjoy her every soughed breath, watch the sensuality brighten her velvet brown eyes, feel her every physical response to him. He wanted this to be as good for her as he knew it would be for him. While he'd always been a solicitous lover, he'd never really cared deeply about his partner's satisfaction.

This felt different. They'd barely escaped certain death. Those flying bullets had come too close. Yet they were still alive, still breathing, their hearts still beating in their chests. He wanted—no, he *needed*—to connect with her in the most primal way, through sexual release. He needed that with Becca.

When she reached for him, he detected a slight shiver in her and he said, "Lie back. Let me warm you."

Before he touched any erogenous zones, he wanted her body warmed and relaxed. So, he took the time to massage and rub her shoulders, her waist, her hips and legs.

She complied, her dark eyes watching his every move.

Finally, beneath the quilts, they were both warmed. Lying beside her, he threaded his fingers through her hair, held her still for his kiss. At first, he merely touched his lips to hers. He wanted to map their shape and texture, and with only his mouth's most tender touch, he felt her lips form a smile.

Pulling back, he smiled into her eyes. "I want you,

Becca. *All* of you."

Her pretty eyes grew heavy-lidded and sultry. "You want all I can give?"

"Yes." He breathed the word, again moving their mouths close together with only the barest of gaps between them.

"I will," she started, but when he touched his tongue to her Cupid's bow, she gasped. "I will give, Rio," she got out, "all of myself to you."

He needed no further encouragement. Taking both her wrists in one hand, he drew them up and held them firmly over her head on the bedcovers. She gasped.

Still holding her, he deepened the kiss. His tongue swept into her mouth, demanding now. Hers responded in kind. When he released her wrists, she dug her fingers into his shoulders. Needing to feel her hands on his bare flesh, in one motion he pulled off his t-shirt. Becca moaned, and squeezed his biceps.

Rio rose on one elbow to watch her face. He touched the hem of the t-shirt she still wore, the one she'd borrowed from his bag. Lifting it a few inches, he let his knuckles drag across her flat stomach.

"You know I want to see you, see your breasts," he whispered into her ear. "After you gave me a glimpse this morning, I've been salivating, hungry for more."

Her eyes lit. She nodded. The need shining in their depths called to him in a siren's song. He could no more stop himself from touching her than Greek sailors could keep from throwing themselves atop fatal rocks.

Lifting the shirt another inch, he allowed his knuckles to skim over her flesh. "And I want to kiss them, and taste them," he said.

Delighting him, she squirmed. "Yes," she breathed. "Oh, yes." She made a little gasp.

Deciding to tease her, and himself, he raised the

shirt another inch, so that only the very bottoms of her breasts peeked out. "I hope you'll let me play with them, toy with them with my tongue." When her breath caught and again she squirmed beneath the quilts, he knew she very much wanted that kind of attention.

Lifting the shirt gently over her head, he tossed it aside and allowed the quilt to fall away from her upper body. Her breasts were as fantastic as he remembered: full, with lovely pink nipples, rounded, and just begging for his ministrations. In the cold air her nipples stood up stiffly. His mouth went dry.

Reaching out, she pulled his head to her chest and he gladly took her between his lips. He rolled his tongue around the nipple, licked it, suckled it. Down below, beneath the quilts, his hard-on raged, hot and insistent. He rubbed it against her hip.

Becca moaned and began to thrash on the bed. He guessed her breasts were particularly sensitive, even more so than most women. He moved to the other breast and tasted her at length. Testing her response, he gave each area of tender flesh little flicks of his tongue, then encircled each one completely. He lapped at her. Gratifying him, her breath escalated and she could not remain still.

As he enjoyed her, he got the sense that she was close to orgasm. Beyond pleased at her responses, he felt blood roaring in his ears. Quickly, he unbuttoned her pants, slid down her zipper. Slipping his hand beneath her panties, his fingers found the heart of her sex.

Drawing a circular pattern on her nub, he heard her gasp louder. Eyes closed, her head moved side to side. She clutched at his bare shoulders, her legs strained to open. Her pants kept her restricted. "Rio," she whispered roughly. "Rio!"

Feeling a wolfish grin spread over his face, he

increased the motion of his fingers, unmerciful, insistent. She could not hold back.

The explosion rocked her in waves. She orgasmed so quickly it caught him by surprise. Shuddering her release, she groaned in pleasure, and the sounds pulsed through him like a wind-whipped ocean current. He luxuriated in her body's vibrations.

Finally now in a hurry, he tugged off her slacks and underwear, tore at his own pants. Kicking the clothing from the bed, he prepared to part her thighs and roll on top. Between his legs, his sex was hot, hard as iron, a demanding sexual tool that needed using. *Now.* He wanted inside her more than anything he'd ever wanted in his life.

Yet she surprised and delighted him again.

With a staying hand on his shoulder, she pushed him onto his back and rolled atop him. Using one soft palm, she took him and guided his hard length to her body's opening. She mounted him. So wet there was minimal resistance to his girth, her body accepted him. In only seconds she was filled to the hilt. She caught her breath.

Rio groaned in pleasure. Her body was welcoming, with a driving and carnal demand of its own.

Above him, her hair in her face, her breasts swaying, Becca rode him, slow at first, and then, gaining speed, she increased the tempo. He reached out and caressed her breasts, staring at them, loving the feel of her wet sex grinding on him. As his manhood grew impossibly bigger, harder, he gripped her small waist.

He couldn't take his eyes off her face.

Showing no inhibition at all, Becca flung back her head, pushed the hair from her face and clasped her fingers together behind her neck. A woman lost in the unafraid, uninhibited throes of sensual desire, Becca embraced her need, and the notion thrilled him.

Rio grinned. She was a wanton wildcat!

Like a little hussy, she gave her breasts a sideways shake. "You like?" Her mouth curved in a sensual smile. Her eyes teased him.

"I like." Again he closed his hands over her breasts' delicious weight. He plucked at her gorgeous nipples, massaged her flesh.

"You want to come now?" She asked the question eagerly, as though his climax would spur another of her own.

When all he could do was nod, she increased the speed, rode him hard. Rubbing against his body, she let out rough gasps. He squeezed her thighs, caressed her waist.

He could tell she was again nearing orgasm. She reached down, took his hands, and placed them back on her breasts.

In answer, eager to please her, he rolled her nipples between his fingers. Obviously, she loved breast play.

The idea drove him mad. She bounced harder, moaning in ecstasy. Seconds before he came in a heated rush, she ground against him in her second orgasm. The knowledge made his own spasm that much more powerful. Lights burst like sparklers inside. He gave a muffled shout.

DORSEY ADAMS

Chapter Thirteen

That night they made love again, and again in the morning. Becca had always known she was a sensual woman, one who enjoyed her own body and harbored few inhibitions. Yet she'd never had a lover of Rio's stamina, with such unwavering interest in her body, or so much tenderness.

The tenderness surprised her most of all.

Mr. Cool wasn't cool beneath the sheets. She'd never known a lover who ran so hot—-from the temperature of his skin to his blazing eyes, to his sexy, whispered compliments.

Becca lay beside him on her back, breathing deeply after her last orgasm. *Phew!*

During the long hours of lovemaking, she hadn't wanted to give much thought to their predicament, to the violent men hunting them. Now, Rio's first words of the morning jerked her right out of her comfortable musing.

"Tonight, we have to move," he said. Beneath the covers he placed his hand on her bare abdomen and gave it a little caress before standing up in all his nude glory. Like a golden mythic god, his broad shoulders tapered to narrow hips and strong buttocks. His skin was tanned all over, as though he sunbathed in the buff. Becca couldn't look away. She'd never before seen a man so physically compelling, so *perfect*.

This incredible specimen of male animal was her lover? It was hard to believe. As she watched him stretch, raise his arms above his head and flex his shoulders, Becca felt herself grow warm. The heavy drag of her heartbeat thundered in her chest. Impossible, after the long hours of lovemaking, but she wanted him again.

As he dressed, obviously his mind was elsewhere.

Tamping down her sexual thoughts, she got up on one elbow. "We're leaving?"

"Soon as it's dark." He pulled on pants and drew a shirt over his head. "Since they haven't found a trail for us yet, those bastards out there will know that we've gone to ground. They'll really concentrate on combing the area. This place is too dangerous to stick around any longer."

"Where are we going?"

"I know a guy. He'll fly us north to Nuevo Laredo, near the Texas border."

"Okay." That sounded good, getting closer to the U.S., closer to her home state of Texas. Closer to home. "So, why Nuevo Laredo? Do you have another, what did you call it, a *hidey hole* there?"

He smiled, revealing his dimple. "No, but I have friends along the border."

"You're so resourceful," she said. "I bet you know a lot of fighting techniques and survival skills."

"A fair amount."

Beneath the quilts, she shivered. "I don't like to think about that mountain lion. I was so scared."

"Me, too."

"I've never been taught any survival skills. Maybe I should take a class."

He sat on the bed. "When confronted by danger, the most important thing to do is remain in control. Panic never helps. When you're in trouble, you should adopt an offensive mindset. If you're scared, the transition from defensive to offensive is essential."

"Offensive mindset," she said, thinking.

"And if you don't have a weapon, keep your mind open to anything in your environment to use against an attacker."

She cocked her head. "Like what?"

"Look around. See anything in here?"

She cast her gaze around the small room. "Just these quilts, your pack."

"No, look like you want to find a weapon."

She sat up in bed. "Okay, there's an old Phillips screwdriver on top of the mantle."

"Good! Anything else?"

"Mmm, not really."

"Do you normally carry a purse?"

"Yes."

"What in there could be utilized? If you have a pen, it can be used to stab someone. A comb can be shoved into a guy's lips—man, that would hurt. See where I'm going?"

"Yes."

"If we were outside, you could scrape up a handful of dirt or sand, throw it into an attacker's eyes. It could buy you time to scream, to run away."

"Okay, I'm beginning to get it." She tried to imagine being attacked and reacting properly.

"What are your strengths? What can you use? Think!"

"I'm thinking, I'm thinking." What was in her purse back home? A wallet. Tissues. Makeup.

He leaned over the quilt and cupped her breasts. "These are weapons, honey, never doubt it. Your confidence makes you wildly hot. To a man, it's very distracting." He gave her a wicked smile.

She smiled back.

Standing up again, he put on his coat and hat. "I'll have a look around. Stay inside."

She had no intention of going anywhere.

****

In deep thought, Rio retraced his path up the mountainside to his lookout point. The sun had come out and melted most of the snow, leaving slush and mud. He'd told Becca he wanted to look around, but he also wanted cell reception. Harrison had better have a good explanation for that fiasco last night.

At the top of his lookout near the outcropping of boulders, he peered through the field glasses. There was nothing going on close but miles to the south he saw unusual activity. Yep, he'd be getting Becca out of there as soon as the sun went down.

Taking out his phone, he waited for his call to connect.

"There was a fuck-up," Harrison said, as soon as he answered.

"No shit," Rio answered. "What happened? Those guys weren't sent by you."

"I can't explain right now. Just know that this thing has become a little complicated."

"What's that mean? They tried to blow my head off, and they weren't careful about hitting Rebecca De Monte, either. Wanna explain that?"

"I just got the report. The team I sent was ambushed by the cartel. Goddamn it, we lost seven men. All killed."

"Somebody told them about the rendezvous point," Rio said. "They were waiting in the right place."

"I know," Harrison said impatiently. "Just get Rebecca to the next location." He rattled off a new meeting point some sixty miles to the west. "I'll have my men there. Get that girl to me now."

"How can I be certain your guys won't be ambushed again? I don't like your plan."

"Don't turn into a rogue character, Lang." Harrison sounded aggravated. "I don't need you going off the reservation. Just do the job you contracted for."

"Maybe I'll take the girl home to her father

myself. That's what I'm getting paid for."

"No! You're getting paid to deliver her to me—to my men. There's a protocol here, a chain of command. And you're at the bottom. Hear me? This is political. Not your area of expertise."

"Yeah? Well, so far on this job I've been shot at *twice*. That sort of thing focuses the mind, you know?" He hesitated. "What do you mean it's political?"

"Just deliver the girl," Harrison growled. "You'll get a big bonus at the end. Double pay." The connection went dead.

Rio stood, his gaze still scanning the landscape. Nothing Harrison said alarmed him as much as the doubling of his pay. That had never happened before. What the hell was going on here?

Obviously he was being given only a small wedge of the information pie. He wanted the whole pie.

He thought of the woman below who waited for him in a warm nest of quilts. In bed, Becca had been sexually adventuresome, eagerly uninhibited, and sexy as hell. She was every man's dream bedmate and he felt his body hardening, just remembering.

But why was her life so valuable that different factions were fighting over her, with some desperately wanting her back, and some apparently trying to kill her?

The bad guys in pursuit weren't going to tell him. Harrison certainly wouldn't.

That left Becca. He had to talk to her.

First, he made a phone call and arranged for a flight to ferry them to a dirt landing strip just outside Nuevo Laredo. The trip was privately arranged, and no flight plan would be filed. The trip wouldn't exactly fall within the narrow parameters of flight law. However, he knew the pilot and would fill his palms with cash. The trip would be covert, with neither the knowledge of the

Mexican authorities, nor Harrison's, to hinder their travel.

Nothing Harrison had told him had given him confidence. He didn't like the uncertainty, or the possibility of yet another double crossing. And more deaths—maybe theirs. His boss had warned him to do as he was told.

He would, and he'd get that double-pay bonus. But he'd do it his own way.

Chapter Fourteen

When Rio got back to the cabin, he found Becca sitting on the edge of the bed braiding her hair. On top of the cooler was food she'd prepared in a simple meal. Granola bars, grapes, and dry salami slices were arranged on napkins. She smiled at him.

He was struck anew by her natural beauty, her dark eyes, her long hair and slim figure.

The homey scene put him in mind of a sweet little wife waiting for her husband to come home from a long day at work. The image was fleeting and for him, fanciful. He would never have a wife. His lifestyle wasn't conducive to marital happiness or longevity. His temperament was too independent, too restless. He wasn't the committing kind.

In seconds, the fantasy evaporated into the ether.

"We have to talk," he said, in a tone rougher than he intended. "Those guys waiting for you last night killed the team that was supposed to get you."

Becca's hands fell to her lap and her eyes grew huge. "Oh, my God. They—they were murdered?"

He took off his coat and sat beside her on the bed. "My boss said something about this being political. Know anything about that?"

She wrinkled her nose. "Political? I-I-"

"What?"

"My dad is currently running for a political position—for a senate seat. He's always been active in the party."

"A senator is a powerful position. What type of business does your dad run? You said you work for him."

"I do. Like I told you, it's a hubcap

distributorship. We sell vintage wheel covers as well as original equipment like manufactured items, alloy and aluminum. They can be bought individually, like to a collector looking for a single product, and also in bulk to car dealerships. I oversee work orders and the shipping department and I make sure the books are balanced. My two brothers are in sales. In recent years, my father has ceded a lot of the day-to-day responsibilities to my brothers and me. He's been spending more time traveling."

"So it's the three of you running the warehouse?"

"Pretty much. We have about two dozen valued employees. We all know what we're doing. Every once in a while, Uncle Tim stops by."

"Uncle Tim?"

"He's not really an uncle, we just call him that. He's my dad's good friend and business partner. A silent partner, mostly. He comes in every few weeks, actually a lot more lately, has coffee, sits around with the guys and asks how things are going. He doesn't really have anything to do with running the company."

"But he invested in it?"

"Originally, when dad started the company, Uncle Tim put up funds. A payment is made to him every month. In another year our debt to him will be paid in full."

"You like him? Uncle Tim?"

"Sure! I love him. He really is like our uncle. When we were young he'd bring us birthday gifts, small toys, ask how we were doing. Like I said, we've been seeing more of him lately. He's so friendly and interested in everything, sometimes he distracts me from my work." She gave a short laugh.

Rio studied her for a long moment. "Which part of your work?"

"What?"

"Which part of your work does Uncle Tim distract you from?"

"Rio, Tim isn't a villain. He's not a criminal or anything, if that's what you're—"

"I'm sure he's an angel. Just answer my question."

"Shipping," she said. "Each afternoon around three it's my habit to see that the orders are filled correctly. Of course I can't look into every container. The men in that department do that and we have pretty good quality control protocols. But I do like—"

"How big are the shipping containers?"

"Different sizes," she answered with confidence. "For smaller orders, we use cardboard boxes. For larger ones, wooden crates. Our big crates measure sixty inches, by twenty-four, by fifteen."

He rubbed his jaw. "A lot of things could fit into boxes of that size."

"Like what? What are you thinking?"

"I don't know."

"Look, my father's business is on the up-and-up." She sounded defensive. "Nothing nefarious is going on there. My brothers are honest, hard-working young men. And my Uncle Tim is harmless."

"Until we get to the bottom of who's so interested in you, nobody is harmless. Everyone is suspect. *Everyone.*"

Becca didn't respond.

"It's clear that some people, bad guys, want you dead. Other people, maybe also bad guys, want you alive. Why?" He gave her his hard-eyed stare.

Becca let her gaze fall to her hands, tightly clasped in her lap. He could see that the idea of militias and armed killers wanting to murder her was messing with her mind.

He didn't have time for that.

"Tell me about your home life," Rio demanded.

"I—I did. I work, go home, go jogging, watch TV. Sometimes I go out with friends."

"What else?"

"My life isn't exciting," she replied. "I don't do illegal drugs. I don't break laws. My one hobby is frogs. I have an aquarium filled with them."

"Frogs," he said curtly, as though they could be the culprits in the whole scenario.

She frowned. "I hope my roommate is feeding them."

"Roommate? I didn't know you had one."

"She's a flight attendant. Almost never there. But when she is, she's good about throwing the frogs some frozen bloodworms or fish flakes." She bit her lip. "I hope they're okay."

Rio gazed at her thoughtfully. "Of all the things you've told me, your work still sticks out. Maybe something is going on at your father's warehouse."

"It's hard to believe … but I need to get in there, look around." A new urgency appeared to seize her. "I need to see for myself what's going on."

"Right, but not during daylight hours. When we get across the border, nobody can know you're back in the States."

"But my dad, my brothers will be—"

He was already shaking his head. "Do you want to get to the bottom of this or not?"

"Yes, of course. But I'm not a detective. I don't know how—"

"I'll help you. I do know how."

She stared at him. "Why?" she whispered. "You owe me nothing. Even after…" She gestured awkwardly at the bed. "Why would you help me?"

He gazed at her coolly. "Don't forget, those assholes shot at me, too. Twice. I don't like that. I'll get you back home, Becca, that's my job. But along the way, we'll also find out why your life is hanging in the balance."

She felt her throat close, both in fear and in gratitude. Of one thing she was certain, her resolve hardened. She must get into the shipping department of the plant. If something was amiss, she'd discover it. If not, they would be able to dismiss any nefarious activity, or anything going awry in her father's warehouse. Alarmed now, she felt a desperate need to uncover the truth.

"One thing's for sure," he told her, "you're safer across the border in the United States. By late tonight we'll be in Nuevo Laredo. Tomorrow, we'll cross into the U.S."

"We don't have passports. How will we do that?" She spread her hands wide.

He winked. "Leave that to me."

****

At dusk, Rio announced it was time to go and Becca bundled up as best she could. She put on her blouse, Rio's t-shirt, and the sweatshirt over that. On her head, she pulled the cap low. Taking the large zip top baggie which had held the grapes, she placed inside slices of salami, crackers, the remaining granola bars, and two water bottles. She didn't imagine they'd be flying first class and served filet mignon and champagne.

He pulled on a sweatshirt, then drew the strap of his oilskin pouch over his shoulder. They were ready.

After a good hour on the Vespa, Rio turned down a dirt lane and motored along until they found a short airstrip. A single engine plane sat parked on the side.

"It's a Cessna 206," he told her. "With high wings ideal for landing on dirt roads, it's also modified so it can take off from short strips like this one." He gestured at the makeshift runway.

Becca gazed at the plane curiously. "What's that metal plate attached to the front?"

"It's another modification hung under the nose. It protects the engine from gravel."

The pilot, a Mexican national with a dark mustache, merely grunted a hello. Rio introduced him as Julio. Julio turned to Rio, and in Spanish he said, "You won't want to go to Nuevo Laredo. Some of the city's police force across the border in Laredo, Texas have been arrested for passing information about military movements to the drug cartels. People are in the streets protesting."

"That's actually perfect," Rio answered. "We can use the crowds and distraction to cross the border and get into the U.S."

When the pilot shrugged, they climbed aboard, and before Becca could orient herself, they were rolling and bumping along the lane and taking off.

They flew through the night sky, leaving the Chihuahua foothills and its mountain range behind. If Becca hadn't been so apprehensive, she would have breathed a sigh of relief.

But they weren't out of Mexico yet, and not yet out of danger. Rio's questions about her father's business made her concentrate. She didn't like the direction of her thoughts, but she must be honest. Uncle Tim had been around a lot lately, far more often than he had ever been before. And it always seemed that his visits were timed at two or three in the afternoon. Exactly when she normally inspected the day's shipping. Did these new visits have any significance?

Uncle Tim always seemed interested in having her attention during those visits, but he never had anything important to say. Why? Were the visits coincidental, or was something happening in shipping?

She wracked her brain to remember if anything else had been different lately and could think of nothing.

What was going on?

DORSEY ADAMS

Chapter Fifteen

The two-hour flight gave Becca more time to fret. She couldn't imagine that if indeed something nefarious was underway at her father's warehouse, that Uncle Tim was involved. Nor could she suspect her brothers. Their family was too close. She'd just know.

During the trip, they did no talking. Halfway through the flight, she took out her cache of food and water and they ate quickly. The last two granola bars she gave to Rio to put in his waterproof pouch.

On another dirt landing strip, if one could call it that, the pilot put down in only a swath of moonlight. At the end, he taxied to a stop. Rio pushed a generous handful of American dollars into his hands, and they disembarked. The pilot pointed to an old sedan parked in the field and flipped Rio a key. In moments, he was back in the air.

The first thing Becca noticed was the balmy air. No longer freezing, Becca sighed in relief. She really hated the cold.

Rio took out his cell phone and muttered a few phrases. Closing the connection, he and Becca climbed into the sedan and he started driving. Over a short hill she could see city lights. "Are we near Nuevo Laredo?" she asked.

"Yeah. But we won't go into town. Tonight we'll stay with some people I know. In the morning, we're in for a long swim."

"A what?"

"You're a good swimmer, no worries."

She was, but how could he know that? On her high school swim team, she'd excelled.

"We're gonna swim the Rio Grande. Cross the

river into United States territory, into Nuevo Laredo's sister city, Laredo, Texas."

Her mouth dropped open. "Like illegals entering the States?" she asked. "Like criminals?"

He looked at her without apology and scratched his chest. "Kinda like that, yeah."

"But—the Americans—they have border security," she protested. "They patrol that river constantly. It's impossible to get past them."

"Not for me."

She looked at him in exasperation. She had no option but to trust him, had to believe his confidence was founded in competency, experience, and knowledge. If he thought they could do it, then she would, too.

"Okay," she said, shaking her head. "All I know is I need to get into the building. If your suspicions are true, there will be something there out of place. I'll find it."

"I'll help you."

Becca slanted him a glance. Never in her life had she been so alone. Deadly killers were after her, and she had no idea why. Upsetting doubts about her family members filled her mind. Were they complicit in some illegality? It felt as though her pleasant life was falling apart. She had no one to rely on except herself.

And now Rio.

Taking a peek at his handsome profile, she felt insanely grateful he wanted to help her. She still wasn't certain why this aloof man was motivated to do so, but she didn't need to question it. For now, it was enough that he was committed to uncovering the truth.

In minutes, he drove down a country lane beneath tall trees. All was darkened, quiet.

"You seem to know exactly where you're going."

"I've made it my business to know my way around these border towns," he said.

She stared into the darkness. Somewhere on a nearby hill, a coyote howled. They went to the door of a small stucco house and it was opened by a middle-aged couple. Speaking in hushed voices, it was obvious they knew Rio. No lights were turned on.

"*Gracias*," Rio said in a low voice. By flashlight, they were shown into a tiny room with only a single twin bed. Backing out of the room, the couple left the flashlight and closed the door.

"We're safe here 'till dawn," Rio said. He gave Becca the small light, sat on the edge of the bed, and started to remove his boots.

Keyed up from the long flight and dark-of-night travel, she didn't move.

"Come on," he said. "Lie down here with me. Sleep. We only have three, maybe four hours before we're gone."

She moved to sit beside him on the bed and shone the flashlight on her loafers. They were scuffed and dirty. So were her socks, her pants, her shirt. She still wore his fleece sweatshirt and the knit cap. She didn't need three or four hours of rest, she needed a good long night of it, plus a hot bath. She needed freedom from worry. She needed peace.

Peace would not be found soon. She knew that.

"Rio," she whispered, "I'm so tired. But I don't think I'll be able to sleep. I'm scared."

He took her hand. "You've been sick, and I've kept you on the move. Of course you're tired. And you will sleep." He brushed his lips across her mouth.

Leaning toward him, she wound her arms around his neck and deepened the kiss. Their tongues met, entwined, danced together. Rio enfolded her in his arms. Taking a gasping breath, Becca found solace in the only person she could trust. In his arms, she didn't know fear, or unrest, or uncertainty. She knew safety.

Gently, he pulled his head back. "That was nice, honey. But, sorry, no sex tonight. Right now, sleep is more important to the mission."

Becca lowered her head. "Oh, the mission."

Rio leaned down, pulled off her loafers, and eased her back onto the bed with him. She curled to his side, his arm around her.

No matter what he said, she knew that no way would she be able to sleep.

****

At dawn's first light, Becca felt Rio shake her awake. "Time to go," he whispered into her ear. He got out his cell phone and made a hushed call.

Groggy, she sat up and tried to orient herself. They were in the tiny room. Outside of Nuevo Laredo. About to swim across the Rio Grande river.

Oh, boy.

Leaving a small pile of hundred dollar bills on the bed, Rio guided Becca down the hall to slip from the house. They walked along a dirt road, keeping to the side. While much warmer and more humid than their snowy cabin near the Chihuahua foothills, heavy fog blanketed the area. Keeping a close watch around them, Rio kept hold of her arm. This early, there were no residents up and about, and they heard only a few dawn-crowing roosters. Within a mile or so, Becca smelled dank water, like that of a sitting pond.

Leaving the road, they wended through trees and close-growing plants, avoiding any of the structures or shacks they passed.

At last they stopped in a heavy thicket. "Nuevo Laredo is connected to the U.S. city of Laredo by four international bridges over the river. We're near one at the end. They're all closely monitored by border security.

But people make illegal crossings every day. Either by water, or under the officials' noses hidden in vehicles. A lot of drugs make their way into the U.S. that way."

"That's awful," she said.

"It's the way it is."

Up on the bridge, early-rising souls drove cars in both directions. Their shapes were barely visible in the thick fog. The banks of the river were choked with brush and green bushes. Across the river, some seventy yards away, three white trucks were parked front end in, their bumpers almost to the water. Several uniformed border patrol agents stood around, chatting and smoking. Each man carried either a rifle or a handgun strapped to his hip.

Although she wasn't cold, Becca shivered.

The dank smell was stronger now and filled her nostrils.

Anxious, she held Rio's arm. "How in the world are we going to sneak by them?"

"We'll have a little help later on. I've hired people to create a diversion. For now, I'm going to make us some ghillie suits."

"Some gilly what?"

"Camouflage," he said. "Stay here. I'll be back in a few." He disappeared into the fog.

Within ten minutes he returned, his arms filled with cut ferns, green fronds, and long bunches of Bermuda grass. Taking a place beside her, he formed a long stalk into a circle and then wove different colored grasses and underbrush into a kind of crown.

Reaching over to pull off her knit cap, he placed the crown of leaves and fronds on top of her head. "The cap stays here," he told her. "That black color isn't found much in nature."

She touched the long clumps of grass sticking out from her head. She felt as though she were wearing a huge-brimmed, Kentucky Derby Panama style made of natural materials. "Wow," she said, filled with wonder at his ingenuity. "Will these really hide us from the authorities?"

"If we move slow, keep our bodies beneath the water, and you do everything I tell you."

She nodded vigorously. "Will do!"

Rio smiled. He leaned over his half-made straw hat and dropped a kiss on her lips. "You're adorable."

Becca wasn't sure about that. Her hair hadn't been washed in ten days, she'd had no shower in all that time, she wore no makeup and she'd been sick. "Do I smell?"

"You smell like buttercups."

She doubted that.

Finishing his own, larger hat, he set them both aside. "Let's have breakfast."

From his pouch, he took out their last two granola bars and handed her one. In silence, they ate.

"Rio," she said finally, "What if something truly horrible is going on at my father's business?"

"Horrible? That's an odd word. I'm thinking more along the lines of illegal."

"What if—" She swallowed the last of her granola bar with difficulty. "What if there are chopped up dead bodies in those shipping boxes?"

He did a double take, and grinned at her. "Little chance of that. Not much money to be made in dead body parts."

"So," she fiddled with her hat, "you think whatever is going on, it's all about money?"

"It always is." He sighed and glanced toward the river. The sun was just beginning to send searing rays through the fog and heat the air. "Time to go." He instructed her to take off her sweatshirt and leave on just her white button-down shirt. He took her loafers and his boots and tied them together using pliant reeds, and slung them to his shoulder. He still had his pouch.

"We'll sneak down to water's edge," he said quietly. "Step in my footprints in the mud. If I pause, you pause. If I sink down, you do it. No fast moves, no talking. Got that?"

"Got it."

"This won't be a quick journey," he continued. "It'll be slow. Very slow. It might take longer than you think it should. Just keep close and do what I do." He handed her a hollow reed.

"What's this for?"

"Once we're in the river, if I squeeze your hand, sink your whole face except your eyes below the waterline. Breathe through this."

"Okay."

"Even if you think someone has spotted you, or is looking in your direction at all, don't panic and don't look back at them. Lower your eyes. Humans can sense when they're being observed."

That made sense.

"Look at the river. See the current?"

She watched as an egret floated by them, and nodded.

"We're just two clumps of underbrush floating along the river, okay? That's all we are."

"Be the clump," she muttered to herself. "I am the clump."

He grinned briefly. "The last phone call I made this morning? I've arranged for a diversion, fifty yards that way." He pointed south and to the Mexican side of the river. A few families had started to arrive and the children were splashing as though in a pool. "When it starts, that'll be our cue."

She wanted to ask him what sort of diversion, but he was already moving ahead of her. Their journey had begun.

A single mantra played over and over in her mind: *please don't let us get shot at again, please don't let us get shot at again, please don't let us get shot at again.*

Chapter Sixteen

With the sun quickly rising overhead, the day heated. After all the freezing days she'd enduring, Becca enjoyed the ambient warmth. On her bare feet, the cool earth felt good. The smell of the river did not. Up to her knees in the water now, she found garbage swirling in eddies on the shoreline. A dead squirrel's body sprawled beside the trash. It stunk. The water was a murky green. She had no idea what lay beneath, and didn't want to know. Balancing their straw head-coverings, they entered the deepening water. Mud squished unpleasantly between her toes.

The last tall bridge of the four leading into Laredo loomed above them, its abutments sunk deep into the river.

Down past all the bridges, local families brought their children to splash in the shallows and picnic on the shores. Apparently it was a local hangout.

Bent almost to the ground, Rio crouched, keeping below the level of tall-growing Carrizo cane plants and out of sight of the border agents across the river. Becca had heard of the invasive Carrizo cane, and knew that it sent shoots up along waterway banks to form an interlocking network of subterranean roots. What she hadn't known was that she'd ever be grateful for its shielding properties.

Still hugging the shoreline, Rio held Becca's hand and slowly they sank to chin-level beneath the water. She waited for him to move farther into the river and when he didn't, she remained quiet next to him.

Deep inside, she was apprehensive, anxious. But infusing her fright was a certain unexpected level of anticipation. She was headed into a real life adventure, with the prospect of possible capture an outcome she couldn't dismiss.

She gulped. She must believe that Rio would protect her and guide her to safety. She must rely on him, trust him, and she did. Implicitly so.

In wonder, she tried to figure out when her shift in attitude had happened and discovered it didn't matter. What mattered now was following his lead, launching herself into the unknown. This was a frightening, hazardous, harrowing journey.

And against all logic she couldn't help thinking also, *this is exciting*!

Atop her hair, the Bermuda grass hung around her head and draped into the water. She could see through the hanging leaves. Wisps of the remaining fog drifted atop the river's surface.

For a good fifteen minutes, Rio didn't move. Under the water and beside him, Becca held tight to his hand. He'd told her to be patient, and to wait, and to be quiet, and not to speak.

She did not. Her heart beat swiftly in her chest.

Suddenly, a tremendous boom some hundred yards south of their position burst through the morning. Becca couldn't help it, she jerked. Instantly she felt Rio's hand press down on hers. She stilled, and that's when he made his move. Slowly, sinking down farther so only his eyes were above water, he moved into the slipstream of the water's gentle current. Swimming now, Becca placed her reed between her lips and tried to breathe.

On the far bank, men shouted, and down the river another, lesser boom exploded. Excited children's voices chattered. As they reached the first bridge abutment, Rio paused, allowing their head coverings to appear to catch on a cluster of tangled branches.

Across and over on the U.S. side, a border agent lifted binoculars. Becca tried to breathe normally. Was he trained on Rio and her? With every nerve on high alert, an alarm shrieked through her. Fighting the instinct to stare back, she lowered her eyes, and forced herself to remain calm and not move.

Above where her pant legs rode up, something slimy slid along her calf. She shuddered. Were there snakes in the river? Was it just a fish, or some biting riverine monster?

Chancing a glance across the river, she saw the man with the binoculars take a step closer. His boots in the water now, he appeared to sharpen his watch. He lowered his hand to his holstered pistol.

Were they spotted?

Near panic, Becca sucked air through her reed, and tried desperately not to strike out blindly for the Mexican side. She grew lightheaded.

As though sensing her panic, Rio squeezed her waist. He allowed their weed-constructed hats to touch. Inches away, she sought out his gaze and he did the unthinkable.

He winked.

If her mouth had been above water, she would have gaped.

Impossibly, inexplicable exhilaration filled her. Now in the middle of this bold journey, she found herself up to the task. She would follow Rio to the ends of the earth. They were in this together. Partners.

Despite all the contradictory emotions swirling through her, she held Rio's gaze … and winked back.

When the lines around his eyes crinkled, she knew he was grinning.

Down the way, three new explosions tore through the morning. On both sides, people ran along the riverbanks. An officer on the American side angrily shouted something through a bullhorn. It sounded threatening.

The man Becca thought was watching them turned away, gestured at others, and pointed at the source of the sounds. They headed upstream.

Rio's hand on her waist urged her forward. Slowly, again they set out across the water. Keeping together in leisurely side strokes, Rio guided their movements to coincide with the flowing current. He swam easily, confidently, at one with the water. His proficiency made her remember his past life: he'd once been a Navy SEAL. Such men were half fish.

She was an excellent swimmer, but her skills were nothing next to his.

His clever movements brought them farther down the river rather than straight across. To any observers, they were merely a few clumps of vegetation among thousands that had broken off from the river's edge and were now floating along on the breeze.

Finally reaching the far side, Rio allowed them to come to rest next to a new growth of Carrizo cane. For several moments, he didn't move. Becca forced herself to remain still and not go wildly splashing up the embankment.

At last, he guided her beneath the water to precede him up the muddy bank. Somehow through his touch, he communicated with her to move with exaggerated care, making no quick moves, and to melt into the surrounding vegetation.

They crept through the cane, keeping low, until they entered a tree line. Beyond the stand of trees, Becca saw a towering chain-link fence. Not far past that, cars dotted a paved road. Rio pressed her to sit beside a thick cottonwood trunk.

"Nice field craft," he whispered. "You followed orders, moved slowly, and didn't panic. Well done."

"Thanks," she whispered back. "What were those explosions?"

"Just fireworks like Chinese crackers. A couple were pretty heavy duty, like cherry bombs and bottle rockets. Airbombs. I paid a couple of the locals to set 'em off."

"Okay. Good idea. But there's a huge fence over there."

He twisted his head to look. "So there is." He rubbed his chin. "Now, how are we gonna get past that?"

Inside, Becca blanched. He didn't know?

By dint of a diversion downriver and tremendous luck, they'd thus far evaded the border patrol. Just yards from their hiding spot and beside the fence, a truck engine fired up and rolled slowly along the line. With the singular attention of roving Doberman Pinschers, the uniformed men inside scanned the area.

When they had passed, Rio grinned at her. His dimple came to life. "Just kidding. There's a breach. I had a kid snip an opening with bolt cutters last night." He took off his crown, tossed it aside. From his shoulder bag, he pulled out his pistol and wallet. He also untied their shoes and handed over her wet loafers.

Becca stared at him, at his grin, and remembered his wink in the middle of the river, right at the very height of danger. "This is like a game to you, isn't it?"

"A game I'm gonna win, baby," he returned easily. He flashed the dimple again. "Fun, huh?"

Becca gazed at him in bewilderment and consternation. Their lives were in danger and he thought this was *fun*?

Taking off her own crown of weeds, she turned it round and round in her hands. After a moment, she thought that on some level, despite her panic and fear, she understood. On some level, *she* was having fun, too.

Chapter Seventeen

With difficulty, Rio and Becca found the breach, crawled through, and began to casually amble down the paved street. People were out in throngs, protesting, just as the pilot, Julio, had told them. Some held signs, NO CROOKED POLICE in both English and Spanish. CUT OUT THE ROT, they said. A man on a makeshift stage shouted slogans and exhorted the populace to keep up the good fight. The people of Laredo would no longer accept a corrupt police force.

Quickly, Rio and Becca were lost in the crowd.

In the warmth of the day their clothes dried. Cars rolled by and people walked to and from the border terminal. Holding hands, to a casual observer, they would appear to be part of the protest.

To cover his bright hair, Rio pulled on his black cap. There had been one dicey moment in the middle of the river when the border agent had raised binoculars and it seemed they'd been spotted. In that instant, Rio had winked at Becca, and bless her, she'd winked back.

Her eyes had been bright with fear, but also excitement. The idea gave his spirits a grand lift. No panicked, mindless female was she! No, she'd kept her wits, followed his every command, and they'd made it safely across. Most of all, she'd shown him that in the moment of highest danger, she was capable, strong, and almost enjoyed the peril. She'd felt some of his same thirst for risk. He'd seen it in her eyes. Now *that* was a real woman. He gazed down at her in pleasure.

"Now what?" she said, keeping her voice low. "We need a vehicle." Three angry women walked by, carrying placards, yelling in protest.

"I'll get us that vehicle," Rio said. "First, I'll give you money, leave you in the shopping mart. Get us some new clothes and shoes. Size twelve for me. Nothing fancy. And buy me some shades, okay?"

"Are you going to steal a car?"

He looked at her. "What do you think I am? A spy? No, I'll rent one." He grinned. "For cash."

"Don't you need ID? Insurance?" She paused. "Oh, I get it. With enough cash, you don't need those."

"You're quick. I like that."

Within minutes they made it to the town, where the crowd thinned. With its two and three story buildings and end-to-end shops beneath, some of the buildings were painted orange, some yellow. Most had long, colorful awnings protecting the store's wares below. The outdoor area featured dozens of vendors hawking trinkets, Mexican sombreros, jewelry, and clothing. Rio pulled her into a small alcove and pressed bills into her hand with a promise to be back soon. "Stay off the street," he ordered. "The fewer people that see you, the better."

****

Within seconds, Becca was lost in the marketplace. She mingled with the crowd. Choosing carefully, she made her purchases and also bought water and hot steamed tamales. She was paying for her last purchase when a car pulled up and she glanced over. Rio sat behind the wheel of a dirty, ancient sedan of indeterminate color. She'd call it *rust*.

He gestured for her, and she hurried out with her packages to climb into the passenger side.

"What? No Vespa?" she asked.

"Naw," he said, pulling into traffic. "We're riding in style."

She glanced around at the torn upholstery,

weathered windows, and beat-up floorboards. "I can see that." From her bag she withdrew a pair of Ray-Ban Wayfarer sunglasses, and he put them on.

"It's about a three-hour drive to San Antonio," he said. "You should rest until we get there."

"I can't rest." She opened her food containers and handed him a warm tamale. "The only thing I can think about is my dad, and my uncle. And my brothers. They can't be doing anything illegal."

"We'll find out," he said, wolfing the food. "Any more?" He pointed at her bag.

Unable to eat, Becca took out more food and watched as he drove and chewed. Now that his hair had dried and he'd taken off his cap, some of it fell over his forehead, lending him a jaunty look. He drove easily, with one wrist draped over the old steering wheel. Even with their dirty-water swim, and in the same clothes for days, he looked impossibly handsome. In his sunglasses, he appeared the epitome of cool. She could imagine him posed like this in a slick retro ad for a men's magazine. Perhaps for an expensive cologne. *Buy this, and you'll look like him*, the advertisement would say. She shook her head at the fanciful thought.

In her mind, like snapshots in time, memories of their long night in bed flashed before her. His slow, luxurious caresses, his obvious pleasure in her body and her delight in his. Warmth seeped through her veins and all at once she wanted him again. She didn't know him well, was only learning his personality little by little. But physically, he was spectacular.

She pushed aside such thoughts. How could she be sexually stimulated during a time of such danger? Why did she feel excitement as much as she did fear?

Perhaps it was her body's way of reminding her of the importance of life, the fragility of it, the preciousness.

"Why?" she asked abruptly. "Why are you doing this?"

"Driving you to San Antonio? Told you. It's my job."

"But it's not your job to help me figure out what's going on at De Monte Wheel Solutions ... if something is," she tacked on.

He shrugged. "Don't have anything else for a few days. I'm sure by week's end I'll have a new assignment, and you'll see the last of me. Meanwhile, I like a good mystery. Especially if it's illegal." He waggled his eyebrows.

She liked a good mystery too, but usually when it was in a novel.

And she guessed his answer was as good as she would get. She shied away from pressing. For now, she desperately needed his help.

"The warehouse is closed at night, correct?" he asked.

"Yes, there's no night crew."

"Good. And you've got keys? Where do you keep them?"

"On a hook in my condo's kitchen. When I leave for work in the morning, I just grab them. Because I'd gone to my college roommate's home in Mexico City, I didn't take them. When we get to town, I'll go over and pick them up."

"You can't," he said. "Your condo is probably under surveillance."

She felt her eyes widen. "I hadn't thought of that."

"Becca, no one can know you're back in the states. Not yet. Not until we find out if you're still in danger."

She breathed in deeply. "Okay."

"I'll get us a no-tell motel room, sneak over to your place and grab the keys."

"But how? Why do you think you won't be seen?"

He didn't take his eyes off the road. "No one will see me."

She thought about how he'd snatched her from the cantina's bathroom right under the noses of her captors. He'd kept her hidden in the mountain cabin, even saved her from certain recapture from the cartel. She reminded herself of how he'd constructed their ghillie suit hats, had successfully maneuvered them past watchful guards and across the river into the United States. For whatever reason, Rio was still assisting her. And he was good at what he did.

"I'm glad you're here with me," she told him. "And I have confidence in you. It's obvious that you know what you're doing. You're the expert. From now on, I'll try to do everything you say."

He did take his eyes off the road then.

She couldn't tell what he was thinking behind his glinting sunglasses, but she gave him a nod and a soft smile.

He took off his sunglasses, and she found that the same blue flames that had animated his eyes during their lovemaking had come alive again. "I want you." Taking a quick glance at the road, his gaze returned to travel over her breasts, down her body. "Do you want me?"

"Oh," she breathed, fidgeting. *Oh, God.* "Yes. Yes, I do."

He slid his shades back on his face. "Good. Man, it's gonna be a long drive." A wry grin twisted his lips. "That part about doing everything I say? That was pretty funny. You're not exactly the meek type."

"I said I'd *try*."

"When we arrive in San Antonio and find a motel, I'll get the keys and late tonight I'll sneak over to your dad's factory, and check it out."

"Sounds like a plan. I'm going, too."

"Becca—"

"I'm going." She set her jaw.

He hesitated, then gave his trademark shrug as though it was her choice and he cared little.

She found it bothered her, his retreat into indifference. During their hours of lovemaking, he'd been anything but indifferent. She wondered if he used the cool attitude to insulate himself from the world, like a shell or invisible armor … or a ghillie suit.

"This evening in the motel, we won't have much to do for several hours. We'll just have to rest…" He grinned wolfishly. "And stuff."

****

As soon as they checked in, Rio left her alone in the low-rent motel room to shower and wait for his return. When he drove away, she locked the door securely, and using the motel's shampoo, washed her hair twice. In the bathroom, she found a room-supplied comb, so she worked it through her long hair until it hung heavy and damp down her back.

Making a pot of coffee with the hotel's equipment, she nursed the black brew. It was bitter and a poor replacement for her beloved Ethiopian Arabica coffee beans, but it was all she had and she desperately craved it.

Putting on new undergarments, white cotton capris pants, and the white embroidered Mexican peasant top felt good. A new pair of white tennis shoes and socks finished her outfit. On the bed she laid out the khaki pants, new T-shirt and shoes she'd bought for Rio. He'd told her he would take a shower when he got back.

Peeking through the motel draperies into the parking lot, she saw that it was beginning to get dark. He hadn't told her how he was going to get inside her condo. She'd only given him her address and a description of the building.

However, now that she'd seen the imaginative way he solved problems, she'd no doubt he'd find a way.

Gazing longingly at the room telephone, she wished she could call her father, reassure him of her safety. She wished she could call Maria, her old roommate, and make certain that during the violent kidnapping, she and her father hadn't been hurt.

Reluctantly, Becca made no calls.

Picking up a newspaper left on the nightstand, she scanned it for news and found nothing about any American woman kidnapped from the Mexican ambassador's home. When she flipped on the TV and watched an entire news cycle, there was no reporting on her case there, either. As Rio had told her, somebody high up was keeping a lid on this.

Pacing the room, she chewed nervously on a knuckle.

At last, Rio pulled into a nearby parking spot.

She opened the door and stood back. "Did you get the keys?" she asked.

He held up a jingling set and locked the door behind him. "Doesn't look like your roommate has been home at all. The place is closed up, no new food in the fridge, all your mail still on the floor from the mail slot in the front door."

"Oh." She thought about that. "It's pretty normal for her to be gone for a couple of weeks at a time. She might not even know I've been gone."

"I fed your frogs," he said. "Found some frozen

blood worms and brine shrimp in the freezer and defrosted it real fast in hot water. Threw that in the tank right in front of their faces. I also gave them some sinking pellets you had there. Little guys were pretty hungry."

Becca gazed at him in wonder. She loved her African dwarf frogs, and knowing that Rio had stopped long enough to feed her pets warmed her heart. "Thank you," she whispered.

Moving to the bathroom to start the shower, he came back and drew his t-shirt over his head before starting to unzip his pants. "Well, I am a frogman."

For a moment she didn't understand. Then, it dawned on her. "Oh, you were Navy SEAL."

"I was a SEAL, but I'll always be a frogman."

With that, he disappeared into the bathroom and she heard him washing beneath the hot spray. In minutes he came out. He'd rubbed his hair and slicked it back with the comb. Around his ribbed waist, he'd tied the towel.

"Way I figure it," he said, lifting her blouse to place a warm palm on the bare skin of her hip, "we've got at least six hours before we can sneak into the warehouse." He caressed her skin. "You tired?"

Becca wound her arms around his neck. "No." She touched her lips to his and caught her breath. Desire snaked through her veins like a flash fire. "Not one bit."

Folding her into his arms, Rio lowered his head.

And he let the towel drop.

Chapter Eighteen

"You fed my frogs," Becca said, as Rio drew her shirt over her head and took her breasts into his hands. "I'm so happy you did that for me."

"I plan to do sweet, sweet things for you, Becca," he said, gently rolling her nipple between his thumb and forefinger. She sucked in air. Pleasure spiraled through her veins, flowed down her body in a languid, fluid river.

When her nipple puckered, he smiled. "Look how fast you respond to me." Lowering his head, he took her into his mouth and she moaned. Thick and insistent, his hard-on dug into her hip.

There was nothing in the world she loved more than having her breasts touched, massaged, licked, kissed. Except perhaps for equal attention paid to her lady parts. As though Rio could read her mind, he whispered, "Lay back, honey," and he guided her to sit on the bed.

She eased onto her back, her legs dangling over the edge as he drew off her pants.

When she was nude, he settled himself on the floor between her thighs. Learning and discovering the contours of her skin, his touch was tender, exploring, worshipping. Excitement shot through her system.

He stroked her thighs, ran his hands over her calves and back up again. Leaning over, his face close to her sex, he breathed in deeply. "God, you smell good. So sexy."

Becca closed her eyes.

He moved a bit of her pubic hair to the side, and when she felt his tongue touch her clitoris she nearly jerked upright. It felt like the best electric shock in the world. Rio delved deeper, licked her, painted her most intimate place with his tongue. His beard stubble rasped against her inner thighs, sending her excitement higher. She shivered in delight. Rio was *all* man, and he wanted her, no other. *Her.*

Thrusting her hands through his thick hair, she caressed his skull, trailed her fingers over his nape. Delirious with pleasure, Becca felt her world telescope down to this single moment. She reveled in their differences, celebrated them, was in awe of them.

Rio paid her rapt attention, his tongue delving into her, then navigating back up to her clitoris. At first with a light touch, he remained there, and his tongue grew insistent, and then firm.

Becca's felt her entire body climb, aching, as she strained against him. Her body lifted off the bed, mindlessly demanding now, and she pressed his head into her flesh. The pleasure built inside in bright, vibrant ribbons.

With his hands, he played with her breasts, squeezed her nipples. In moments she was gasping for air and thrashing on the bed.

The climax rose like a great wave speeding to shore. "Rio," she exclaimed in a guttural whisper. "*Rio!*"

When the wave crashed, sending currents through her, quickly he covered her body and pushed inside. She was wet, ready for him, and even while the reverberations of her orgasm were fading away, she found a new excitement in his movements.

He watched her face, and rocked her inevitably toward another orgasm. Wanting to give him as much pleasure as he'd already given her, she used her sexual muscles to squeeze him. When he groaned, she knew he enjoyed it. Giving him better access, she spread her legs wide and drew her bent knees up high.

"That's so nice, Buttercup," he said in a low

growl. As he quickened his tempo, she knew he was getting close. "That's real *nice*." Placing both his hands beneath her buttocks, he pumped harder. The bed squeaked from his rhythmic thrusts.

She came again on nearly his final push, sending him over the edge.

"Becca," he breathed, sucking in great lungfuls of air.

****

He stayed inside her for a long time. Longer than she would have imagined, but she liked it. The intimacy between them was a thing to be cherished. She knew there would be no future relationship for them, and she must enjoy what he offered in the here and now.

Drunk with spent passion, she had no wish to move anyway.

Finally, he rose and retrieved a damp, warm washcloth from the bathroom. Carefully, he cleaned her, and then himself, giving her little kisses on her nose, her cheeks, her eyes.

"Sleep," he commanded, taking her into his arms again. "I'll wake you when it's time for us to go."

Four hours later, Rio woke her with a kiss. "Time to head out," he said.

Instantly Becca awoke. Outside the motel room, it was pitch dark and near midnight. She sat up, pushed her hair from her eyes and hunted around for her clothing. "You know what I hope? I hope we don't find anything suspicious at all. I want everything to be normal. Legal. Above board. None of my loved ones involved in anything terrible."

Pulling on his pants, Rio did not respond.

"Maybe those Mexican bandits were simply opportunists and discovered I'd be visiting Maria in Mexico and kidnapped me, hoping for money. Maybe this has absolutely nothing to do with my dad's business."

Rio gave her a wary glance. "Yeah, maybe." It was clear he didn't think so.

Becca stubbornly continued to believe she was right. Her entire family had always been law-abiding, with no black sheep, no criminals or shady characters. Yanking her shirt over her head, she set her chin. Of course they must investigate. Kidnapping was not a thing to be taken lightly. She shivered, remembering that violent evening, and the following days and nights of awful captivity. This would be a chance to exonerate her father, her brothers, her uncle. She'd show Rio. They were all innocent.

Driving across town in the old beater Rio had rented in Laredo, he followed Becca's directions through San Antonio and pulled into a parking spot some two blocks away from her father's warehouse. In an industrial section of the city, there were many complexes, factories, and manufacturing plants. Here and there night crews arrived for or left work, but most of the buildings were dark. A few cars rolled each way down the streets.

Although both Rio and Becca wore light-colored clothing, there was no helping that now, so they didn't try to hide. They walked, hand in hand, like a happy couple out after a late night on the town.

At the corner of the building, Becca indicated the correct two-story building and showed him where a side door led inside.

Rio glanced left and right, and then nodded. Together they slipped down a concrete walk between buildings until they found the door. He slid the key into the lock and it opened.

Holding the door, he ushered her inside and closed it quietly behind them. He pocketed the key.

Inside the building, it was dark.

"This the front of the business?" Rio whispered.

"Yes, the receptionist area, then behind that, cubicles for sales people. Our offices are just past this area." She pointed past rows of desks down a wide hallway.

He hesitated in an open doorway. "What's in here?"

"That's the day care room. It opens to an outdoor patio where the children can ride tricycles, get a little sun."

"Children?" He raised a brow.

"Yes, for our employees who are parents. Rio, we don't have time—"

"You provide day care?"

"Yes," she said impatiently. "When I came to work here after college, I noticed our employees rushing off to pick up their kids. Some of the moms were sad, and they missed them. So, why not provide care here? The mothers and fathers can visit their kids any time, have lunch with them, and when their shift is over, they don't need to drive anywhere to get them. Simple. Now, let's go."

Moving with her down the hallway, Rio said, "How does this business work? You said it's a distributorship."

"I wish you could see the warehouse on a normal work day," she said in a low voice. "It's so busy, with people working hard both in the shop and here in the offices. But right now there's no time for that. We need to get moving, okay? There isn't time for a tour." Didn't he understand the need to hurry?

"Just a mini-tour, then."

"Argh!" Frustrated, she clasped her hands together. "Okay. Real quick, De Monte Wheel Solutions is a distributorship, and more. We sell hubcaps both in bulk to car manufacturers, and also if a private customer wants just one special wheel cover. We stock vintage, as well as new. Also, we have a reconditioning division." She hesitated, then said with no small amount of pride, "We strive to beat our competitors. That's why I keep such close tabs on shipping. Those costs can rise pretty fast."

Something akin to admiration came alive in his eyes. "You really care about this place," he stated softly.

She blinked. "Of course I do. It's my family business."

"Understood. And I can see why it's important to you. Right now, I want to see the floor itself," Rio said. "We can look into the offices afterwards. One day, I'll want a full tour of the place. Got any flashlights in here?"

"I think my brother has a little penlight in his desk."

"Grab it."

"Okay. The machinery is in back. There's one big shop with different staging areas and a loading dock." She opened the second door, went to the desk and found a small flashlight.

Rio nodded, and she led the way past the offices to the warehouse. While the hallway leading into the shop was dark, Becca was startled to see light emanating from the rear of the building.

Behind her, Rio must have seen the same thing. He squeezed her arm in warning. Did she hear voices?

Moving silently along the wall, they entered the shop, a large single area of some eighty thousand square feet. Steel i-beams loomed with rows of product stacked high between them. Machinery, tooling, and wooden pallets containing hubcaps were arranged with pathways zigzagging neatly through the labyrinth.

They kept the penlight low. A ramp along the wall led to an upstairs viewing station and restrooms. That area of the floor was dark. Rio squeezed her again, and when she looked at him, he thrust his chin at the ramp.

Together they crept upward, well concealed by darkness. At the viewing station they stopped, and knelt below the top railing to peer downward.

At the rear of the shop, the large doors opened and Becca gasped.

Lights in the back were turned on, spotlighting a man directing three others to load up a forklift and move crates to a waiting flatbed on the loading dock. Recognizing the man giving directions, she froze. Her heart rate skyrocketed.

"Let me guess," Rio whispered in her ear, "The sweet and innocent Uncle Tim?"

Numbly, she swallowed hard and nodded.

Quietly, they watched the process and stayed low while her Uncle Tim and the other men pushed some of the wooden boxes to a corner and piled tarps and equipment on top. They closed the doors and locked them from the outside. The truck's engine rumbled to life and it was driven away.

Becca couldn't imagine what her uncle might be doing there at this time of night. Confusion filled her.

Rio stood. "Let's go down there, see what's in those boxes they left behind."

Hurrying down the ramp, the small light affording just enough illumination, they made it to the floor, and wove around equipment to the back of the shop.

The men had piled steel bars and handheld machinery on top of the boxes.

Rio took them off, then the tarp, and set them all aside. "Camouflage," he said, "so no one looks in here until they can move the boxes. I'm guessing they're moving whatever it is in small lots. Less noticeable that way."

"If Uncle Tim is coming here at night, why distract me during the day?"

"Maybe he's ramping up deliveries and needs to double them."

She helped him lift the last item off the top crate. Hunting around for something to crowbar it open, Rio found a steel rod, wedged it under the top and it popped free. Becca held the light over the top.

Inside, long black rifles lay side by side. Becca gulped.

Rio lifted out a weapon and studied it with an expert eye. "Gun running," he said. "Some nice AK-47s here. Lucrative."

"But illegal." A sudden outrage took hold of her. "Damn him! I didn't even know Uncle Tim had a key! I can't believe he put us all in danger like this. And for what?"

"Money." Rio fitted his eye to the sight. "But I've got a bigger question."

Still fuming, Becca said, "What?"

"Is your father involved?"

Chapter Nineteen

"Oh my God," Becca murmured. "I can't imagine that my dad would do anything illegal like this. Sell weapons, of all things."

Rio set the rifle aside and inspected the wooden crate. "No markings except for a number. Wonder if there's any clue about where these puppies are going. The number should correspond to a purchase order, right? Maybe there's a paper trail."

"Yes, in fact any purchase order should go through my office. I see them all. Let's go. I'll show you."

Carefully. Rio put everything back as they'd found it, and moved to follow her up the ramp and down the hallways.

At the first door, Becca opened it and Rio pushed inside. He used the penlight to search the room. A typical office, it featured a desk, a tall fiddle fig plant in the corner, and a few framed photos of her family.

Pinned to a bulletin board, he saw notes in childish scrawlings. *Thank you*, Miss De Monte, one said, and beneath that was a crudely drawn dark-haired woman with a big smile. Becca. He guessed it might have been made by one of her employee's kids. He figured that for working parents, this hubcap business must be a great place. Becca appeared to be an understanding and flexible employer. That was pretty cool, her attention to detail. She was incredible.

Becca took a seat at her desk … and found nothing. "Where's my desktop?" she asked, looking around.

"Your computer is gone?" he asked.

"It's not here."

Rio met her gaze. "Can you get into your brother's computer files?"

"Yes, I know the passwords." They went into the next office and she sat at the computer. Typing in a few commands, it took only a moment to discover there were no purchase orders that looked unusual or different.

"Bet those crates are going to Mexico," Rio said. "To the cartel that grabbed you."

"But why kidnap me?"

"Maybe the cartel took you originally for ransom money. But for whatever reason, they didn't want you getting away, going back home. If they think you stumbled on your Uncle Tim's extracurricular activity here, you might know too much for their comfort."

"But I didn't know anything."

"They can't afford to take that chance. Better to take you, even kill you before you possibly blab to the authorities. They've got a sweet deal going here."

Becca shook her head, overwhelmed. Unexpectedly, her eyes filled. "Does Uncle Tim want me dead?"

Rio squeezed her shoulder. "We don't know how deep he's in this. It looks bad, but let's not draw any conclusions yet."

She sniffed. "Okay."

"We need a face-to-face, Becca. With your dad. It's vital to know if he has any connection to the gun running happening in his own business."

"Is it safe for me to call him now?" She wiped her eyes.

"Let's not tip him off ahead. Do you know where he might be tomorrow? In town?"

"I can check his schedule. His campaign keeps it online and I know that password, too." In a hurry, she pulled up her father's day-to-day appointments. "He's due to speak at a political fundraiser tomorrow night. It's here in San Antonio at a private residence. A mansion belonging to a local bigwig businessman."

"An outdoor rally? Casual? That type of thing?"

Again, Becca scanned the website. Before she could answer, he asked, "Tell me it's not a dress-up event."

"Black tie champagne reception."

He groaned. "I hate getting stuffed into business suits."

"It won't be a business suit," she said. "It'll be a tuxedo and tails."

With his thumb, Rio rubbed a spot between his eyes.

At his obvious discomfort, her tears dried and she suppressed a smile. "Something tells me you'll look okay in a tux."

****

Rio didn't look just *okay* in his black tuxedo. He looked fabulous. Using his cache of money, they'd gone to a clothing rental shop and while she found a stretchy fitted black dress and heels, he'd been outfitted in the formal suit.

Now that he was clean shaven, with his hair brushed back from his forehead, she saw that his muscular body nicely filled out the crisp white dress shirt and black jacket and trousers. A satin detail lined the lapels. With his tanned skin, vivid blue eyes, and blond hair, he would have outshone any movie star on an Academy Awards red carpet.

When he presented himself, Becca was momentarily speechless.

"I look all right?" he asked, fastening a gold cuff link.

"More than all right." Reaching up to straighten his bowtie, Becca took in every facet of his appearance, from his neatly brushed hair to his gleaming dress shoes. She decided it wouldn't do any harm to tell him the truth. "You're a gorgeous man, Rio."

"Think so?" He grinned. "Does that mean I might get lucky later tonight?"

Becca shrugged, deliberately allowing her breasts to sway. The stretchy black sheath dress fit her every hill and valley down to her lower calves. The mermaid style covered the bandaged wound on her leg and plunged scandalously low in front. Her slim arms were bare. She wore no bra and when she moved, a tantalizing curve of side breast showed.

Instantly, Rio's gaze dropped to her cleavage. "You've got a little exhibitionist in you. Don't you?"

Her cheeks pinkened. "I don't know." She glanced away.

He pulled her close, ran his finger down her neckline and drew a pattern over the tops of her breasts. "It's okay, Becca. I don't mind."

"Really?" She sought his gaze. "My other boyfriends didn't like it. You know, if I wore something revealing. Or if … if I wanted to flash someone. Just for fun, you know? They were threatened."

"As long as all of this," he cupped her breast, "is just for me, I'm not threatened."

Becca caught her breath, and met his gaze. "I'm just for you."

Rio placed his hands on her rear and pulled her close to kiss her thoroughly. Lifting his head, he gave her a wicked grin. "Promise to flash me every once in a while?"

She nodded.

He fingered the black dress. "If we don't go right

now, this scrap of fabric is coming off."

Becca hesitated, tempted. After their visit to her family business, and Rio's insistence on what he called a mini-tour, she appreciated his intellectual curiosity. It was a trait sorely lacking in her recent boyfriends. He'd expressed genuine interest in how things were done at the warehouse, and seemed to admire her efforts. He'd made her feel good about her drive, her attention to detail, her hard work. He *understood.*

Unfortunately, they couldn't afford to miss her father's political event. Sighing, she picked up her bag and headed for the door. With even greater reluctance, Rio followed.

****

Their cab pulled smoothly up to the gates of the grand San Antonio mansion. Since Becca's car was still parked at her condo carport, and the rusty beater Rio had rented wouldn't do, they used a car service.

The home's Spanish Colonial architecture created a mood of charm and grace. White, with a barrel tile roof, the house featured carved stone columns wrapping around windows and porches. Soaring stone arches rose gracefully from the ground floor to a high second story. Mature Monterrey oak trees grouped around the curved driveway flanked by well-trimmed hedges. Every light in the house and gardens had been turned on and the compound blazed.

As their driver wheeled away, they approached a man guarding the gate. As part of her father's security detail, Becca realized he was someone she knew.

"Can you get us by him?" Rio muttered into her ear.

"I think so." She greeted the man. "Hi, Gill. How are you? How's Emily?"

"Good evening, Miss De Monte. Emily is well."

He glanced over a clipboard and looked troubled. "I— I'm sorry, but you're not on the list tonight."

She squeezed Gill's arm. "I know. I'm surprising my dad. He doesn't know I'm coming. Don't radio up to the house."

Eying Rio with clear misgivings, Gill hesitated. "I don't know, Miss De Monte. It's against policy."

Rio returned his gaze coolly.

Becca took Rio's hand in hers, and leaned her head on his shoulder. "Come on, Gill. My date and I will only be here for a little while. I just want to surprise Daddy. He won't be happy with you if you stop us. Now, don't say a word and I won't tell him about this."

"I'm not sure…"

As though he hadn't answered, Becca casually walked past him, still linking hands with Rio.

Gill looked confused.

When they were several yards past and he made no move to stop them, Rio whispered, "Nice work."

At the soaring front door, they were greeted by two men dressed in black directing guests into the main salon. Expansive stone-cut travertine flooring led to stone wall plaster finishes and cathedral ceilings.

A crush of cocktail-attired people chattered amid the chink of champagne flutes chimed against each other. Servers passed with trays of oyster-on-the-half-shell. In one corner, a cigar roller was busy at his craft. The women were all in fashionable, glittering dresses, and the men in tails and coats. Eagerly, Becca scanned the room until her gaze fell on her father, holding court in the middle of a knot of men across the room. Well groomed, in an expensive suit, the handsome fifty-year-old seemed in his element.

Intent on making a beeline for him, she was stopped by Rio's hand on her elbow.

"Wait a second," he said. "He'll be pretty surprised to see you. We don't need a scene. Remember, he doesn't know you've been rescued. We need to get him into a private room."

"Got it." To the left she spotted a pair of closed doors, presumably a library or guest room. That would do.

As they approached, she saw Daniel De Monte's gaze stray from the men in front of him and he caught sight of her. His mouth dropped open. He gasped. "Rebecca?"

"Dad!" She flew into his arms. Rio stood back.

Hugging her tight, the older man exclaimed, "Oh, God, I can't believe it! You're safe!"

The people surrounding Daniel looked on curiously.

Rio came forward. "Since it's been a good two weeks since you've seen her, I'm sure you'll want a private word with your daughter," he said, indicating the closed doors.

Before he could react, Becca urged her father toward the room. "Yes, Daddy, come talk to me for a minute."

One of the men standing beside Daniel faded back, stepped away from the others. He was bald, with lightly pocked skin and a reserved manner. He said nothing and Becca barely noticed him.

Looking confused but relieved, Daniel De Monte allowed himself to be herded into the room. When a tall, rather muscular man who appeared to be a bodyguard tried to follow, Becca said to her father, "Just us, okay, Dad?"

He waved the bodyguard off and Rio closed the doors.

Inside, the paneled room was walled by

hardbound books and featured a broad desk and groupings of club chairs. A fire crackled in an enormous fireplace.

Daniel took his daughter by the shoulders, and searched her face. "I'm so happy to see you. You can't imagine how worried I've been. Are you all right?"

"I'm fine now, thanks to Rio." She broke the embrace to look at her rescuer, standing behind her. "He got me away from the Mexican cartel. This is Rio Lang."

"Mr. Lang, I'll assume you work for Black Eagle?" He held out a hand.

In the fireplace, a log snapped and briefly blazed. Sparks flew upward into the flue.

Rio took the shorter man's hand, perhaps with a firmer grip than strictly necessary. "That's right."

"Allow me to express my deepest gratitude. I've been worried sick."

"Uh-huh." Rio dropped the other man's hand. "So worried you still needed to continue your political fundraising?"

"Rio!" Becca scowled at him. The fire behind her climbed higher.

Daniel blanched. "I—I had to! I realize it might look bad, but I was advised to keep the matter quiet. We needed to continue on our regular schedule. Nobody wanted an international incident." He spread his hands wide.

"Of course not, Dad," Becca said. She patted his arm. "Rio, please." She cast him a warning glance.

He ignored her.

Daniel said, "The Black Eagle people assured me they'd send their best."

"They did. They sent me." Rio leaned toward the man and allowed his superior height and bulk to loom over the other. The fire in the grate raged. "So, tell me, what kind of man puts his daughter's life in danger? Did you know she was shot?"

DORSEY ADAMS

Chapter Twenty

The library door flew inward and a florid, overweight man entered. Like the great prow of a ship, his girth preceded him. His perspiring forehead shining from the overhead chandelier, he smiled and held out his arms. "Daniel! You can't hide yourself away in here. The donors are all waiting to have a word with you." He smiled at Becca. "I didn't know your lovely daughter was coming tonight! Hello, you're Rebecca, aren't you?"

A visibly shocked Daniel came alive. Rio guessed he was truly surprised by the bomb he'd just dropped, that Rebecca had been struck by a bullet.

Daniel managed to find his tongue. "Maynard Ward, may I present my Rebecca. And ... her friend ... Mr. Lang?"

Rio stepped forward to pump the other man's hand and herd him toward the doors. "Great to meet you, Ward. But Rebecca hasn't seen her father in quite some time. She's requested just a moment alone with him. If you don't mind?" He opened the door, and pushed the other through the portal.

Blinking, Maynard Ward looked confused, but as a gracious host, he allowed himself to be ushered out. "Of course, of course. But only for a moment. Daniel is needed out here. The donors are waiting."

Closing the door, Rio crossed his arms and leaned back against the wood.

Daniel took Becca's elbows in concern. "You were shot? My God, are you all right?"

"Yes, it's just a graze on my leg."

Rio tired of the small talk. "Go ahead, Becca. Ask him."

She drew a deep breath. "Dad, tell me about

149

Uncle Tim. What's he been doing at the warehouse?"

Daniel frowned. "What do you mean?"

Rio pushed off the door. "Look, De Monte, Becca has been kidnapped, nearly killed twice. Now, your partner is illegally gunrunning out of your business, probably to criminals across the border. And that's at the very least. I think you know something about what's been going on."

"Did you say *gunrunning*?" Daniel blanched. "What is all this about?"

"Dad," Becca caught his arm, "we found proof. We caught Uncle Tim late at night shipping big boxes of rifles from the warehouse. He didn't see us, we were hidden, but what we saw is irrefutable."

Daniel's gaze slid from side to side, as though casting about for understanding. "I just can't believe that."

"Believe it," Rio spat. "It's true. And it's your business, with your name on it. If the authorities discover this little operation, you'll be the one indicted."

Daniel paled. "Any hint of a scandal will torpedo my senate race," he said. "And the campaign is going so well."

With difficulty, Rio suppressed a spurt of anger. Rebecca's own father had not only discovered his daughter had been placed literally in the line of fire, he was now thinking only of his political career.

Politicians were unreal.

****

Out in the salon, the reserved man with the bald head and pocked skin, the one who hadn't spoken, took his whisky highball and slipped onto the rear patio. He needed the privacy. Harrison hadn't spoken, because while Rio Lang didn't know his face, he'd surely recognize his voice. They'd talked many times by telephone.

Harrison chewed the end of a fine, unlit Cuban cigar and studied the gardens.

In no way could Harrison allow the observant former Special Forces expert to know that he was intimately involved in Daniel De Monte's senate campaign.

Rio could only know him as his contact with Black Eagle, the deeply hidden government entity that employed them both. Harrison had set up a sweet operation in Daniel De Monte's warehouse. And he'd easily recruited a willing Tim to facilitate it. The products—weapons and fentanyl—they were shipping were bringing in a *lot* of money, and no one knew he was the brains behind the outfit. All the while he'd carefully kept any hint of suspicion off himself. It had been gratifying, secretly pulling the strings all this time.

Harrison studied his cigar. Because Rio had thrown a monkey wrench into the mix, he would have to act. His superiors at Black Eagle didn't know what he was doing and they wouldn't have stood for it. Tough shit. The allegiance he felt to them was nonexistent.

In his younger years he'd served the government as a proud Green Beret. While the life was exciting, the pay was terrible. Harrison had long ago decided it was past time to enjoy a little of the world's wealth and power. After all, he knew how to accomplish difficult tasks. He also knew how to prevent others from asking too many questions.

The main thing was results, and Harrison *always* got them.

Rio Lang shouldn't be here. He was supposed to deliver Rebecca De Monte to the new meeting place and be on his way. Instead, he'd smuggled her back across the border and brought her straight to her father.

Why he'd done that had become abundantly clear after observing the two together. Even in that short amount of time, Harrison spotted Rio's obvious sexual interest in the alluring De Monte woman. Slim, with long gleaming hair, huge eyes, and an impressive rack, Rebecca De Monte was a hot young thing, and he could understand it. The way they'd entered the house, holding hands, whispering together, their physical connection was obvious.

This complicated matters.

Rebecca De Monte was never supposed to make it out of Mexico alive.

Chapter Twenty-One

Trouble, much bigger than he'd initially thought, was brewing here. Rio felt the foreboding conclusion seep into his brain. And one thing was clear: Becca was still in danger, and while he didn't know the exact reason beyond the illicit gun running, he was certain that her father would not, or could not, adequately protect her.

After Becca had shown him her office the night before, explained the business in further detail and her role in it, his estimation of her grew.

Though she stood to one day inherit a fortune from her father, she hadn't lived the life of a dilettante, of a lazy rich person. She'd apparently used her business degree and loyalty to passionately throw herself into work. She'd become an integral and important part of that company. Rio was certain she didn't need to labor away forty hours or more a week, but she did.

He admired her work ethic. Becca's life had meaning.

In direct contrast, he was footloose, with little of the gratifying sense of purpose she had. A strange jealousy rose in him and instantly he pushed it down. In a lot of ways she was a better person than he was. That was a no-brainer.

He already knew her wonderful body. Or, at least, he was beginning to learn its contours. That delicious expedition might never end. Now, she was beginning to fascinate him, to impress him with her diligent motivation to keep their family business successful. He found his appreciation for her devotion rising. She definitely wasn't the spoiled heiress he'd first assumed.

Briefly, Rio closed his eyes. After all he'd seen

and done, with various women in far-flung countries around the world, he didn't mind Becca's bent toward exhibitionism.

Actually, he liked it. A staid, prudish female could never interest him.

It seemed only right to remain with her for a few more days, to do a little snooping, and make certain she stayed alive until the felonious Uncle Tim was stopped or arrested. When Rio felt confident that the business had been restored to its old lawful practices, he could return to his own life. Surely Harrison would have a new assignment for him soon. When he'd told Becca this was his life, he'd meant it. For him, there was nothing else.

"There's no point in hiding at the motel anymore," Rio told Becca in the cab. They'd left the mansion, and her distressed father, only moments ago. "Now, the bad guys will know you're back in the States. I'll grab our things from the room and we can go stay at your condo."

When Becca nodded, he knew she wanted to go home. There, she could feel safer, see her little frogs, return to some semblance of her former life. Meanwhile, he planned to stop at an ATM machine, withdraw more cash, and buy a few monitoring cameras. If anything further was going on in that warehouse, he wanted to know. At the very least, he'd get video evidence of Uncle Tim doing his dirty work.

****

The following morning, Becca woke in her own bed, thankfully, with the reassuring presence of Rio right beside her. She made him a homey, house-wifey meal of bacon and eggs. The eggs in her refrigerator were a little old but not past their expiration date. Happily, she found bread in the freezer for toast. It felt odd and somehow … wonderful to perform this most basic of services.

Preparing food for a man she was beginning to care for felt both good and frightening, all at the same time. Becca chose not to delve too deeply into her feelings. He'd said nothing about their future, and she dared not think about it.

Rio used toast to sop up the eggs. As usual, his hair fell casually over his forehead. She marveled at him. Only Rio could make messy bed head look like it had been carefully tousled by a photo shoot hairdresser. She really needed to stop staring at him.

"Becca," he said, "I know you don't like contemplating that your family could be involved in shady crap, but we've got to consider something."

"Consider what?" She held her coffee up to her nose and inhaled deeply. The rich Columbian roast smelled delicious. Thank God for coffee. Right then, she needed it.

"The money. Why does your Uncle Tim—or your dad—need more money? How's the business doing? Any financial troubles there? Any at all?"

"No," she said. "None. I keep careful tabs on our profit and loss ratio. It's running at a fine profit and always has." Today she'd donned a white baby t-shirt and black yoga pants.

"Then, for some reason, it's not providing enough. You know, running a senate campaign takes a *lot* of funding." He paused and let her work through the ramifications.

"You think my dad is illegally adding to his war chest?" She frowned at him. "Like … as in funneling money to those accounts? I don't know much about running a political campaign, and I haven't been a part of it. But it seems that would have to be done by a complex routing of the cash through various financial institutions. It's totally illegal."

"So it is. But these campaign funds never seem to get big enough. And what are your dad's chances of winning that seat? Fair? Pretty good? How are his contacts in Washington, D.C.?"

She shifted on her stool uncomfortably. "Well, he has the ear of the President," she admitted. "They're good friends."

"You know him? The President?"

"No, I've never met him. Dad goes to dinners and stuff when he's in the capital. I stay out of politics. It's not my thing."

"Mine, either," he said. He added, "Usually."

Frowning, she pushed aside her half-eaten plate.

"Buttercup," he said gently, rubbing her back, "I've gotta be honest."

"About what?"

"I think this thing is much larger than just a few guns making their way south of the border."

"Larger?" She took a deep, alarmed breath. "What do you mean?"

"That, I don't know. But my plan is to head over to the warehouse tonight and install a few cameras, see if there's anything else to deal with."

"I'm going, too," she said. "I'll help you."

"Sure," he replied.

He didn't look thrilled at the prospect, but she ignored that.

Jumping to her feet, she grabbed an open-top hobo-style handbag, and started rummaging around in its depths. Onto the table she spilled a sunglasses case, a package of gum, and a fistful of make-up items: tubes of lip gloss, and a small pot of powder.

"What are you looking for?" Rio asked.

"Think I have a flashlight in here. We'll need it. That little penlight of my brother's is too small." As she dropped her make-up onto the table, a tube of lip gloss rolled to the edge.

Before it could fall he caught it. Another container with a screwed-on lid slid toward him. He caught that, too. The vagaries of women's potions and facial products had always mystified him. Turning the little pot around in his hands, he asked, "What is this?"

Becca looked up. "Oh, that's loose foundation powder. You're supposed to apply it to your face with a brush. Only I keep losing the brush."

"You don't need it," he said. "Your skin is perfect."

She smiled. "I don't know about that. But I always forget to use it anyway. That container is full." At last she took out a flashlight. "Aha!"

And she brandished it high in triumph.

****

At midnight, they drove Becca's small SUV and left Rio's old rental parked at her curb. The cameras were placed as Rio wanted them in different and hidden locations around the shop floor. One camera was pointed at the loading dock, one on either side of the floor, another outside.

"We'll have live feed and watch from your condo," he told her, setting the lens of the last camera in just the right location and concealing it in a jumble of parts. "Since your Uncle Tim isn't here tonight, maybe tomorrow he'll be back."

"Okay," she said. Glancing around the dark warehouse, she didn't like the deep shadows. At night everything looked different; it felt different. Creepy. All she wanted to do was leave. "Are we done? Let's go. In the morning I want to visit my brothers."

"Ah, your brothers," Rio said. "I'll have a few questions for them myself."

DORSEY ADAMS

Chapter Twenty-Two

Becca's younger brothers, John and James De Monte, were twins. They lived together in a residential condo. Like most bachelor pads, the place was messy. The sink was piled with dirty dishes and old laundry was strewn across a chair.

When the door opened and Becca and Rio stepped inside, before she'd even introduced them, she immediately began to gather the clothing and eye the dishes. He guessed as an older sister, it had become her custom to clean up after *the boys*, as she called them.

An enormous television screen, fronted by gaming controllers and scattered boxes of video games, had been placed on the living room carpet. Apparently they were avid gamers.

After their initial greeting and hugs, she gestured at Rio. "John, James, this is Rio. You won't believe this, but he saved my life."

The boys, actually men in their early twenties, gaped at him in surprise. They were dark-haired, brown-eyed, and slight. Both were in shirtsleeves and jeans.

"Saved your life?" John said to her. "What are you talking about?"

"Yeah, and where have you been?" James cut in. "You were supposed to be back from Mexico days ago."

They shook Rio's hand and he could see a resemblance to Becca in their hair and slender builds.

"Your sister," Rio told them bluntly, "was kidnapped from the Mexican ambassador's house by some nasty cartel guys. And she was caught in gunfire. Shot."

Both identical faces swiveled to their sister. John burst out, "Are you okay?"

"Shot!" James said. "What—what happened? We didn't know."

"Does Dad know about this?" John asked, scowling.

They both looked her up and down, but since she wore a white oxford shirt and black slacks, they couldn't see a wound.

Becca stuffed an armload of clothing into a laundry hamper and sent Rio a frown. "I'm fine," she told them. "It's just a graze on my leg. Rio has a melodramatic way of blurting things out." She closed the hamper lid. "And yes, Dad knows."

In clipped tones, Rio told them the rest of the story: the kidnapping, the lack of ransom demand, even about Uncle Tim moving contraband in the warehouse.

In unison, both sank onto a leather couch. Their faces revealed shock, and, to Rio's practiced eye, their innocence. They were young, naïve, and probably didn't know what was happening right beneath their noses. He didn't think they'd be much help.

"Have you two," he asked, "seen anything different going on at your warehouse? Anything unusual at all?"

The boys exchanged glances. Rio noticed they did that a lot. It was beginning to annoy him.

James spoke first. "Seems like a lot of extra crates have been ordered by the shop foreman."

John stroked his jaw. "You're right. Crate orders have gone up."

Rio tried not to jump on them. They weren't stupid, but yeah, he'd nailed them from the outset: they were naïve. "Did either of you think to find out why the shop suddenly needed more crates?"

"Not really." James scratched his armpit. "That's Becca's job and she was still out of town."

Rio fought the urge to bash their heads together. Maybe they could be useful in another way.

Cutting to the chase, he asked them, "Either of you proficient with firearms? Do you own guns?"

Once again, they glanced at each other. John said, "We played paint ball one time."

Rio raised his chin and stared at the ceiling. Becca had told him that their mother had passed years ago. Now, as he watched her rinse her brother's dishes at the sink, he understood that she'd become the caretaker of the family.

She was the important center of both the family *and* their business. It was increasingly apparent that the company was successful because of her. She was the linchpin.

No woman he'd ever been involved with before had such importance within her own world. The concept was outside his experience, and he needed a moment to process the alien notion.

And he was left with one thought: Becca was amazing.

"We're digging for the truth now," he told the boys. "So, don't tip our hands. Go to work each day but say nothing to anyone else. Got that? Not a whisper."

They both gave solemn nods.

Apparently neither would be of use in protecting Becca any more than their father. As he'd thought, his protective services were much needed. Still.

Becca needed a keeper.

****

Returning to his city penthouse office, Harrison paced by the expansive window and studied the bustling traffic and people moving below. Concentrating hard, he barely saw them.

Rio Lang had become a problem.

It wasn't unheard of, although unusual, for one of his own to turn from an asset into a liability. It happened. And he was philosophical about the matter. In his business, operators came and went. It was a difficult decision to make, because in terms of smarts, ingenuity, and just plain expertise, Rio Lang had been right at the top.

The man had gone off the reservation. He'd gone rogue. Harrison hadn't heard from him in days and when he'd unexpectedly turned up at De Monte's senate fundraising party, dragging Rebecca De Monte with him, it was obvious he would no longer follow Harrison's orders. Now he knew too much. Clearly, a new element had come into play for Rio Lang, an ingredient as old as humanity itself.

The power of the pussy.

Too bad. Three days prior, Harrison had sent a new team to the Mexican valley rendezvous point, to the place where they were to receive Rebecca from Rio, and this time he'd chosen them more carefully. He made sure they looked more like professional operators than the ruffians he'd sent before.

Despite that, obviously Lang had been spooked, had run with Rebecca, and they'd lost themselves in the vast Mexican forests. The new team reported that they'd gotten away.

When the two later appeared at the fundraiser, Harrison knew exactly what had gone wrong. Lang had fallen under the woman's spell.

Now, Harrison walked to a small wet bar and tossed a few ice cubes into a highball glass. Opening a crystal decanter, he poured himself a hefty serving of whisky. His doctor had told him to cut back on the alcohol. Way back. His doctor had also told him to cut out the cigars. The nagging hadn't ended there. He was supposed to get exercise, eat right, lose weight.

He'd done none of it.

Hell, he wanted to enjoy life. Nobody lived forever. And neither would Rio Lang. This was just business.

It was time to take him out.

DORSEY ADAMS

Chapter Twenty-Three

As had become his new habit, in making the rounds of Becca's small condo, Rio examined every door and window lock. He peered through blinds for any movement on the street, rechecking the view and checking again. The man was excruciatingly careful, Becca realized, as she watched him perform his security measures.

Her tablet computer served as their video monitor, and was propped on the kitchen table. It received live feed from their hidden cameras at the warehouse. So far, there had been no change.

As the hour grew late, Rio took up a pacing routine. Too nervous to sit, Becca kept busy by using her stackable washer/dryer machine to wash their clothing. Since most of her things were either black or white, she only needed to run two washes. Later, she fixed a simple meal for them, and then fed her frogs. All the while, Rio paced.

At last, near midnight, Rio took a seat at her table to stare at the monitor. Becca sat next to him and reached for his hand. He gave her an absent smile and squeezed her fingers.

"You think Uncle Tim will be back tonight?" she asked.

"Bet he will." He stared at the screen. All was quiet.

"I don't like thinking about the purpose of those guns." She shuddered. "That the weapons might be used for murdering people. It makes me sick to my stomach. And it's all being shipped from my place of work!"

"Whatever happens, we're putting an end to that," Rio promised. He gave her a look. "Becca … your Uncle

Tim is going to prison."

"Prison." She whispered the word.

"It could be worse. If he isn't careful he could be killed either by the guys paying him, or by the American authorities. This is a dangerous business he's gotten mixed up in."

Childhood memories flowed into her mind: her father's business partner bringing birthday celebration toys, she and her brothers riding on his shoulders, his bright affectionate smile. Tim and her father were close friends as well as business partners. If she hadn't personally seen him directing those men to ferry away illegal products, she'd never have believed it.

"Bingo," Rio said suddenly. He pointed at the video screen. A single light went on in the warehouse and the automatic bay doors opened. Men hurried inside. A truck backed up to the dock. With the camera's audio capability they could hear voices, but the men spoke very little.

Uncle Tim ducked inside, pointed at the boxes Rio and Becca had checked, then watched them being loaded onto a forklift. His face was clearly captured by the cameras.

Although she'd witnessed this before, Becca moaned.

"Easy, Buttercup," Rio said, still holding her hand. "This is hard for you to watch, I realize that. But it's better to face the truth. Your Uncle Tim, who isn't really your uncle at all, is crooked."

"I know."

As they watched, the sliding door of the truck opened and suddenly they saw several young girls, perhaps six teenagers, crammed tightly together.

Becca gasped, and she felt Rio tense.

Some were manacled to rings attached to the

truck. Some were handcuffed. All were dark-haired, dressed in peasant blouses and flowered cotton dresses, Mexican native clothing. Many of their feet were bare. Their heads hung down. Becca heard soft crying.

"This just took an ugly turn," Rio said, anger infusing his voice. "Looks like *Uncle* Tim is also into sex trafficking."

"Oh god!" Becca felt her head go light. "This is horrible! Pure evil!"

The wooden gun crates were shoved into the truck behind the girls, and the back was closed. The truck rolled away.

Uncle Tim was left behind.

"I can't believe it," Becca said.

Another truck backed up to the dock. As Rio and Becca watched, Tim and the driver unloaded armfuls of AK-47 rifles and placed them into open crates.

"I'm going down there," Rio said, standing up. "Right now. It's only a couple minutes drive and I need answers." From his pants pocket, he took out his Glock pistol. Holding the slide with one hand, with the other he pushed it back and looked into the ejection port.

Becca saw a round inside. His weapon was definitely loaded.

Fury enveloped her. Those poor girls! They'd been shackled like animals. How dare Tim—she'd never call him *Uncle* again—do something so nefarious, so evil?

Just as suddenly, a new thought drenched her in dread. "My dad said he knew nothing about this. He can't have known about those girls, either."

"One thing's for sure. Tim's gonna tell me."

"How can you be certain?"

"By the time I'm done with him, he'll be singing his life story. Don't worry about it." He grabbed a pen, studied the video monitor, and jotted down the truck's license plate.

Becca recalled a fact about the Navy SEALs she'd read somewhere: as part of their training, they were required to attend survival school. The days-long ordeal included capture by the 'enemy,' 'imprisonment,' and some sort of 'torture.' It was meant to simulate what might happen in the event of true capture. It trained the men to withstand hardship, to never give up on escape.

She imagined such training must have taught Rio several forms of enhanced interrogation. When she thought of Tim and the nasty business he was carrying on, it made her blood boil. If Rio tortured him, she would not intervene. No doubt he'd deserve whatever he got.

"I'm ready." She shoved to her feet to stand beside him. "Don't even think about telling me to stay here. Not happening."

He sighed briefly, and shook his head in resignation. Picking up his oilskin shoulder bag that seemed to accompany him everywhere, he said, "It won't be pretty."

She showed him her teeth. "I'm counting on that."

Chapter Twenty-Four

"I'm gonna crush your skull." Taller by several inches, heavier by thirty pounds, Rio gripped Tim's shirt collar and shoved him up against the warehouse wall. The fabric bunched in his fist and was gripped so tightly the older man's face turned red.

Choking, Tim wheezed.

Becca stood in the shadows of the open doorway where Tim couldn't see her. At his obvious pain, she grimaced, but kept her arms tightly crossed.

Tim held both hands high. He was already sweating. "No, don't—"

"Then I'm gonna break your arms."

"Stop—I—"

"Next comes knee-capping."

"Who are you—"

"Then I'll sell *you* into sexual slavery. How's rape every day and all night sound? Your life will become just like those girls you're hauling at night." Rio shook the other man. "Sex slaves."

"No, no, they're not!" Tim tried and failed to dislodge Rio's fist from his neck. "They're going to work as maids and kitchen help."

Rio banged Tim on the stucco wall. His face close enough to Tim's that their noses nearly touched, he bared his teeth. "Maids and cooks don't need to be shackled. Now before I beat the ever-lovin' shit out of you, tell me where they're going. And the drugs and guns." He shook Tim again. "Where?"

"To Juarez," Tim babbled. "We deliver the stuff—pick up more girls."

"Where do the girls end up?"

"I don't know! Some here in the U.S. Some in other countries, I guess. People want maids—"

Rio grabbed Tim's throat and smashed the side of his head into the wall.

Tim's head wobbled and his eyes fluttered shut. He began to sink down the wall, but Rio hauled him back up. "Don't," Rio said through gritted teeth, "Say. Maid. To. Me. Again. I don't like liars. Tell me another whopper and I'll smash your teeth so far back into your head they'll end up chewing up your brain."

Semi-conscious now, Tim moaned. Blood ran down the side of his face onto his shirt. An egg-sized contusion rapidly rose on his jaw.

With clenched teeth, Becca watched it all and felt conflicting emotions roiling inside her. Many years of good memories of *Uncle* Tim now fought with the reality of his illegal, immoral activities. The mix was both bewildering and enraging. Keeping her arms tightly crossed, she was determined not to interfere because now everything had changed. Her past memories counted for nothing.

"No, you don't," Rio told Tim. "You don't get to pass out." Hauling him over to a three-foot concrete ledge beside the dock, Rio shoved him into a sitting position, and kept his hold on the other man's shirt.

Becca came out of the shadows. She touched Rio's sleeve and he straightened, but didn't let go of his prisoner.

"Hey, Tim." She moved close. "Surprised to see me?"

With effort, Tim raised his head and looked into her face. His eyes widened. "Rebecca? You're alive?"

Grimly, she met Rio's frowning gaze before accusing Tim, "So, you are surprised. You wanted me dead!"

Rio gave the other a rough shake.

"No!" Tim cried out.

Rio got into the man's face. "People have been shooting at Becca. Somebody made her a target. All fingers point to you."

"No, I'd never." The man held his bloody face. "They were just supposed to hold her for a few days, not kill her."

"So you could do your dirty work here and I wouldn't know?" Becca demanded. "What for, Tim? Just money? What's all the money for anyway?"

In spite of his injuries, a sly expression overtook Tim's face. "Since you're here, I guess you already have it figured out."

Again, Becca met Rio's gaze. She couldn't speak.

"The political campaign?" Rio demanded. "That's it, isn't it?"

"Does my dad know about this? About the guns and drugs and the girls?" Becca's question was anguished.

"He doesn't want to know, but his new position will be so unique, so formidable." Tim's knowing look deepened. "Without me, he'd never have gotten this far." He held out his hands. "Think about it, Becca. Think how important this senate race is. If Daniel can get into office, imagine the influence! He's close to the President. He'll pass so much legislation, he'll make amazing deals."

"Deals." Rio spat the word as though it were an epithet.

"My life is worth more than that," Becca said. "More than your *deals*."

"Don't you see?" Tim entreated her. "This is bigger than all of us. More important than any one person."

"Want to ask those stolen girls if they agree?" Rio

asked. He raised a fist as though to do further violence. "Maybe they won't like their sacrifice."

Becca nodded. She noticed Rio didn't tell Tim that it had taken only moments on their way over for them to buy a burner phone and call in the truck's description and license plate. As soon as the report was made, Rio tossed the phone into a trash can. That particular batch of girls and guns wouldn't make their destination. By now, the authorities would have stopped it and arrested the driver, and freed the captives.

Abruptly, from behind them both, a man's voice rang out. "Move away," the man said.

Becca whirled, and a stranger with a drooping mustache appeared in the open doorway, his handgun aimed at her and Rio. His eyes were cold. She shrank behind Rio. In a lightning fast move, Rio pulled Tim up and held him in front of their bodies. He crammed his Glock into Tim's temple. For an interminably long moment, they faced off. "Sure you want to take this chance?" Rio asked. His voice was calm, nearly casual.

The man's gaze went from Rio to Tim. He didn't move.

"Carlos," Tim said, "put your gun down before this guy shoots my head off. Go back outside."

With obvious reluctance, Carlos backed through the doorway, lowering his weapon.

Rio let go his hold on Tim and took Becca's arm. He kept the gun on Tim.

Tim stood, swaying and holding his jaw. "Remember what I said, Becca. This isn't just about you or me. It's more important than any of us. Can't you see that helping get control of the legislature and thwarting the powers that be is essential? Now, if you're smart, you'll keep your mouth shut—you and your boyfriend." He let his gaze cut to Rio.

When she might have responded, Rio squeezed her elbow. As she'd told Rio, she didn't consider herself a political being. But she didn't like Tim's argument. People should be able to do what they wanted. She didn't like the idea of people being *controlled.*

"You want your dad to succeed, right, Becca?" Tim asked. "You care about him? He's going to do good things for the electorate, better things than most senators even dream about."

"And kill me in the bargain," she said. "Anyway, how does all this help my dad? I'd gladly work for him, but—"

"But nothing," Tim cut in. "You don't need to do anything, Becca. Nothing beyond looking the other way. That's all. You can do that, right?"

When she opened her mouth, Rio squeezed her again. She knew enough to stall. "Is it worth what you're doing, Tim? Is it?"

"Of course it is. You know it is. Just think about all the good that can come from your dad's incredible ascension up Washington's hierarchy. Just keep focused on that."

Becca dropped her gaze.

Tim backed carefully out the open doorway, joining Carlos outside to drive away.

"Shit," Rio said. "It was hard to let him go." He shrugged. "Guess it's better I did."

"At least they didn't kill us." Becca folded her arms around her waist.

"Two dead bodies in America are a lot harder to hide than one small female in Mexico," Rio said. "They were smart to let us go."

"Not really. For all they know, we'll go to the police, have Tim arrested, stop all this."

"Tim doesn't know me. He thinks I'm just your

173

boyfriend. Fact is, he's counting on you caring more about your history with him and your love for your father to stay quiet. Remember, he's already had you kidnapped and nearly caused your death. He can always revert to that."

Becca shivered. "You think you know someone. But you don't. Tim's different. He's not the man I've known."

Rio shook his head. "Come on. We're out of here."

He drove Becca's car as they headed back to her condo. She remained silent, processing the difficult scene.

Finally, he interrupted her thoughts. "How far do you want to push this thing, Becca? There are several felonies being committed here and your Dad, like it or not, is up to his neck in this shit. Even if he's exonerated, his business ties to Tim will destroy his campaign."

As he turned the wheel to pull into her carport, Becca didn't answer right away. She needed time to think.

Getting out, they moved together up the walk.

Only thirty yards from her door, Rio went rigid. "Get down," he said, low and harsh, and he threw himself in front of her.

Shots rang out, and in a tumble of arms and legs, they both fell behind a block wall.

Chapter Twenty-Five

Drawing his Glock, Rio knelt and peered around the wall. He opened fire. On the ground by his side, Becca couldn't see who or what he was aiming at. She couldn't see anybody or anything, only heard gunfire coming from somewhere near her front porch. One thing was certain: she was fervently glad Rio was there.

He turned to Becca. "Get the car," he commanded, tossing her the keys. "Get going."

Panicked, Becca scrambled backyards and around the corner through the darkness to the carport. With shaking hands, she unlocked her SUV and threw herself inside. Suddenly she realized that Rio hadn't followed. With squealing wheels, she backed out and sent the car leaping forward to where he slumped, his back against the wall.

But he didn't move.

In a frenzied rush, she rolled down the passenger window. "*Get in the car*!" she screamed.

He was looking down, his hand pressed to his side.

She leaned across the seat and opened the passenger door. "*Get in*," she shouted again. A hail of bullets struck the car's front right fender.

Peeking around the corner, Rio lifted his gun and sprayed rounds. Bent over, one hand on the ground to steady himself, he half-crawled to the car. Awkwardly he climbed inside and slammed the door. "*Go*," he told her. Holding his gun out the window, he aimed his weapon and fired off rounds.

They flew around the corner. When Rio told her to turn, she did. When he wanted her to double back, she did. They drove through the city in zigzags until finally he decided they weren't being followed. Becca noticed his breathing was heavy.

"Are you hurt?" she asked, and felt a pang of fear.

Hunting around her car until he found her old college sweatshirt, he didn't answer right away. Pressing the fabric to his side, he said, "Guess it's my turn. You got it in the leg. Now I got it in the side."

She gasped. "You're hit! We have to get you to a hospital."

Lifting his shirt, he examined the area with gritted teeth. "No hospital," he said. "Physicians are mandated by law to report gunshot wounds to law enforcement. Can't have that."

When Becca saw the open gash and seeping blood, she felt faint. With both hands she clutched the steering wheel. "Rio," she said, "you need medical care. We don't have any choice. I'm taking you to the hospital right now."

"Lucky for me, the bullet went clean through the fleshy part of my skin," he said. "No hospital."

Becca wondered if he was thinking straight. After all, he'd been struck by a bullet! "I know you're lucky," she said with all the calmness she could muster. She spoke slowly, in case he wasn't in his right mind. She took her eyes off the road long enough to muster a reassuring smile. She had to get him on the right track. "You're Lucky Rio, right?"

"No, I'm bad. I'm Bad Rio."

"Huh?" With no time to sort out his meaning, she said, "Don't worry about anything. I'll take you to a walk-in emergency medical clinic, not a big hospital, okay? We'll get you fixed up."

Rio leaned toward her, grimacing. "No. There'll be too many questions, long interviews, and nosy investigators. We can't afford that. Not now. Take me to Mexico. To Nuevo Laredo."

"*What*?" She couldn't have heard him correctly.

"Just drive. We're American citizens. You have your I.D., don't you? We can go to Mexico legally. Just drive me there, Becca. Remember where my friends live? Across the border? The ones who gave us a room that last night?"

"Of course I remember—"

"Take me there. They'll get me a doctor who won't blab. I need antibiotics and a few stitches, that's all."

"Are you insane? It's a three-hour drive!"

"I'll make it. The bleeding's already slowing."

"Rio." She had to take this situation in hand. "I'm not driving you hours into a foreign country. You could die along the way. From blood loss. Or … or lead poisoning. Or, I don't know, shock."

"Hurts like hell," he said. "But I won't die from shock." He fumbled on his back for his shoulder bag. "Fill the tank." He pulled out bills.

Becca frowned at the money in his hand. "Who was shooting at me, Rio? Was it Tim? Or one of his men? If he wanted me dead, why didn't they kill us both at the warehouse?"

"Wasn't Tim," he said. "That guy back there is a pro. He was lying in wait. And this time, nobody was aiming at you."

"What kind of pro? Like a professional killer?" Her mind was a mass of confusion and half-formed thoughts. "Who's trying to kill us now?"

"Not sure. But I have a suspicion. Now get some gas. And take us to Mexico."

Becca rubbed her forehead, now wondering if *she* was the one who'd lost her mind. In two blocks, she pulled into the bay of a filling station.

Oh God, oh God. They were going back to Mexico.

Chapter Twenty-Six

The filling station featured a mini-mart, and Becca used the extra money Rio had given her to buy packages of beef jerky, granola bars, packets of nuts, and four bottles of water. At the counter was a bowl of oranges, and she picked up six. She also grabbed a container of ibuprofen.

As she drove through the night, she cast Rio fearful glances. He said almost nothing, and despite the four ibuprofen tablets she'd gotten down him, she knew he was in terrible pain. After an hour she nearly turned around. That roused him and he growled at her to keep going.

"Just get me to Mexico," he commanded. "Just do it."

The border crossing was simple and went without mishap. Rio managed to sit up and appear normal. She handed over their driver's licenses and after inspection, was waved through. When days ago she'd left to visit Maria in Matamoros, she'd taken only her passport, and left her driver's license behind in her bag. Fortunately, now she had it with her.

"Thank goodness they don't currently require birth certificates to cross," she said to Rio. "Or we'd be doing the backstroke in the Rio Grande again."

Her small joke got no traction; he didn't reply. Anxious, she noticed splotchy patches of color in his cheeks. He began to slump. Was he running a fever? Oh, God. Infection. When his eyes drifted closed, Becca was afraid he'd lose consciousness. She touched his arm. "Don't pass out. I need directions to your friend's house."

He roused enough to point the way, but she could

tell he was nearing his limit.

At last, she pulled her car into the dirt drive of the couple who'd been so kind to them before. Switching off the engine, she ran to the door and rapped sharply on the wood.

"Por favor," she called out, low and urgent. "*Por favor, abre la puerta. Mi amigo esta herido!*" Please open the door, my friend is hurt!

After that, everything went by in a blur.

The couple came out and helped Rio into the house. They put him in the same room where they'd stayed only days ago and sent for a doctor. A man arrived carrying a black bag, examined him, gave him a shot of something, cleaned and stitched his side. Before he left, he pressed two bottles of antibiotics and pain meds into Becca's hands with instructions for Rio to take them over the next ten days. In the deep of night, the doctor hurried away.

For a brief moment, she left the room to find their host. She touched his arm. "Please," she said in Spanish, "can you contact the pilot who flew us here? Julio? I want to go back, back to where he picked us up, to the Chihuahua Mountains. Also, we need coats. And food. I'll pay."

The man nodded.

Unable to safely return home, unsure of who their enemy actually was, Becca made the best decision she could, a desperate one, but at the mountain cabin at least they'd be safe.

Before falling into bed beside Rio, she plugged both their phones into wall chargers so they'd have full batteries.

They slept and spent the morning resting.

Late the following evening, the wife pressed heavy coats and a full bag of food into her hands. The husband gave her short driving directions to the dirt runway. It was dark when she found it. The pilot and his modified Cessna waited. Julio asked them only a single question. Where did they want to go?

They flew south, and on landing, Becca touched the pilot's arm. "Come back in ten days," she said. "We'll be ready to fly home then."

His answer was a wordless wave.

In moments, she found the scooter exactly where Rio had stashed it in the brush. The plane and its laconic pilot took off.

As dawn broke, she bullied a half-conscious Rio into swinging his leg over the seat. He was exhausted and wounded, but she exhorted him to hang onto her as she wended her way up back roads and through trees. Fortunately, she remembered how to find the cabin.

All the snow had melted, and even most of the mud had dried. The weather had eased and rather than the bone-chilling cold it had been before, the air was merely cool and mild.

Later, she didn't know how she managed to get the food, clothing, medicine, and Rio through the close-growing trees and into the cabin, but she did it.

Barring the door, she turned on the lantern and helped Rio to the bed. For the first time in hours, she was able to take a deep breath.

At least for now, they were safe.

****

"Water," Rio croaked, hours later. "Need water."

Beside him and under the quilts, Becca woke with a start. It was early afternoon. She put her hand on his forehead. No fever, thank goodness. He tried to sit up, grimaced in pain, and sank onto the pillow again to close his eyes.

Pushing back her mussed hair, she scrambled off

the bed and went to the cooler. The night before, she'd carefully placed their food and water bottles inside. In the bag of food the woman had generously given her, she was surprised to find a new pistol magazine, and guessed it was for Rio's Glock. She set it aside, next to his gun. In the bag was also, happily, a pound of ground coffee, a trial-sized shampoo, and toothbrush and toothpaste. Bless that woman.

At the bottom of the cooler, she found blue ice freezer packs that were still cool and packed them around the food. Inside, she found peanut butter, crackers, and more tinned peaches. Even a couple of cans of soup. Good. Not all of their food would be perishable.

She brought Rio water and held the bottle to his mouth. Weakly, he sipped.

"How are you feeling?" she asked.

"Great," he said. His voice sounded gravelly. "Ready for some tackle football."

She smiled. "Sure thing, tough guy. I guess you won't need the painkillers the doctor gave me for you."

He opened one eye. "You have drugs? Gimme."

"First, we have to get some food down you so you won't throw them back up." Back at the cooler, she dug through the various packages. "How about some *carnitas* in a soft tortilla? I don't have any way to heat them, though."

"I don't care."

She eyed the cold fireplace. On the mantle was a screwdriver and a box of matches. "Do you think it'd be safe for us to use the fireplace now?"

On the pillow, he moved his head. "Nobody knows we're in this country, right? Even if they find out, they won't know where we are. And the cartel isn't looking for you anymore. We'd just be another cabin in the woods burning wood."

That made her happy. "I'll go out and gather up a big bunch of dry tinder a little later. Now, let's eat and I'll give you a pill."

She got him up in bed and propped against the wall. Like a companionable old couple, they ate together. After he drank more water, she gave him a powerful painkiller and a dose of antibiotics. He lay back, thoroughly exhausted.

"You rest," she told him. "I'm going to scout around, get some firewood." Already he was falling asleep.

Because the air was still nippy, she put on her borrowed coat and ventured outside. The sun shone brightly and the sky was blue and clear. Exploring around the cabin, she moved carefully but saw no mountain lion tracks. Hopefully, the big cat had moved on. As she checked the area, she had new appreciation for how hidden they were. Walking through the trees below the ledge, which had been ice-covered only days before, she came to the choke point and peered at the mountainside.

Several hundred feet up in altitude, she could see snow and ice. That was good.

Not far from the shack, she found abundant dry wood. From her childhood days at sleepover camp, she remembered that wood burned fast. They'd need a lot of it. For an hour she worked, gathering sticks and short logs she thought were small enough to fit inside the tiny hearth. She built up quite a pile beside the door. To get the fire going, she also collected armloads of dried pine needles.

Carrying in enough to last through the coming night, and making a pile on the floor, she saw that Rio was sound asleep. Quietly, she set a new bottle of water beside him and took one for herself. Into her coat pocket, she stuffed two plastic bags and the blue frozen packs.

On the mantle beside the matches she found the screwdriver, and slipped it into her jacket.

She planned to climb the mountain and get some of that ice. Their cooler wasn't cold enough to preserve their food and she was determined to stay for as long as it took, nursing Rio until he was recovered. With ice, their cache of food would last days. At the last minute, she stashed one of the small nut packets in her pocket. It would be a long climb.

Rio slept on.

Quietly, she let herself outside and began the trek. She climbed, step after step.

Halfway to her goal, she nearly quit. The countryside was rough, the mountain steep, and the snow and ice seemed just as far away as it had when she'd started an hour before. At times she had to use her hands to claw her way upward.

Only the thought of all their food decaying and of Rio unable to care for himself pushed her on. Glad of her nuts, she stopped to rest for a few minutes, ate them hungrily and drank half her water bottle. As she pushed on, at last the air cooled and she saw that the tree line had changed. Tall coniferous pines and fir trees now grew and snow collected on their upper branches.

She wasn't there yet. Still Becca climbed. It became cold, as cold as it had been when she was at the cabin before. Even in her coat, she shivered.

Finally, she got high enough to crunch on snow underfoot. She didn't want snow, however, she wanted ice.

Taking the screwdriver and plastic bags from her pocket, she found a rock crevice frozen over and hacked at a hunk of the frozen stuff until she had large chunks for her bags. Within ten minutes she had enough to satisfy her, and slung the heavy bags over her shoulder. The blue ice packs she buried in the snow, and left them. Later, when she needed to replenish their reserves, she'd return for them. If they would freeze again, they'd be far more valuable than the ice, which would melt too quickly to last.

Descending the mountain was easier than climbing it, but with her added burden, she slipped and slid on loose soil. The bags of hard ice banged into her back and she cursed. Thinking of the ibuprofen down in the cabin, she decided her muscles would be sore. She would need a few.

In less than half the time it took to go up, she reached the shack. Wanting to be prepared for anything, she took a few moments to use Rio's gas cans in the brush to refuel the scooter and then hide it beneath the tarp. The skies were darkening into dusk.

As she was gratefully building their first small fire in the hearth, Rio awoke. She turned to him and smiled.

"Buttercup," he said. "Come here. Please."

Moving to his side, she crouched beside the bed.

He raised a hand to smooth her hair. "Thank you. For everything. For getting me here—it was a good decision. You didn't have to do that. I'm nothing to you."

She opened her mouth to protest, then decided to change her answer. "You saved my life a few times. I'm just repaying the favor." And he was *something* to her. She just wasn't sure yet what that something was.

"Yeah, well, I was getting paid for that."

"You can pay me." She laid her index finger beside her mouth. "The price is … one million dollars."

He cracked a small smile. His eyes moved to the fireplace. "The heat feels good." After a minute he closed his eyes. "I'm so tired. And I gotta pee."

"Can you make it outside the door? I'll help you."

"Yeah." With effort he sat up, groaned, and rested

a moment.

Becca helped by swinging his legs over the side of the bed until his feet were flat on the floor. She slipped his tennis shoes on his feet and helped him up.

He swayed, shuffled to the door, and she unlatched it.

Outside, she wedged herself under his arm and waited while he did his business. Back inside, he fell onto the bed and didn't move.

"You can't go to sleep yet," she told him. "First, more food, and then another pill."

Sorting through the now ice-filled cooler, she pulled out an orange, two enchiladas, and more water. While she peeled the orange, she set the two foil-wrapped enchiladas close to the fire.

Within an hour they'd eaten, he'd taken his pill, and had fallen into a deep, peaceful slumber. Becca was glad, because she knew his fit, healthy body was healing itself.

Turning off the lantern, Becca unearthed the package of ground coffee and poured a healthy measure into a battered percolator coffee pot she found beside the hearth. She filled it with water and set it into the coals. When it was ready, she raised a chipped cup to her mouth and sighed in pleasure. Rich aroma wafted to her nostrils and she inhaled deeply. How she loved coffee!

Nursing the hot drink, she watched the firelight play over Rio's face. He was truly handsome, with his sun-god good looks and strong body. Her heart squeezed.

Over these past days of danger and uncertainty, she didn't know what she would have done without him. Probably she'd have been killed. Whether he was being paid or not, she owed him her life. There was no doubt in her mind that he'd gone over and above any professional obligation.

All at once she realized that she didn't want her time with him to end. She didn't want him to move onto his next post. In some capacity, she wanted him in her life. She wanted him.

Their explosive attraction would never be lasting. She knew that. Like a winter bonfire, flaming brightly and then dying with the cooling advent of spring, it would expire. She knew their relationship, such as it was, had been born of a woman in need and of a man doing a job, nothing more.

Two people had been thrown together into harrowing circumstances and turned to one another for comfort. Their coupling was transitory, temporary, fleeting.

Still, watching the play of light on his features, she drew in deep breaths. Whatever time they might have together, she would make the most of it. She wanted to help him get better, to enjoy his company, to make love again.

On that thought, Becca felt a familiar warmth creep into her lower extremities … and she felt a soft smile steal over her face. Oh, she wanted him better again. Soon.

DORSEY ADAMS

Chapter Twenty-Seven

In the morning, Becca was thrilled to find that Rio's body temperature remained normal, with no return of his fever. He was still weak, but coherent. After changing his wound's dressing with fresh gauze and tape, she prepared food. He took his pill, and she sat beside him in bed and asked about his home life.

"Guess there's no harm in telling you." He rubbed his jaw. "My dad—or at least the man who raised me—is Jim. Big Jim. And he raised my sister, too. Sarah. They're my family."

"Where are your real parents?"

"Don't know."

Becca decided prying wouldn't be prudent. "Do you see Big Jim and Sarah often?"

"Not much."

Thinking of how close she and her brothers were, she wondered why not. "Where are they?"

"Cattle ranch," he said. "In Montana. I don't go home much," he offered. "In my line of work, I've made some enemies. It's best if my connection to them is kept quiet."

She frowned. "You think your family is in danger?"

He shifted uncomfortably. "Honestly? No, but it's not smart to take chances." His mouth curved up at one corner. "Anyway, my dad's a rancher and a hunter. He's sharp, proficient with guns. And Sarah's tough. Anybody tangling with them might wish they hadn't."

Becca thought about how she'd like to meet the people who'd influenced Rio. But she dared not speak those thoughts aloud. The subject was too personal. It didn't seem appropriate to keep probing.

"Where's your mom, Becca? I've met your father and brothers. She still around?"

Becca lowered her gaze. "She passed. Six years ago. Lymphoma."

"That's too bad," he said. "I'm sorry."

Accepting his condolences, she thought about the year-long ordeal her family had endured while her mother sickened and died. She didn't like thinking about it.

Instead, she asked a pressing question. "Do you know if there are any clear water streams or creeks nearby? We're getting low on water."

"Sure, only maybe a hundred yards to the west there's a pretty creek. The water's drinkable." He yawned, tiring.

"All right." She began to scoot off the bed. "I'll take our empty bottles and refill them."

"Wait." Still flat on his back, he put a hand on her leg. "I'm not up to doing anything more right now, but how about a little kiss?" He smiled at her and her heart melted.

Leaning over him, she pressed her lips to his. "Get better and we'll see about doing something *more*." With a deliberate movement, she brushed her breasts across his chest.

His eyes alight, he leaned up an inch, groaned in pain and fell back. "Are you trying to kill me?"

She giggled, delighting in teasing him. "I'm off to refill our water, and maybe wash my hair in your creek. While I'm gone, you sleep, okay? The sooner you get better, the sooner we can get busy."

His eyes briefly flamed, then his lids drifted closed, and she could tell she was already losing him to sleep. "Kiss me again, Becca," he whispered. "Kiss me."

"I'll kiss you when I get back," she promised. "Now, you just rest." Gathering empty bottles, her coat and the shampoo, she eased out the door.

Taking her time, she made a wide-ranging tour of the area. She wanted to familiarize herself with the surrounding landscape, have a better understanding of their location. She learned where the taller trees leaned into the wind, where the squirrels chittered and ran across branches. She discovered a flock of green-feathered, redheaded, thick-billed parrots roosting in a wild oak. Across the mountainside, she saw a single, small gray fox trotting along his way. The mountain was breathtaking.

At last she found Rio's creek, wending its way down the mountainside, cold from melted snow above, and clean. First, she refilled their bottles, capped them, and then leaned from the side to wash her hair.

It felt heavenly. Fluffing it with her fingers, after sitting in the sunshine for a bit, she had it half-dry before returning to the shack.

Rio was awake and propped up in bed against the wall.

"Honey, I'm home," she sang out, smiling.

He grinned. "Welcome back. Your hair looks pretty."

She swung its heavy weight, still damp from the washing. "Thanks! You have a severe case of bed head." He didn't, though. His hair just looked artfully tousled, as though for a romantic film scene in a chick flick. How did he do that?

He ran a hand though the blond strands and rubbed his three-day stubble. "Sorry. Do I look like hell?"

She nearly burst out laughing. Since she'd already decided he belonged in Hollywood, or in the pages of *Gentleman's Quarterly* magazine, she couldn't imagine him looking *like hell*.

But she wouldn't tell him. "You look like a hot

mess," she said instead. Setting the water bottles on the floor, she hid a new grin.

"At least you think I'm hot," he said, showing his dimple. "I'll take that."

She busied herself rebuilding the fire and replenishing their wood from the huge pile she'd made just outside the door. At last lowering the latch, she turned to him. "Rio, who was trying to kill us, back at my condo? If not Tim, who?"

"I've been working that out," he said. "Trouble is, my brain isn't operating real well. Feels like mush."

"I'm so upset about those poor girls, chained in the truck. Hopefully the authorities were able to rescue them."

"No doubt they did. I gave a full description of the truck and the license plate."

"But there must be others."

He didn't answer.

"Okay," she said. Perhaps she was pushing him too hard. "Don't worry about any of this right now. You're getting better. We'll be here for a few more days. Maybe all week. I want you much improved before we go back."

"I need to talk to my boss. Haven't called him in days. I gotta see what's going on." He scowled.

"Both our phones are charged, but I turned them off." When he continued to frown, she asked, "What?" She'd grown intuitive to his moods. "What is it?"

"Not sure. Maybe I'll call tomorrow."

"Or in a couple of days," she said, correcting him. There was no way he'd be able to travel far enough to get cell reception for at least that long.

"Can I have some food?" he asked. Clearly he wouldn't discuss whatever was bothering him.

Becca went to the cooler and pulled out a can of

nuts, peeled another orange, and unwrapped granola bars. She didn't mind waiting on him. Doing things for him felt nice. It seemed ironic, how the first time they'd come to the mountain shack she'd been the one cold, sick, needing care. Now, their roles had reversed and she was taking care of him.

Happily so. If she weren't careful, she could get used to it.

That day they spent the time chatting and napping, only venturing outside to go in the trees, or take a short sunbath. Rio tired quickly and needed a lot of sleep. When he slumbered, Becca watched his face, knowing he was improving each hour, and would continue to each day that she managed to keep him quiet. There'd be time for action later, when he was better, and when he could think properly again.

Meanwhile, she decided to enjoy this interlude. It seemed an idyllic time, when no one knew where they were, couldn't contact them by phone, couldn't shoot at them. There in the mountains, there was no intrigue, no threat, no fear. There was only Becca, and Rio.

Was she falling in love?

She didn't know, but found taking her eyes off him for more than moments seemed painful. At every opportunity, she ran her hands over his back, through his thick hair. She touched him, petted him, and caressed him.

He appeared to enjoy the attention, and when he could, he held her hand and kissed her back.

That night she lay facing the wall, and he curved his body to hers, his wounded side facing up, his arm around her. Before falling asleep, he brushed his fingers over her breasts, and predictably her nipples responded. She felt the rising of his desire against her bottom. In seconds, he was asleep, but she smiled to herself.

Rio was getting better.

****

On the fourth day, Becca told Rio she intended to hike back up the mountain again, to fetch the blue ice packs and more ice. In the cooler, most of it had melted. They still had a good store of food, and with careful management, enough left for a few more days. She wanted to make certain it remained safe to eat.

"I'll go with you," Rio said, swinging his legs over the bed with care. He grimaced.

"The trail is almost straight up," Becca said. "You stay here. We can't have your stitches pulling out." She put on her coat and collected the plastic bags.

He studied her for a long moment. "Take the Glock. I don't want you going out alone anymore without it." From the floor, he picked up the gun, checked the chamber. "You know how to shoot, right?"

"I've been to the shooting range a few times." She wouldn't tell him it was with an ex-boyfriend. "But I won't need the gun."

"With the break in the weather, that mountain lion has probably moved on, but I don't want you taking any chances. We don't know who or what could be out there." Showing her the gun's safe action system, he explained that to fire it, she must depress both the trigger safety and the trigger itself at the same time. He pushed the weapon into her hands. "You're taking it."

Not liking to argue with him, she tucked the gun into her coat pocket and brushed her lips over his mouth. "Be back in a few hours."

With difficulty, he got off the bed and followed her to the door. "Be careful," he said.

"Yup!" As she let herself out of the cabin, he surprised her by coming with her, and although he moved slowly and carefully, he walked a few yards. After a dozen more steps, she stopped him with a hand on his chest. "I'll be fine. Now go back inside. Rest."

He scowled down at her. "I don't want you to go."

"You'll probably die of loneliness," she said, and gave him a saucy smile. "You'll miss me something awful."

"I'll miss you something awful," he repeated, searching her eyes. "I should be the one getting ice," he said. "I should be taking care of you."

Something inside her warmed. "For now, I want to take care of you."

"*Becca*," he said, and pulled her to him. His eyes lit to shimmering blue flames. Bending his neck, he kissed her thoroughly.

Her body flooded with pleasure. She pulled away an inch. "You're feeling that good, huh? Well, when I get back, if I'm not too tired, and if you're up to it, I could take care of you in a more interesting way." With that, she deliberately ran her tongue across her upper lip. She allowed her eyes to half close with *come-hither* allure.

His gaze glowed. "I hope you're thinking what I'm thinking."

"Oh, I am," she promised. "I am." Turning, she walked away, toward the incline, and allowed her hips to gently sway.

Over her shoulder, she gave him a last smile.

"Hurry back, Buttercup," he said, looking stronger than he had in days.

DORSEY ADAMS

Chapter Twenty-Eight

Within three hours, Becca returned, tired but gratified. The blue ice packs were frozen solid and the additional ice chunks she'd lugged down the mountainside should keep their food cold for days.

She had barely a hundred yards to go before reaching the shack when she saw it. The mountain lion.

It perched on a rock not fifty yards away, absolutely still except for its twitching tail. With feline menace, its yellow eyes watched her, unblinking. Startled, Becca lost her footing on the steep, loose terrain and slipped. She fell to her backside, landing hard. Digging her heels into the sliding dirt and rocks, she stopped her momentum and dropped the ice bags. Her hands shaking with fright, she scrambled to find the Glock in her pocket. A cold sweat broke out on her forehead, under her arms. For long seconds, she struggled with the heavy fabric of her coat, but finally freed the weapon.

The enormous cat got to its feet and lowered its head. It was the same lion, she could tell by its tawny markings and huge size.

Gasping for breath, Becca raised the gun, and pointed it at the animal.

During long, tense seconds, they stared at each other. Becca held her breath. The cat didn't move.

For some reason, she didn't shoot. It had threatened her before, bounded menacingly toward her over the ice until Rio had scared it off. Obviously it had no fear of her. It was just as clear now that it could reach her in a flash, tear her into bite-sized pieces.

Yet still, she didn't pull the trigger.

Time stalled.

Moments later, the cat turned away and took trotting steps in the opposite direction. Instantly she saw that it wasn't nearly as thin as it had been in the snow. With the break in winter, it must have found prey.

From behind the rock, two cubs emerged, frolicking, playing, and when they saw their mother's exit, they gamboled after her. The family of three kept moving.

Becca slumped, and gasped for breath.

Phew.

With a shaky grip, she collected her ice bags and made the last few yards down the mountain without further mishap. She was glad she hadn't orphaned the cubs.

When she came into the cabin, Rio woke from a light doze. He struggled to sit up in bed. "Any problems?" he asked, studying her carefully.

"I saw the mountain lion," she told him, shrugging out of her coat and placing his gun beside him on the floor. "It has two cubs."

Rio sat up straighter in alarm.

"I showed it the Glock." She pretended nonchalance. "It ran away." Kneeling at the cooler, she settled the food so it was beneath the cold packs and ice.

"You did good, honey," he told her. "You're smart. You figured out how to keep our food fresh, and you brought enough to eat for us both. You even intimidate wild animals."

She smiled at him, got to her feet and dusted off her hands. "I do what I can." Moving to his side, she sat on the bed and took his hand. "I can't believe you were a Navy SEAL. It's not something I would have ever guessed."

"Have you ever met one before?"

"No, you're the first."

"You can usually tell where a SEAL is because the earth trembles in his presence."

She rolled her eyes. "I've heard they're an arrogant lot. It's making more sense all the time."

He chuckled. "I miss the lads."

"You've mentioned something like that before. But you've been out of the service for years, haven't you?"

"Sure, but in the SEALs, it's a brotherhood. A lifetime bond is formed with teammates because we have to rely on each other to stay alive. It's a trust thing, and a guy in the Teams has to prove himself reliable and honest before anybody *will* trust him. Once that connection is made, there's no breaking it."

She thought about that. "Sounds intense. And … important."

He nodded, pleased. "You understand."

Becca enjoyed his approval. She liked his dry sense of humor. In fact, she appreciated everything about him. He was just as he'd described his SEAL teammates to her: reliable, honest, and trustworthy. Hadn't he proven those things to her time and again? Never mind his gorgeous good looks. Rio was good inside, too.

A deep need rose up inside her, a desire to give back to him, to give something of herself. This was Rio, her Rio, at least for now. And for now, he needed her to care for him. She felt a connection with him that demanded expression, physical expression. And she knew exactly how that connection would be realized.

Placing her palm on his chest, she gently pressed. "Lean back, sweet man." She smiled into his eyes. "I'll relax you."

Already maneuvering his body to slide down onto the bed, he looked hopeful. "Now?"

She plumped a pillow beneath his head. "Now."

"You're not too tired? You climbed that big mountain."

"Just thinking about what I want to do for you is giving me new energy." She waggled her eyebrows, then a new thought occurred. Hesitating, she asked, "Are *you* up to this? I don't want your side to hurt or break open the wound."

"Baby, the whole time you were gone I thought about nothing else. Trust me, I'm up for this." He cut his eyes downward to his pants and she saw his rising erection.

She trailed her hand down his belly to squeeze him. Heat pooled in her sexual organs. She felt her nipples stiffen. "Mmm," she said. "Proud."

In a small surge he came off the pillow to take her in his arms, but instantly he let out a harsh groan, and teeth gritted, sank back down. "Damn it."

"You're going to have to let me do all the work today," she said, bending to lift his t-shirt. She took care to skirt his bandage wrappings and place her mouth on his warm belly.

Indulging herself, she traced each ribbed muscle on his abdomen with her lips. His body was fantastic, better than any professional athlete, and she felt fortunate to have him all for herself.

"How awful for you, to have to cede authority to another," she teased. "To have to follow someone else's orders."

"SEALs are trained to lead and to follow equally," he said. "Trust me, I'll do anything you say right now."

"Good. I command you to allow me to do what I want with your cock." Sliding her hand beneath his waistband, she closed her hand over his thick length.

He groaned, but with gentle hands, he held her

head, caressed her hair. "Yes, ma'am."

Rising up to peel off his pants, she threw them to the floor. "I like you submissive," she said, eager to begin. "It's a nice change." With that she pulled her shirt over her head, unlatched her bra, and stepped out of her pants. He watched, unblinking, his expression alive, his eyes flaming. When her clothing fell away, she lay beside him and cupped his testicles. His hand found her breasts and squeezed her nipples.

They kissed, and she played with his hardness. Their hands were everywhere, all over, discovering, exploring. There was so much to know, Becca realized, so many places on his body she wanted to learn.

Taking control, she angled down his frame, ran her lips over his chest, his belly. Finally addressing his straining cock, she used her tongue to lick him from his base to his tip. She took care to wet all sides.

As she stroked him with her soft hands, his breathing thickened. At last she took him into her mouth, took him far back in her throat, in and out, as she caressed his balls and stroked the base of his penis.

All the while he held her head, trailed his fingers over her nape, and tenderly stroked her hair. Within minutes he was sweating, moaning. He reached down to play with her breasts. "Feels so good."

Encouraged, Becca crouched closer between his naked thighs. Leaning over him, she sucked him, enjoyed his pleasure. Lifting up for only a moment, she whispered, "Rio, wanna come now?"

"Oh god, yes!"

Bending to him again, she let her tongue swirl around his tip, let her breasts slide back and forth on his inner thighs. Upping her tempo, she stroked him faster and more firmly. His excitement fueled hers and she was incredibly pleased to bring him to this level. Never before had she enjoyed a lover more. This man was different. Special. Lovingly, she suckled him.

She could tell he was getting close when he arched his back. He came on a low shout of exultation, ecstasy tightening his features.

As she settled against his good side, he wrapped his arm around her, breathing heavily. She snuggled into him, put her face into his neck and made a line of kisses along the column of his throat. How very gratifying it was to bring Rio such pleasure. She enjoyed it immensely … because it was *Rio*.

"You're amazing," he said, panting, and pulling her closer. "The best ever."

"Glad you think so," she said. "Does your side hurt?"

"It's on fire," he said. "But I don't care. It was worth every second."

She frowned, and began to sit up. "Let me check the stitches."

He wouldn't let her up. "Later. I wanna cuddle."

She smiled into his neck and pulled his face to hers. "I know you're a tough man, Rio Lang. But I like this tender side of you, too."

He kissed her, his lips lingering on hers. "I like tenderness with you. Just don't tell my old teammates."

The chances of her ever meeting any of his old buddies, of ever being part of his life seemed low. The idea saddened her.

Disliking the direction of her thoughts, Becca came to the conclusion that now was not the time to dwell on them. She needed to enjoy Rio while she had him. This was her time, she decided. Tucked away as they were, hidden in the beautiful mountains, for this moment in time while he healed in the remote cabin, she would live every moment. It wouldn't last, it couldn't.

But for now, he was all hers.

DORSEY ADAMS

Chapter Twenty-Nine

Two more days passed, and Rio grew stronger. He was able to walk normally, if slowly, to go alone outside for bathroom business, and to spend ever-greater amounts of time awake. He quit the pain meds.

In the morning, he said, "Becca, where's my phone? Gonna make that call to my boss."

When she handed it over, he turned it on and ignored everything except a message from Harrison. The voice commanded, *Check in, Lang. Now.*

Sure, Rio would check in, but this time he'd be the one getting answers.

He insisted on driving the Vespa, and when Becca wanted to go with him in the hunt to find cell service, he didn't see a problem. Although the mild weather barely required it, they put on their coats, and headed out. Because of his injury, he drove slowly, avoiding as many ruts and rocks as possible. Mindful of his bandaged wound, Becca clung to him with care. He could tell she was being solicitous and he appreciated that. He appreciated most everything about her.

It was a sign of his improving health, but he relished the feel of her full, fabulous breasts pressed to his back. With her legs spread across the Vespa seat and snug against his rear, her position put him in mind of her warm sex, and how unbelievably good it felt to take her. He didn't think he'd ever before enjoyed a woman's cries of pleasure so much. The luscious memory of the oral pleasure she'd given him had blown his mind.

Predictably, he felt himself harden. While he was pleased at his body's return to normality, he greatly regretted they had no time to pull over so he could pay her the proper attention she deserved. A shame. He'd have to make up for it. Soon.

The rough travel took its toll, and by the time they'd ridden down the mountainside, over back roads, and found reception, his side was burning and his mood had soured.

Pulling the Vespa off the asphalt road, he drove a few dozen yards into the trees and left Becca with the scooter. Some distance away, he found a tree stump, sat on its top, and made the call.

Harrison answered on the first ring. "Lang, where the fuck have you been? I've called three—"

"This time I'll ask the questions. First, I want to know who put the hit on me?"

"What hit? There is none. What are you talkin—"

"The guy shooting at me a few days ago was lying in wait. That's just not nice. Now, what's the truth?"

"Are you suggesting I sent someone to take you out? It didn't happen. Now, listen. I left your pay for the Rebecca De Monte hostage grab at the usual drop location. Pick it up when you can. Meanwhile, Rebecca's gone missing again." He paused as if thinking. "Do you have her?"

"Why would I have her?" Rio prevaricated. "I fulfilled the contract, took her back home in one piece."

Harrison sighed. "All right. Where are you?"

"That doesn't matter," Rio said. "Why don't you level with me? Tell me what's really going on."

"I need you to come in." Harrison said it impatiently. He sounded agitated. "I'll brief you on a new contract. It's a job requiring your special skills." *Coming in* meant Rio should travel to a pre-determined location for a face-to-face meeting with Harrison.

"Come in? Why is that necessary?" It never was before. In fact, they'd never met in person. "Just email me the details."

"Lang, don't give me shit. You have to—"

"Sorry, you're breaking up. I'm losing the connection. Get back to you later." With that, he ended the call, opened the phone's back cover and removed the battery. He'd learned enough. Swiveling his upper body to throw it like a baseball into the forest, the sudden pain in his side made him decide instead to underhand it away.

Finding a good-sized rock, he set the phone case down, grabbed another rock and smashed it. The broken parts fell into the weeds.

Becca approached. "Boy, you must really hate that phone."

Rio wanted to smile at her attempt at humor, but his thoughts were too dark. "I've had a bad feeling about our situation," he told her, "and I don't want to be tracked by my phone. I knew this was bigger than I first thought. Now, new angles are coming into play."

"What does that mean?" She sobered.

"What's the connection?" He asked the question aloud, not expecting an answer. "To you, to your uncle and dad's dirty business, and now … to me? It's a triangle that makes no sense."

She raised her palms.

"Give me your phone." He held out a hand.

"Don't break it," she said, alarmed.

"No, I'll just take the battery out. Nobody should know where we are."

"Oh," she said.

Clearly she didn't know that a person could be tracked by his phone, even if it were turned off.

"I'm operating blind," he said, "not knowing exactly who the enemy is, not even sure my boss can be trusted any more. I need answers—and I need a safe place to communicate while I send out feelers."

"What safe place?" she asked.

"Home," he said, abruptly making the decision. "We're going home. To my family, to Big Jim and Sarah. I can control things there, and gather information. We're going to Montana."

Chapter Thirty

After flying north to Nuevo Laredo, Rio explained to Becca that they didn't dare try crossing back into America openly—he said the authorities might discover where they were and they couldn't chance that. He'd lost faith in Harrison, and by extension, Black Eagle. It was, after all, a government entity. There was no telling what they might do.

Besides, they had no passports with them. At the border, they would only run into trouble. With his open wound, this time he couldn't risk infection from the dirty Rio Grande water.

In the end, he hired *coyotes* to smuggle them into the U.S. He arranged for a local man to drive Becca's car over the border and leave it near town.

The *coyotes* put them into a secret compartment of a tall transport truck. After they were in, a false door was closed and the truck was loaded with mangoes. At the crossing, Rio whispered to Becca that since money had changed hands, given his bribe, the truck would only be cursorily inspected, a mere formality. Indeed, they heard the rear doors open, and someone apparently glanced inside, saw only the fruit, and didn't investigate further. The doors closed.

In Laredo, Texas, they were delivered to a nondescript warehouse. It was a mere mile from where her car had been stashed, and hand in hand, they walked down a quiet country lane, found the key beneath the seat, and were on their way headed farther north. Sighing in relief, Becca leaned back in the passenger seat.

Rio took her phone, replaced the battery, and made a muttered call. In moments he hung up. "Big Jim's expecting us."

When she accepted her phone, she saw a dozen missed calls and voice mails from friends, her brothers, her father, and a two from Maria, the ambassador's daughter. Sighing, she turned it off, and again removed the battery. Her friends and family might be worried, but there was nothing she could do.

They took turns driving while the other dozed, stopping only for food and fuel. Within twenty-four hours, they drove into the outskirts of Billings. When they pulled into the city limits, Rio was at the wheel.

"Montana is beautiful," Becca said, admiring the long, rimrock cliffs, and beyond, the majestic shadow of the Bighorn Mountain range. It seemed as though she could see for miles in any direction. The air was crisp, clean. It was so open and free. And she liked the idea that no one knew where they were.

"I've been to different places around the world," he said, "some amazing places. But this is home. Feels good to be back."

Instead of driving into downtown, he kept to the outskirts, taking them into the foothills. The countryside grew lonely and wild. At last, he pulled through gates over a cattle guard and onto a mile-long driveway. He stopped the car at a sprawling, two-story ranch house. White-faced cows grazed in the fields. A hawk soared overhead.

Already walking toward them from the house, an older man approached, tall and lanky. Two gray and tan cattle dogs trailed after him. He wore a battered straw cowboy hat, worn Wrangler jeans, and beat-up boots. His skin was weathered, his manner calm in the way of an old cowhand who knew that with the rhythms of country life, there was always work to be done, and always another day in which to do it. A hurried, frenzied attitude would never define him.

On the driveway, Rio surprised her. Instead of a manly handshake between father and son, or perhaps a shoulder slap, they greeted each other with a hearty hug.

And to think, she'd first thought Rio was so detached!

"Dad, this is Rebecca De Monte," he said, drawing her forward. "Call her Becca."

Beneath the cowboy hat, observant and wise eyes studied her. He was taller than Rio by a couple of inches. That put him at a good six-foot-five. His gnarled hand engulfed hers. "Pleased to meet you, ma'am."

She smiled up at him. "Allow me to return the compliment, Mr. Lang."

"Jim," he corrected. "Come inside. Sarah's waiting."

Together they walked into the two-story clapboard house and a small, old-fashioned kitchen. With a linoleum floor, simple tiled countertop, and gingham curtains at the windows, the room was cozy and inviting. A woman in an apron was pulling a blue-speckled pan from the oven.

The dogs followed, sniffing the air and looking hopeful.

"I made supper," Sarah called out, not looking up from her oven. Delicious smells of roast, potatoes and vegetables wafted from the pan. Becca was instantly starving.

"Rio, get your friend something to drink and have a seat," Sarah instructed. "We can eat now." She waved at Rio as though she'd seen him only an hour before.

Rio grinned at Becca. "She's bossy. Always barking orders."

Sarah did look up then. She snapped out a kitchen towel. "I'm not bossy! Maybe you'd rather wear this roast, huh? Now, get the drinks."

"And she's spunky," Rio said to Becca. He moved to pull Sarah into his arms for a big hug.

After a moment, she pushed him away. "I'm not spunky," Sarah said. "I'm sweet and kind. Now, sit down."

Becca hid a smile. "I'll be happy to follow your orders, Sarah. Thank you for making us this meal. It looks heavenly. I'm so hungry."

Rio went to the doorway. "Jim and I'll get some wine," he said and the two men disappeared into the next room.

Untying her apron, Sarah faced Becca for the first time. In her early thirties, she was tall, at least five-foot-ten. A thick, dark blonde braid fell to her waist and enormous green eyes under darker winged brows fastened on Becca. "I'm so glad to meet you," she said. "At last, a woman has lassoed Rio."

With that she threw her arms around Becca and gave her a close hug. Surprised again, Becca returned the embrace. When they parted, she said, "Um, I'm not sure I've lassoed him at all. He was sent to rescue me in Mexico when I was kidnapped. He saved my life."

Sarah appeared unsurprised. "That's what he does." She reached into a cabinet for dinner platters. "And he's very good at it." She also took down four salad plates.

"Can I help?"

"Utensils are in that drawer," Sarah said, and they worked companionably to set the table. In the center Sarah placed her roast, and then from the refrigerator a wooden bowl filled with fresh salad greens. "And I made an apple pie for dessert," she said. "It's Rio's favorite. He doesn't come home often, so I wanted to do that for him."

"I love apple pie, too," Becca said, "but I've never

made one."

"I'll teach you." She smiled and Becca saw that her white teeth were perfect. In fact, she was truly a stunning beauty. "Tomorrow," she said confidently.

With that, Becca was at home. She marveled at how easily Sarah accepted her, and was grateful for Big Jim's hospitality. She wondered how an astoundingly beautiful young woman remained hidden out here in this remote place. Like Rio, Sarah was Hollywood gorgeous.

In consternation, Becca glanced around. Maybe there was something in the water?

Over dinner and glasses of red wine, Rio and Becca filled the other two in on their predicament, on her father's political aspirations, and their ignorance of who, exactly, was trying to kill them.

"You'll reach out," Big Jim asked Rio, "to your old contacts?"

"Tomorrow," Rio confirmed. "I'll make a few calls, send a few emails. I don't like running blind, and on this one, we need a little help."

Jim stretched out his long legs and folded his hands over his lean belly. "Gonna call in the Feds?"

Rio cast a wary glance at Becca. "Maybe. We'll see what new information my contacts dig up."

Becca gulped. "The Feds? As in … the FBI?"

Rio reached out, took her hand. "We'll see, okay? Now's not the time to worry about that." He sent a warning glance to his father.

"Pie?" Sarah said brightly, getting up to fetch the expertly made dessert, the top layer basket-weaved in an intricate pattern. As she took a tub of vanilla ice cream from the freezer and cut generous slices, she said, "Tomorrow, you guys will be busy. So, we're going to bake another pie, and then I'll take Becca for a ride into the meadow." She glanced at Becca. "You ride, don't you?"

"You mean on horseback? Yes, I love horses." As a child in private schooling, proper horsemanship was part of the curriculum.

After dinner, she helped Sarah clean the table while Rio washed dishes. Eventually, the men went onto the screened veranda. Big Jim smoked a fragrant cigar and Rio took a tall whisky on ice. Their low voices rumbled.

When the last dish was being put away, Sarah looked sideways at Becca. "Rio's smitten," she said, "with you. It's obvious."

"Oh, I don't think—"

"Trust me. I know him. He's my brother and he's crazy about you. He's never brought a woman home before. Never. And he looks at you as though he'd like to eat you for lunch."

Becca didn't know what to say.

"Are you in love with him?" Sarah demanded. "Just tell me."

"I—I don't know." She met the other woman's eyes anxiously. "I'm … safe with him. He … makes me feel beautiful and valued. It's just so soon. We only met days ago!" She rubbed her brow. "I'm grateful he's helping me solve this terrible mystery my family is mixed up in."

Sarah waited, and so Becca whispered, "All right. I'm crazy about him."

"Good enough," Sarah said briskly. "That's all I need to know. He's a fine man. He deserves the best. Looks like he found it."

Becca flushed. She hoped so. She really, really hoped so.

Chapter Thirty-One

That night they slept in his childhood bedroom, a simple room with a queen bed, an iron headboard, and a patchwork quilt. Becca curled to Rio's side, her arm across his chest. He pulled her close and within moments, he was out. For a little while longer, Becca lay awake. This man had come to mean a great deal to her. She trusted him. She needed him.

While he seemed just as taken with her, she really didn't know. She couldn't see inside his mind, couldn't tell what he might want from her later. Gently, without waking him, she stretched up to place a soft kiss on his neck. His skin was rough, warm. Under her lips, she could feel the steady beat of his heart. Her own heartbeat joined his, and it seemed to her that they thrummed together. Slowly closing her eyes, she drifted off with that wonderful thought.

In the morning, Rio used Big Jim's laptop to send emails. He made a series of hushed phone calls, and while waiting for answers, he helped his dad haul away a fallen tree, and later tinkered with a broken tractor engine.

On a ranch, Becca learned, there were endless chores. She warned him to be careful and not stretch the skin too much over his wound. He waved her away.

Becca helped Sarah prepare breakfast. Afterward, together they made a new apple pie and Becca enjoyed learning the skills of rolling out dough and mixing chopped apples with butter and sugared spices. The kitchen filled with the smell of cinnamon.

In the afternoon, they tacked up two saddle horses and went riding into a green meadow where deer grazed.

A stand of Douglas fir trees shaded a fawn at its mother's feet.

Becca held the leather reins in her left hand and leaned her forearms on the saddle horn. From Sarah, she'd borrowed jeans and an old straw cowboy hat. The jeans were okay through the hips, but were so long she'd had to roll them up at the hem.

As a child, she'd ridden enough times to be comfortable on horseback. Her mount was a paint quarter horse gelding. She patted his neck. His tail swished at a fly.

"Big Jim's not your real dad, right? Or Rio's? How'd you two end up here?" she asked Sarah, who sat close by on a bay mare.

Sarah raised her shoulder matter-of-factly, and resettled her straw hat. "We were both orphans. As an infant, Rio was left on the firehouse doorstep where our dad volunteered. That night he took Rio home."

Becca felt her eyes widen. "Somebody left an infant at a firehouse?"

"Happens more than you might think. As for me, my mom was homeless. She didn't want me anymore. Rio was about eight at the time. I was five, so I got an instant brother. Big Jim brought me home. Dad never married, never had kids of his own. We became his instant family. He formally adopted us both."

"Wow."

"We grew up here." She gestured at the landscape around them. "Riding horses, taking care of the cattle, doing chores. Every year Rio and I would show a pet goat or a pig at the fair. When we were a little older, I competed in barrel racing. Rio team roped."

"Rio can rope?" She couldn't have been more surprised.

"He's one of the best, a heeler. Coulda gone on

the circuit, but he wanted to join the military."

"I had no idea." Becca fiddled with her horse's mane. Add yet another talent to Rio's already impressive skill set.

"On a working ranch, there's always something to be done," Sarah went on, "and while we were busy, we never had a lot of extras. But we had happy childhoods. Big Jim is a great man."

"Sure sounds like it." When Becca thought of her own posh, privileged upbringing, she couldn't imagine that she'd had it better. While she, too, had a happy childhood, the best that a fat wallet could buy didn't seem superior to this bucolic life.

By the end of their third day at the ranch, Rio called a meeting. At the kitchen table, Big Jim and Sarah took chairs next to Rio. They'd eaten the evening meal, and the last three slices of Becca's apple pie. Everyone said it was delicious. After the dishes were cleared, Rio's manner became serious.

"Okay, enough answers have come in for us to draw some conclusions. Becca," he put his hand on her nape and rubbed, "are you sure you can handle this?"

She nodded, instantly tense. Somehow, after all they'd been through, it felt like they'd come to a crossroads. "I need the truth, wherever it leads."

"Okay. Remember I said before to always follow the money? That's what I did. Turns out your dad's senate campaign is definitely leaking cash. It takes a lot of dough to run for high office. He's getting donations, but they're not enough. Just as we suspected, he's been supplementing his war chest with a separate slush fund, which, by the way, is illegal as hell."

At last facing the full truth, Becca swallowed hard. "That's why Uncle—sorry, he's not my uncle— that's why Tim started the gun running out of the shop."

"And the sex trafficking," Rio added.

She bobbed her head. *Ugh!*

Big Jim's eyes grew hard and Sarah stiffened. "That ain't right," Jim growled.

"Sounds like," Sarah observed grimly "the definition of *dirty money*."

"As soon as we discovered it, I contacted some operatives I know," Rio went on, "gave them the video link to the shop from those cameras we placed. They have the evidence. They took up surveillance and followed the trucks hauling guns and young females to the border at Juarez."

Sarah gasped. "Oh, no! Those poor girls."

Rio held up a hand. "Don't worry. They were stopped. The guns and fentanyl were quietly confiscated, the driver arrested and the girls released. Another guy I've worked with, a tech expert, hacked into Daniel De Monte's campaign accounts. The extra money has been laundered, and then deposited, and then spent. You know what that means, right Becca?"

"It means my worst nightmare. That my dad is well aware of all the illegal activity." She spoke woodenly. Her head buzzed.

Sarah reached across the table to touch Becca's arm. "I'm sorry, Becca. I'm so sorry."

"What about my brothers?" she asked Rio, anxiety squeezing her chest. "Is there any evidence that they were involved?"

Rio shook his head. "That was checked out. They're not in the loop. They're clueless."

Becca slumped. "That's a relief, but honestly, I'm not surprised. I love the boys, but they are kind of … clueless in an all-around way. At work, they're fine salesmen, but once they leave, the remainder of their day is usually spent video gaming."

"The games saved their lives, Becca."

"What?" She squinted at him.

"Their general lack of attention. Their devotion to each other and to their video games. It meant they were never in danger like you were. It's why the bad guys didn't kidnap *them*."

She considered that. "It's my job, not theirs, to keep track of the shipping department. They wouldn't have been responsible for that aspect of our business anyway."

"Mmm." Leaning back in his chair, Rio crossed his arms and gazed at her. Big Jim and Sarah both stared downward. When at last Sarah stole a glance at her face, Becca realized they were all waiting for her.

She straightened and cleared her throat. "It's time to call in the authorities, isn't it? The Feds?"

Rio nodded in approval. "I don't know what will happen to your father's business," he said. "But it looks like your dad and Tim will be arrested, indicted, and most likely serve prison time. It's the smallest issue in all of this, but you'll probably lose your place of employment."

Becca frowned. "Maybe not. My brothers and I can run the business," she said slowly. "We've been doing it for a long time. I'm not concerned about that part." She may or may not have a job when the dust cleared. So what? Right then, it was hard to care.

Abruptly, her eyes filled. She put her hand to her forehead and bit her lip. "It's so difficult to accept," she said, "that my own father could go to such evil lengths. And do it for *money*!" She paused. "Was he ... did he know they were trying to kill me?"

"I doubt it," Rio said. "He went along with the crookery. He probably never saw you as a problem. That part fell to others. You might say there are degrees of evil."

She sighed. "Do what you have to, Rio."

"That settles it, then," he said. "We're gonna bust them."

He took her cell phone, went out onto the screened porch and made a phone call. Becca could hear him explaining everything. The following day, men in black arrived at the ranch.

The Feds.

Chapter Thirty-Two

"Multiple serious felonies are being committed," Agent Webster said, frowning. An experienced man in his mid-forties, he'd taken off his suit jacket, loosened his tie, and sat down at the kitchen table. He'd told Rio, Becca, Big Jim, and Sarah he'd been with the Bureau for twenty years. Ticking points off on his fingers, he said, "Unlawful possession of firearms, trafficking them across the border. Selling those firearms to neo-paramilitary criminal gangs in Mexico—"

"The Bureau of Alcohol, Tobacco, Firearms and Explosives will be notified," the second agent said. Agent Thompson, the other man and also in his forties added, "The ATF will be interested in the gun-running. The drugs. Meanwhile, there'll be charges for kidnapping, particularly in which the victims are willfully transported in foreign commerce. Those crimes carry mandatory prison sentences. Usually long."

Rio had shown them a video on the laptop computer of Tim moving the guns, and of the bound girls. "All right," Rio said. "It's in your hands now. You have all the information we know."

"We'll set up a broad sting, with our objective to nab all the perpetrators at once." Agent Webster's frown eased as he glanced at Sarah. "Ma'am, I'd sure love another piece of that wonderful pie." When she got up, his gaze lingered on her.

Uninterested, she set a plate before him and moved to the sink. Becca figured she must receive more than her share of male attention. If she hadn't felt so tense, she'd have smiled.

Then, Agent Thompson picked up his plate and

met Sarah at the sink. "I'd like to help you wash these, ma'am," he said hopefully.

Sarah plucked the plate from his hand. "No, thanks."

Chastised, he walked back to the table.

Rio and Big Jim got to their feet. The two agents shook hands all around. "We'll be in touch," the first one said to Rio. "It would simplify matters for us if you and Miss De Monte stayed out of San Antonio until you hear from me." With lingering glances at Sarah, they drove off.

Sarah didn't even notice.

"We'll stay here," Rio told Becca after they left, "until it's all finished. You're safe at the ranch, and I won't have to worry about you."

Sarah set aside her kitchen towel. Addressing Rio, she said, "You need to lay low, too, and keep that wound healing properly. Those stitches have been in your side long enough. It's time they came out."

"Ah, no, not now." He grimaced.

"Yep, now. They're coming out. I'll get my medical kit." She pointed at a chair. "Sit."

"Is Sarah a nurse?" Becca asked in wonder.

"Naw," Rio said, defeated. "But on a ranch you learn how to stitch up small cuts, and how to take 'em out. Out here, we don't run to the doctor for every little thing." Resigned, he sank down.

"It's going to hurt, isn't it?" Becca bit her lip.

Big Jim grinned. "Don't worry about Rio. He'll live."

As Sarah came back with a kit and a pair of tiny curved scissors, Becca admired her deft fingers. She wasn't only beautiful, but able.

While Sarah worked, Becca had time to think.

The federal agents were now in charge of

stopping the criminal acts that Tim and, unfortunately, her father were committing. She hated the idea of her dad's involvement. It would mean the end of his political dreams, and likely the end of his freedom. The worst part was knowing he'd made such poor decisions. He'd done it to himself, and he would pay the price.

Also, unfortunately, he was hurting his two sons, and hurting Becca, too. Why hadn't he considered his own children in all of this?

She didn't know. There was nothing to do now but wait.

****

Harrison ran a hand over his bald pate and blew out a frustrated breath. It had been a long time since he'd done wet work himself, preferring these days to delegate that sort of thing to his operatives.

However, it had now become mandatory. The careless assholes he'd assigned to do the job in Mexico had blown it badly. Then, the man he'd sent to ambush both Rio and Becca at her condo had failed. At least he'd managed to plug Rio in the side. A wound like that would be painful and perhaps debilitating. It wouldn't kill him, but should slow him down. At the proper time, it might help Harrison.

The situation had reached critical mass.

He took a fast turn around his spacious, penthouse office. This time, he'd have to do the job personally. He couldn't afford to have anyone know about his ties to Daniel De Monte's senate campaign. He was a behind-the-scenes guy. The one pulling the strings, not someone who got hung out to dry when things went south.

His wide net of underground sources had informed him that Rio had been contacting others to dig into areas he shouldn't be. Familiar with Rio's resourcefulness and persistence, Harrison knew that it was only a matter of time before the trail led straight back to himself. Not good. Besides, it was evident that Rio had already become suspicious of his motives.

Opening a desk drawer, he took out a Beretta M9 semi-automatic pistol. The weapon employed an open-slide, short-recoil delayed locking-block system, which yielded a faster cycle time and delivered exceptional accuracy and reliability. It was his favorite.

One by one, he fed 9mm rounds into an empty magazine. When it was loaded, he inserted the magazine into the weapon and tapped it home with the heel of his hand. Lastly, he placed a bullet into the chamber.

The gun was now hot.

While the Beretta M9 might not be as muscular or have the stopping power of a 45, Harrison preferred its lighter weight. He examined its sleek lines and admired the smooth black finish. It would do the job. Sighting down the barrel brought back memories of long ago days when he'd been a Green Beret. In the service and on wildly dangerous missions, he'd learned to fight. And he'd learned to kill. Although he'd aged, a man never forgot a skill like that.

It would not serve him well for Rio Lang to uncover his part in the moving of drugs, guns, and the stealing of young girls. The woman, Rebecca, would have to go, too. Of all the people working at De Monte Wheel Solutions, Becca was the only one with intimate knowledge of the shipping department, its deliveries, its transport. And by all accounts she was smart. It wouldn't have taken her long to figure out the scam.

They were the only two outsiders who knew the truth, and the only ones who presented a threat to his plans. He must eliminate the threat.

The system he'd brilliantly set up using De Monte's shop as a shipping hub was making them a lot of money, keeping the campaign machine running on the mother's milk of cold hard cash.

So long as he didn't have to personally see it happen, Daniel De Monte had agreed to it all, and Harrison enjoyed exploiting the other's overweening need for political influence.

For a moment, he indulged in thinking about that. Having a sitting senator deeply beholden to him, and one so cozy with the President himself—now *that* was influence and authority. At the prospect of such a marvelous outcome, Harrison smiled. Finally, he'd be the one pulling the levers of power in Washington. He'd waited and schemed a long time and the opportunity was ripe. No one could stop him now.

He picked up the phone.

"Our trucks," Tim said on the other end, "are being stopped, at least half of them, damn it! The authorities are confiscating the goods and setting the girls free. What the hell's going on?"

"Calm down, Tim," Harrison said, lighting a cigarette. He didn't care if Tim took the fall, because if the worst happened and the operation blew up, he planned to take the money and just disappear. Perhaps to Rio de Janeiro. The idea made him smile again. Rio would have a good laugh at that one, not that he'd ever get to know. "So what if the police grab a couple trucks? Others will get through. At this point the authorities don't know about the warehouse. The drivers won't talk, not even if they're convicted. They're too well paid, and they know a wad of cash waits for them when they get out. If they talk, they'll get a bullet. Trust me, they know that, too. Just keep doing what you're doing."

"Rebecca hasn't come back from wherever she went," Tim said. "Her brothers don't know where she is. Tell me you didn't have the cartel snatch her again. You said she wouldn't be hurt."

"Haven't touched her. She must have run away for a while, scared. Can't blame her. I'm sure she's fine."

"Yeah, well if she's with that boyfriend of hers then I'll worry. He's a mean sonofabitch. He really roughed me up. Think he broke my nose."

"Don't worry about him," Harrison said smoothly, hiding his disgust at the whining. Tim was weak, and he wasn't too bright, either. "He'll be out of the picture soon," he assured the other man. "Just keep those deliveries rolling, hear me?" Fondly, he fingered the grips of his Beretta. "Everything's working out great."

Chapter Thirty-Three

For three days, Rio and Becca waited for word. Sarah was unfailingly kind, and took Becca on more horseback rides. She was quick, funny, and tough. Becca liked her.

At night, she slept warm and snug in Rio's arms, his big body curved around hers. It felt right. And it felt good. Becca never wanted her time with him to end. She couldn't bear to face the day when he might wish to part from her. So, she didn't think about it. When those thoughts arose, she pushed them firmly aside.

On their fourth afternoon, she and Rio sat together on the screened porch, enjoying a cool glass of white wine. Sarah was busy with chores and Jim had gone to town for a tractor part. Beyond the porch, the alfalfa fields gave way to the towering mountain range. Two blue jays winged past.

Rio held Becca's hand, their fingers linked. He smiled at her.

"Sarah shared with me how you two came to have a home here with Big Jim," she said. "I hope you don't mind."

His smile didn't falter. "I don't mind."

His easygoing attitude encouraged her. "Well, I'm curious. Do you ever wonder about your mother and your true father?"

"Big Jim *is* my true father." His smile abruptly faded.

"I'm sorry," she rushed out. "Of course he is. I meant your natural father."

"The sperm donor?" He scoffed. "Why should I spend a second thinking about him? I don't even know if my mother told him she was pregnant. For all I know, he has no idea I'm even alive."

Becca nodded, and squeezed his hand. She'd gone plenty far enough with her probing. Time to drop the subject.

"You'll make a good mother," he said out of the blue. "You're responsible, logical, affectionate. Any kid of yours coming into this world will grow up lucky."

"Thank you," she said, touched by his praise. He sounded sincere.

To hide her pinkening cheeks, she sipped her wine. She felt certain that a child of Rio's would also be lucky, but she couldn't voice that thought. If they had children together, how blessed they'd be as parents.

She couldn't say that aloud either. She imagined, only briefly, nursing a little boy of his. He'd be blue-eyed, with golden baby curls. How adorable he'd be. How wonderful. Awed at her own thoughts, she marveled at herself. Until then, she hadn't even known she wanted children. But she did. Suddenly, she was certain. Stealing a glance at his handsome profile, her heart pounded.

To keep her thoughts private, she took more sips of wine. Because he'd never mentioned any promise of a future relationship, he could never know her fantasies. The glass quickly emptied.

"You're swilling that wine like a sailor on leave," Rio said with a laugh. "It's only afternoon. Maybe you'll want to slow it down a little?"

Becca managed an innocent smile. She held out her empty vessel. "This country air is invigorating. I'll slow down after the next one. Another glass, please?"

****

On the fifth day, Agent Webster phoned to tell them it was all over. Rio, Big Jim, Sarah and Becca gathered once again around the kitchen table. Rio put the phone on speaker so they could all hear.

"The sting went down without a hitch," Agent Webster said. His voice came through the speaker sounding tinny but loud. "Tim has been arrested together with his aides in the commission of illegal gun and drug transport and kidnapping."

Her hand at her throat, Becca leaned toward the phone. "And my father?"

"Daniel De Monte has been brought in for questioning. He made incriminating statements and was arrested. Big surprise, he's already lawyered up. Now, his senate campaign will be suspended. I'm sorry."

Hearing this, Becca's heart ached. Naturally she knew her father's attorney, his name and office address. At least he was in sound legal hands.

Rio pulled her to his side and stroked her arm.

"We have temporarily shut down operations at your father's hubcap distributorship and sent the employees home," the agent said. "However, I don't expect this to be for long. We have the perpetrators in custody. Now, the wheels of justice will begin to turn."

"Thank you, Agent Webster," Becca whispered.

"Eh, just a minute. We're not finished, Miss De Monte. We'll need both you and Rio Lang to come in for a thorough interview. The branch office in San Antonio will be fine."

She pushed hair out of her eyes and met Rio's steady gaze. "Of course. We'll do that."

Rio spoke up. "We'll leave here tomorrow."

She didn't object. The call was ended and abruptly she got to her feet. "I'm going for a walk," she told the surprised table.

Rio began to stand up and she held out a hand. "No, I need a little time alone."

He sank back down.

****

During a private walk around the corrals, she made a long phone call to her shocked brothers, explained matters, and told them to stay strong.

"Dad has been arrested," she told them. "And so has Tim."

Both were thoroughly bewildered. She could tell they had a hard time believing their father could have stooped to such lows.

"Where are they holding Dad?" James asked in a tight voice. "We have to go see him."

Quickly, she gave them the attorney's contact information.

"But where are you?" John asked. "We've been worried sick. Are you okay?"

"I'm in a safe place and I'll be home in a day or so. Don't worry. You won't be able to go into the office for a few weeks, but the authorities are working things out. We three will have a sit-down and decide what to do with the company. Personally, I think we can run things ourselves."

"We've been doing it right along anyway," James offered. "I think we should keep it running. You know … for Dad."

She agreed, and promised to be home soon and tell them more.

Becca leaned on a fence post and watched the placid cluster of Hereford cows chewing cud just on the other side. This whole nasty predicament was almost over. It felt anticlimactic, as though something else should happen first but she couldn't imagine what.

However, she was glad to see the end of the violence. If Tim and her father were convicted, and it was clear now that they should be, she must accept that. They had chosen to break both the laws of the land and the laws of morality. Sex trafficking! Becca shuddered. How could they? For political gain? For power? It was inconceivable, and something she realized she would have to deal with for a long time.

One last concern nagged at her: Rio had still made no mention of a future between them. He hadn't asked her about her plans or said a single thing about what might happen between them once they arrived back in San Antonio.

He'd given her no reason to believe he'd thought about it at all. Beyond his caring for her safety, which was his job, and even including their incredible sex, what ties might he feel to her? Very few, she concluded miserably. She clutched the fence so tightly her fingers ached.

If she were honest, she couldn't allow herself to be surprised. He'd told her that first time in the cabin that "no woman would have him." He was wrong about that, but he'd also said he was an adrenaline junkie, used to being in the scrum, on the move, part of the action. He implied it would last forever.

She wouldn't beg. She wouldn't abandon her dignity, and even if she wanted to, it wouldn't work. Rio would move on to his next job, his next hostage rescue, his next mission, and she'd become a memory. She wondered if, in time, he'd forget her.

The possibility knifed through her.

She was now about to lose the man she'd loved as an uncle, and about to see her father face ruin and shame. Most likely, he'd be incarcerated. Her life was imploding.

Would her heart be broken, too?

****

LATE THAT NIGHT WHEN Becca was asleep, Rio eased out of bed, picked up Becca's phone, and padded barefoot downstairs. Letting himself out into the night air, he took a seat on the front steps. In the pasture, moonlight shone on the cattle's white faces. A light breeze ruffled the trees. An owl began a solitary hooting. He punched in a number.

The man answered as though it were a reasonable hour and not two AM. "Ben Paxton," he said.

"Hey, Ben. It's Rio."

"Hey, fucker," Paxton replied easily. "How's it hanging?" He and Rio had served in the Teams together. These days, they didn't talk much, but the hairy missions in Afghanistan they'd barely survived had forged their friendship into a rock solid, unbreakable bond.

"Can't complain," Rio said. "Could use a little assistance."

"I'm here for you, brother. What do you need?"

They spent an hour talking and at the end of that time, Rio was satisfied.

"We've got work for you here," Paxton offered. "If you want it." Like Rio, he was now in the private sector. He and a few of their old teammates had formed a successful security business.

"Thanks. I'll consider it," Rio answered. They hung up.

Still on the steps, he examined every angle of the matter and decided he had it pretty well figured out.

At last, he made his final call. First, he made certain Becca's cell number was blocked from view.

"Where the fuck are you?" Harrison practically shouted into the receiver. "I told you that you have to come in."

"Sorry. I'm ready now. I'll be in San Antonio soon. You said you've got a new job for me and I'm a little low on funds. I need the work. Where do you want to meet?"

"That's more like it. By the way, have you had

any contact with Rebecca De Monte? The family still doesn't know where she is. She doesn't answer emails or her phone. It's been turned off."

"Yeah, I do," Rio admitted. "She's been in hiding and scared to death until she can talk to the Feds. She's going in day after tomorrow. They want to ask what she knows about some illegal crap going on at her father's hubcap business."

"She's talking to federal agents in two days?" Harrison's voice sharpened.

"That's what I said."

There was a short pause. "I'll get a hotel room there in San Antonio—tomorrow—so we can have privacy when we meet." He named a hotel and a time. "If you've got the girl, bring her."

"Sure," Rio said. "She'll be safer with me."

"Good thinking. You don't want to leave her behind. There's a bad element lurking out there. Make sure you bring her along."

DORSEY ADAMS

Chapter Thirty-Four

In thirty-six hours, Rio and Becca were indeed back in San Antonio. Rio's wound hadn't completely healed. That would take time. However, it hadn't become infected and the sides were slowly knitting together. Unless he forgot and bumped it, or moved too fast, he was in little pain. Certainly he couldn't be considered in combat effective shape, but he didn't expect further trouble.

To get the ordeal over with, they went straight to the authorities for their hours-long interview. Both told all they knew, and were finally allowed to leave.

Back at Becca's condo, they found where the shooter had hidden on her front stoop. The lock had been broken, but it didn't appear that he'd had time to go inside.

Rio spent a few hours replacing her old lock with a solid dead bolt, and he put new sturdy latches on her windows. No way was he going to leave her alone without adequate protection. The cartel would have no further interest in her now, he was certain, but there were a lot of bad guys out there and he believed in keeping honest people honest.

Besides, he had something to take care of and it didn't involve her.

Inside her condo, it was evident that her roommate had arrived home, stayed for a few days, and flown out again on a new work trip.

In the kitchen, Becca was happily preparing a roast chicken dinner, and had promised him an apple pie just like the one Sarah had taught her to make. He figured the female part of her needed to stir around the kitchen, find a sense of normality after all the stressful events. His new locks would help her feel secure in her home again.

Tomorrow she'd be interviewed a second time by the authorities, and her brothers would need to go in, too. The sooner the matter could be put behind them, the better. Another issue entirely was dealing with their disappointment in their father.

At five o'clock, he put aside the few tools he'd bought to install her locks and made sure his Glock was tucked into the small of his back. He wore a t-shirt and over that, an open button-down shirt to conceal the bump. "I have to go out for a while," he told her. "Be back in a few hours."

In surprise, she glanced up from seasoning her chicken. "Where are you going?"

He went to the door. "Got some business to take care of."

"What?" She put down her spoon. "What sort of business?"

"Don't worry about it." He walked back to cup her cheek and brush a kiss over her lips.

"Rio." She clutched his arm, her brow creasing. "You *are* coming back. Right? You're coming back?"

He marveled at her intuition. Somehow she seemed to know he was going into danger. But he couldn't admit that.

"In a couple of hours. I'll take the old rental car and leave your SUV here." He moved to the door. "Looking forward to that chicken and pie."

Worry clouded her features. "Wait. You're taking your gun?"

She must have seen the telltale bump on his back. There was nothing he could do about that now. "It's just habit."

Before she could protest further, he moved into the night. No way could he tell her that in the next few hours, somebody might be killed. He couldn't tell her there was a chance that somebody could be him.

DORSEY ADAMS

Chapter Thirty-Five

Rio sat half his butt onto a barstool in the hotel lounge, and stretched out a leg to leave one foot on the floor. Without appearing to search for anyone, he had a look around.

One of the nicest hotels in San Antonio, the Magnolia Inn was eight stories high, featured two restaurants, the bar, two pools, three conference halls, and a few hundred guest rooms. In the early evening, the place was busy with patrons enjoying a pre-meal drink, checking in at registration, and coming and going from their rooms.

An old establishment, it was built in the Spanish Colonial Revival style, with soaring arches and heavy iron lanterns. Giant potted palms against the walls sprouted from huge ceramic containers. The ceilings were cathedral-high. Flickering torches on rough-textured walls gave the feel of ancient Spain.

On the lounge stage, a hot Latina in a thigh-slitted sparkling dress crooned a love song, her legs sexily crossed. Behind her, an accompanying guitarist strummed away. As she sang, she caressed the microphone.

From the bartender, Rio ordered plain iced tea. "Put it in a highball glass. Lots of ice." When the drink arrived, he casually held it to his chest as though it were straight whiskey. Taking Becca's phone from his pocket, he again made sure her number was blocked and placed a call. "I'm in the hotel lounge," he told Harrison. "Come on down, have a drink."

As expected, he got an argument.

"Lang, I need you up here, in my room. I've got sensitive documentation to show you for the contract. I can't bring that out of my room. Just come up. You've got the girl, Rebecca, right?"

"Aw, c'mon," Rio said. "We've never met before. Let's have a drink. I'll go up to your room and see your papers after that. What do you want? I'll order it."

"No, you need to—"

"Bartender," Rio raised his voice at the worker behind the bar, "another one of these." He raised his glass. Into the receiver, he said, "Come on down. One drink. There's a hot chick, a lounge singer. She's sexy as fuck. You'll like her. I'll wait." And he hung up.

In a careful perusal of the room, he thought about the job waiting for him. He sure needed the work.

All seemed normal, with people chatting, moving around the hotel, going about their business. He liked the reassuring weight of his pistol sitting in his waistband.

Moments later, a bald, tall, overweight man approached. His skin was pocked, with the sallow hue of a person who was not particularly healthy. With a singular purpose, he walked toward Rio. His eyes were dark, bloodshot, and cold.

Harrison.

For a brief moment, a wispy memory slid through Rio's mind. Had he seen this man before? He couldn't place him, couldn't remember where.

"Lang." Harrison sat heavily on the next barstool. "Only one drink." He signaled to the bartender for gin. "Where's the girl?"

"Chill out, man." Rio studied the other. "She's in the ladies room." The familiar voice was the one he'd heard over the telephone many times when he'd been awarded Black Eagle contracts. Now, he could put a face to the man.

On the stage, the singer worked her way to the middle of her number, her voice growing in volume. She sang of lost love, of heartbreak, and the dangerous emotion of a lover spurned.

When Harrison's drink arrived, he downed it in three gulps. Getting off his stool, he gestured sharply at Rio. "Let's go. Get Rebecca."

"In a minute." Rio swigged his own drink. Casually, he looked around. Ben Paxton's men should be in position by now but he didn't see anyone. Catching the bartender's eye, he raised two fingers and pointed at his and Harrison's glasses. The man nodded.

"Listen, I'm flying out tonight." Harrison remained standing. Impatience underlined his words. "I have an important contract for you. A lotta money. You said you need it. Right, Lang? The details are in my room. Names. Dates. Locations that you'll need. We're going. Now."

On stage, the singer belted out her number, her voice rising. Her vibrato echoed off the stone walls in soaring notes. The torches seemed to flame brighter.

"Sure thing. Lemme finish this." Holding his drink, he pointed at the singer. "She's good, huh?" He glanced around again. Where were Paxton's men? They should make their move. *Now.*

The woman on stage allowed her voice to rise and it drowned out all other sounds.

Suddenly, in a subtle, efficient move Rio hadn't anticipated, Harrison pulled a Beretta pistol from his coat. Beneath the bar top, and out of sight of anyone observing, he shoved it hard into Rio's side.

The barrel crammed right into Rio's injury. Pain burst through his system. He doubled over in agony. Harrison couldn't have known about his gunshot, could he? Was it pure luck that he'd hit the weak spot? He felt part of the newly-healed skin tear open.

Beneath waves of pain, the truth flooded his mind. So, he'd been right: he'd become a liability to Harrison, and by extension, to Black Eagle. Now, Harrison planned to punch his ticket.

Where the hell was Paxton?

"Think you're going to mess up my plans?" the other hissed in his ear. "Those young girls and drugs funneling through De Monte's warehouse are funding the senate campaign nicely. We need that money to win."

Rio drew in enough air to wheeze, "That's *your* operation?" He wasn't surprised. He'd figured on some sort of connection, but *damn*. Rio wasn't really the one who'd gone rogue. The one who'd turned to the dark side was Harrison, with money at the root of his drive. Big shock.

Still bent over, he grimaced and hunted around the lounge for the help that should be there. Sweating, he struggled to breathe. The pain was debilitating. He could barely keep his seat on the stool.

Gripping Rio's arm, Harrison muttered, "Hold your hands in front of you where I can see 'em. If they leave my sight even for a second, you're dead. Got that? I'll come back later to get the girl. You're coming with me. Get up."

****

Making sure her hair was completely tucked up inside the beige bucket hat she'd pulled onto her head, Becca slipped inside the elegant hotel and tried to act like a normal guest. She wore black jeans and a long white sweater over a white camisole. The sweater opened at the front and hung nearly to her knees.

Rio's behavior had been so strange she hadn't even tried to resist the urge to follow him. What in the world was he doing at the Magnolia Inn? She sensed it had something to do with her miserable situation. If so, she should be part of it. If he thought she'd stay home fussing like a ninny over a chicken dinner, he was mistaken. She stiffened her spine. Besides, maybe she could help.

Setting her open-top hobo bag onto the end of the registration desk, she smiled and shook her head at an approaching receptionist and pretended to be searching for something. The receptionist returned the smile and moved away. In Becca's purse, her fingers absently brushed over her wallet, tissues, and makeup containers. As she did, she cast surreptitious glances around the lobby.

In her second pass, she spotted him in the adjacent lounge. A singer on stage in a sequin gown wailed away. Rio perched on a barstool, leaning awkwardly to one side. A man she didn't know stood close beside him and held his arm.

Instantly she sensed something had gone wrong.

Who was that strange man? And why was Rio's body canted to his side like he was favoring his healing wound? Had he somehow re-injured himself? He was in trouble, she just knew it.

Hotel employees scurried by, carrying trays and going about their business. Guests milled. Nothing else seemed amiss.

The man kept his grip on Rio's arm and appeared to be urging him to stand up. Rio's features were screwed up tight. She knew immediately he was fighting tremendous pain.

To others observing, little might indicate impending danger. But she knew about Rio's injury, and now he seemed to be favoring it. She could tell the other man's grip was not friendly. He had a coat draped over his arm and she couldn't see his hand. This didn't look good.

Like a blinding flood of lights in a dark room, panic lit her brain.

She had to do something. But what?

In the mountains, Rio had taught her a few survival skills. She tried to recall them now. *When in trouble,* he'd said, *adopt an offensive mindset. Transition from defensive to offensive mindset is essential.*

Casting her gaze about, she saw waiters, a broad reception desk, potted plants—nothing to use as a weapon. Yet she needed to go on the offensive. She needed something!

What are your strengths, he'd asked her at the time. *What can you use? Think!*

And then he'd cupped her breasts. *These are weapons, honey, never doubt it. Your confidence makes you wildly hot.*

And all at once, she knew.

Pulling off her hat, she shoved it into her bag and shook out her long hair so it spread around her shoulders in all its thick glory. Shrugging out of her long sweater, she left only her fitted camisole. With her arms bare, the tiny top revealed her small waist and the rounded rising of her full breasts. She draped the sweater and hobo bag over her arm, making sure her chest was on full display.

Pasting on a smile, she threw back her head and told herself in a repeated mantra, *I'm sexy. I'm hot. Men want me.* In order for this to work, she had to believe it. *Sexual confidence is wildly sexy*, Rio had told her.

Walking in a swaying strut, she struck out for the two men, strolling with confidence.

****

"There you are," Becca trilled at Rio. "You're not going anywhere, are you? I thought we were having a drink." In her last couple of steps, her breasts bounced.

Shit! Rio grimaced. She must have followed him to the hotel. Her presence now made his task exponentially more challenging. Damn. It was difficult to think over the searing pain in his side.

The other man half-turned to her. His scowl eased. "Rebecca De Monte? How nice. Rio was just telling me about you. He and I are old friends."

"*Becca.*" Rio said her name in a low and husky warning. Past her shoulder, he spotted two men staring at them suddenly start their way. Finally! Paxton had at last sent them in.

Yet, now with Becca unexpectedly in the line of fire, he couldn't allow it.

At his side away from Harrison, he clenched his fist, the signal to stop. Seeing his sign, the team veered off. He had to get rid of her. "Becca, you need to g—"

"You never told me about meeting a friend here," Becca said to Rio, smiling seductively at the older man. Perching herself onto the next barstool, she crossed her arms over her lap, causing her breasts to lift and swell over her top. Her nipples stood out against the top's thin fabric. "I thought we were just here for a little drinky poo."

What the hell is she doing? Rio groaned.

Predictably, Harrison's gaze fell to her deep cleavage.

Fishing a single ice cube from Rio's drink, she drew it across her neck and down to the tops of her breasts. Water beaded on her smooth skin. "Is it hot in here? I swear, sometimes I get so overheated." She giggled.

The older man's dark eyes lit in appreciation. He grinned, showing all his teeth.

As though suddenly noticing Rio's slouch, she asked, "Something wrong?" Like a woman who couldn't bear to stop touching herself, she trailed languid fingers over her chest. Idly, she glanced again at Rio. "Are you feeling well?"

The other man spoke up. "Rio's a little tired. We're headed to my room so he can rest, catch up, and have a couple of drinks. It's too loud in here. You'll join us, of course."

"Sure, I'll join you." She giggled again, a brainless female. "A private room sounds so much nicer than a public bar. If you're Rio's friend, then I can be your friend, too. But I didn't catch your name?"

"Harrison," he said.

Rio sent her a hard glance and gave a slight shake of his head. Gruffly, he told her, "Harrison and I have business. Private stuff. Go back home."

"Nonsense." Harrison tightened his grip on Rio's arm.

He pushed the barrel of his Beretta deeper into Rio's side. A new pain shot through him and he grunted. For long seconds, his brain went black.

"She'll go with us." Harrison leaned in and whispered to Rio, "Remember, keep those hands out front or she'll get it." Pulling Rio to his feet, he moved toward a bank of elevators. To anyone watching, Harrison appeared to be helping a drunk friend to his room. Becca slid off her stool and walked on Rio's opposite side.

"This will be a cozy party," Becca said, as though they were headed for a *ménage a trois*. Tugging her camisole top lower, leaving her breasts nearly bare, she leaned past Rio and gave the older man an impudent grin. When he boldly viewed what she offered, she smiled into his eyes. Taking advantage of his distraction, she slipped her arm across Rio's back.

He knew instantly that she felt something sticky on his waist, his blood. His wound had reopened, begun to soak through his t-shirt, but not yet through his open button-down shirt.

He felt her fingers trace the outlines of his pistol.

Rio caught her gaze and held it. *Take the gun*, he tried to communicate silently. Had she gotten the message?

Harrison yanked Rio away from her and closer to him. "Don't worry, I've got him. He'll feel better once we get to my room."

She smiled in agreement. "Do you have vodka up there?"

"You bet, honey." His eyes glittered, and dropped again to her chest. She curled a lock of her hair around a finger and gave him a saucy smile.

An elevator opened, filled with people.

Their little party pressed inside and faced front.

With Harrison on Rio's right, Becca maintained her position to his left. As the elevator doors closed, they jostled among others.

In the tight confines, Becca again wormed her hand around Rio's back and eased up his shirt. Her fingers closing around the grip of his Glock, she slid it from his pants and held it close to her side. It disappeared into the folds of her sweater, still hung over her arm.

On the seventh floor, the elevator pinged and the doors opened. They stepped off, and behind them the doors *whooshed* closed. A long hallway stretched out. It was empty.

Rio scanned the area. With Harrison's pistol still rammed in his wound, he could do little. He needed Becca to get him the weapon.

Had Paxton's men followed them up? Where the fuck were they? If Harrison managed to get Rio and Becca into his locked hotel room, it would be too late. Harrison was bent on murder.

He needed his Glock.

Beside him, Becca had her hand down her shoulder bag and seemed to be scrounging around the bottom for something. He tried to catch her eye but she was looking into her bag. At the closed door, Harrison stopped and fished out a room card.

Alarm bells clanging, Rio knew they could not go into the enclosed place. Not with him bleeding and weakened, and absolutely not with Becca. In this state, he wouldn't be able to physically overwhelm Harrison. Although an older man now, Harrison had been a Green Beret. He knew nasty moves they didn't teach at boot camp or academy. His grip on Rio was strong, punishing. The pistol he kept shoved into his wound was agonizing, and kept him immobile. Harrison was no fool, and he'd be expecting Rio to try something.

Becca chose that moment to act.

Chapter Thirty-Six

At the bottom of her handbag, still hung on her arm, Becca scrabbled her fingers around until she found what she wanted. She had no pen with which to stab Harrison, no folding knife, not even a comb to jab into his face.

But she did have her full container of loose make-up powder. In her other hand she clutched the Glock and wished she could use it herself. However, with little confidence in her shooting skills, she was certain that the instant Harrison saw it he'd kill both her and Rio. He'd be faster on the uptake than she could ever be.

No, she must get the weapon into more capable hands. Rio's hands. Right then, she needed a distraction—a diversion—if only to buy her an all-important beat in time.

At the cabin, Rio had said that throwing dirt or sand into an enemy's eyes could temporarily blind them, could buy vital seconds. Wouldn't make-up powder do the same? Her fingers still deep inside her purse, she worked to unscrew the top and managed to dump its contents into her palm. Her shaking fingers curled around the precious, fine grains. She bit her lip.

Just as Harrison was sliding his card key into the lock, she drew her hand from the bag and threw the powder directly into his eyes.

"Damn you!" His head jerked back and he released his hold on Rio. He clawed at his eyes.

She thrust the Glock at Rio. Taking it, he shoved her away. Stumbling back to the wall, she cried out, and caught her balance.

Harrison roared and raised his Beretta. He bared

his teeth.

Gunshots boomed. Her heart in her throat, Becca hugged the wall.

Not three feet away, Harrison twisted this way, then that, his body riddled with bullets. He fell back, and landed twitching on the carpet. Then he stilled. From two holes in his forehead and three in his chest, blood dripped on the floor, and made small pools.

Rio stood, bent to the side, panting. His Glock was still raised.

From down the hall, men ran past Becca to approach the man on the floor. They first kicked the gun away from his lifeless hand, then turned to Rio. "You all right?"

"Yeah. But that was close, Paxton. Not sure if I got him first or you did. Where the fuck have you been?"

"Sorry, got hung up on the elevator. Had to use the stairs. And you hit him first. You got the head shots. I got him center mass." The man was tall, burly, and carried himself with the same poised self-confidence as Rio.

Lightheaded, Becca gaped at them all, mostly at the dead man. She'd never seen anyone shot before. Never seen anyone die. Her fingers went to her mouth. With the smoke already dissipating, the acrid smell of gunpowder filled her nostrils.

Still leaning to his side, Rio moved to take her arm. "Are you okay?"

Unable to speak, she wobbled her head in something resembling a nod.

The men quickly secured the area and kept hotel patrons from the hallway. She and Rio were taken downstairs to wait for the police. Paxton, apparently the man in charge, said to them, "Don't worry. We have a pretty good working relationship with the authorities.

They're gonna have a lot of questions, and it'll take a while, but we'll get matters straightened out. I'll be back down in a few."

Downstairs, the hotel had erupted into a panic. The gunfire had echoed through the floors and people were running, scrambling for cover, locking themselves into their rooms. Women screamed and hotel employees shouted conflicting instructions.

Rio led her through the milling crowd to the lobby and an out-of-the-way grouping of sofa and chairs. They sat, which was a good thing because Becca was sure her shaking knees were about to give out. Unsteady, she sank down.

Rio pressed his hand to his side. Blood soaked through both layers of his two shirts. He pulled Becca to his other side, and stroked her arm.

In minutes, the man Rio had called Paxton joined them. He was muscular, with a short, military-style haircut and a self-possessed manner.

Rio said, "Ben Paxton, this is Rebecca De Monte."

Paxton inclined his head. "Miss De Monte."

"Nice to meet you," she managed, her voice quavering. "Thanks for saving our lives."

He cracked a small smile. "It looked like you two had things pretty well in hand. What was that stuff you threw into Harrison's face?"

"Make-up powder," she managed to get out, teeth chattering. "From my handbag."

"Genius move, blinding Harrison." He gave her an admiring glance. "Your timing was spot on, too. Just now, we went into Harrison's room, checked it out. It looks like he'd prepared a kill site. A lot of plastic laid out on the floor."

"Plastic?" She blinked. Her brain felt like wet

oatmeal. It seemed to be barely working.

"To contain the blood," Rio explained. He kept his hand pressed to his bleeding side. "To hold our bodies. No evidence left behind."

Becca shuddered, suddenly very cold. Harrison was planning murder.

She couldn't look away from Rio. "We need to get Rio medical care," she told Paxton. "His wound has reopened."

"We'll see he gets attention," Paxton said, getting out a cell phone and calling for a doctor.

Scooting closer to him, Becca leaned into Rio. "Who was the man, anyway? That—that Harrison?"

Rio grimaced. "Believe it or not, he was my boss."

Chapter Thirty-Seven

Drained and exhausted, Becca stumbled into her condo, saying she could think only of sleep.

Rio understood. They'd spent hours at the police station explaining matters, being interviewed. The federal agents they'd worked with before were called in. It was past dawn before they were released. Finally, he'd had to sit for a nurse, called in to re-stitch his injury and give him a new shot.

Behind her, Rio flipped closed the new deadbolt locks and followed her into the bedroom. Without talking, they stripped off clothing, and dropped it to the floor where they stood. He took two painkillers. Carefully minding his newly-stitched wound, they made love quietly. Their orgasms came in a short rush, and soon Becca fell into a deep slumber.

Holding her in his arms, Rio found sleep elusive. Now that Becca was safely out of danger, he was confident she would no longer need his protection. The threats had been neutralized and he was glad.

He guessed he'd go back to work for some government entity that could use his talents. He wasn't a doctor, didn't have a law degree, what else would he do for a living? Dig ditches? No, his skills earned in the elite Special Forces had served him well in civilian life, and he'd made money utilizing them. That was where his talents lay, and he'd continue on. He was a mercenary. His expertise was bought and paid for.

With a grim fatalism, he realized that his sort of life left no room for a woman like Becca. She'd expect, and she'd *deserve*, someone reliable, someone steady. Not a man often sent to far-flung lands, constantly putting his life at risk.

Rio knew she and her brothers would figure out a way to continue running their father's business. They liked the work and were proficient in that industry. The corporation would become theirs. Becca would be all right.

She wouldn't need him anymore.

One day she'd find someone who answered to a nine-to-five, a nice, good guy who'd be home for dinner. He'd take care of her, take care of their kids.

The notion of her bearing another man's children stabbed into him, and he took a hard breath. He didn't like considering such an outcome. In fact, he hated it.

Without thinking, he tightened his hold around her naked, sleeping body. She stirred, and he made a conscious attempt to loosen his grip. The effort actually made him grimace.

In a moment, he got his head back on track. That other guy he imagined for her was the sort of man she needed, not a nomad like him. Not a man unaccustomed to a placid life devoid of interesting predicaments he must solve using both his brains and his brawn. He was a loner, a man apart. It was time to move on.

Tomorrow.

The break should be made clean, without a lot of uncomfortable hanging around, no second-guessing himself, and absolutely no talk of *feelings*.

He wasn't the type of *good* man Becca needed. After all, he was bad. He should face facts. He wasn't the decent guy she should have. He'd proven that. Over and over.

He was Bad Rio.

****

They slept nearly around the clock, and Becca woke to see Rio pulling on his pants. It was nearly evening. His movements were necessarily slow. Re-opening his wound again was not an option. Sitting up, she rubbed her eyes.

"Hey, sleepy head." He glanced at her. "Feel okay today?"

The events of the night before flooded back and she groaned. The scene at the Magnolia Inn ... the images of Harrison frog-marching a weakened Rio into an elevator ... the moment when she acted ... the gunshots ... the blood. She shuddered. "I'm not sure yet. Are we still alive?"

"Alive and kicking." He sat on the bed to pull on socks and tennis shoes.

From the pillows, still nude, she smiled at him. "Hungry? I could eat a horse. I don't care what time of day it is, I'm thinking about making pancakes, eggs, bacon. And maybe breakfast potatoes. Sound good?" Pushing her arms into the air, she arched her back, and stretched.

"Can I have a rain check?" He shrugged into his button-down shirt and picked up his shoulder bag.

Puzzled, she stopped in mid-stretch. "Are you going somewhere?"

"Yeah." He picked up his oilskin bag. "Time for me to leave."

She watched as he slipped the strap across his neck. Perhaps it was the dullness of her just-waking brain, but she didn't understand him. "To leave for where?"

"Just time for me to go. You're safe now, with no further threat. All the bad guys are neutralized." He turned and left the bedroom, stopping in the kitchen to fill a quick glass of water from the faucet.

Bewildered, she grabbed a light wrapper and followed. As he drained his glass and set it in the sink, she pulled on her wrapper and tied it at her waist. "Sorry, I just woke up, but I'm a little foggy. What's going on here? You're leaving … like … for good?"

He went to her front door and disengaged the dead bolt. "The job's done. Time for me to head out."

Her jaw dropped and the mists of sleep fled. A hideous shock spiraled up her spine. "You're heading out as in *moving on*?"

Coming back to her, he cupped her jaw. "I'll miss you."

Her eyes round, she heard herself repeat him like a stupid parrot. "You'll *miss* me? I—I thought. Well, I figured—" Stopping herself, she felt unexpected tears well in her lower lids. Growing frantic, she searched his eyes. Hadn't she always told herself he wouldn't stay with her? Hadn't she long ago realized the hard truth— that he wasn't going to be her man?

"You didn't figure I'd stick around," he scolded her gently. "I never made promises. Never said we'd get married or anything crazy. You knew that."

All at once she found standing before her the old Rio, the one who'd first confronted her in the cabin. He was again the aloof, uncaring, detached man she'd once discovered him to be. Had she been right about him all along? Was he truly cold? Was he incapable of emotionally caring for another human being?

She felt her throat working. Pain took hold, grew in her chest, stabbed like a hundred sharpened knives. She jerked her chin from his hand. "You never promised to stay with me," she acknowledged. "Actually, I didn't think you would." She gave an awkward laugh. "I just thought … silly me, that you'd want to."

A shadow passed over his face. He rubbed the back of his neck. "I'm tempted, but I'm just not the committing kind. I gotta keep moving, you know?"

"You're tempted," she repeated. Why did she keep echoing everything he said? She was having trouble understanding. "You're walking out on me—away from *us*?" He was abandoning their deep connection, their intense relationship, and he was doing it like it was *nothing*?

A new anger mingled with the heartache.

His hand went to the knob. He was just walking out. Going to the next job, and naturally the next *woman* as though the magic between the two of them had no more importance than a casual fling. As though what they had wasn't incredibly intense, or valuable, or life changing, or something to be honored. Something *precious*.

"Rio," she whispered. "Please."

He stiffened, turned to face her. His features hardened. "You'll be all right, Becca. You have your family. You'll find somebody else. You've got your business. Your damn hubcaps."

"My *damn* hubcaps?" That stung. She felt her trembling lips firm. "I realize my wheel cover business isn't curing cancer, but we do provide a service and products people need and want."

"Yeah, well, when it cures cancer, give me a holler." He opened the locks. "They're not that important in the world, your hubcaps. Don't make a big deal out of them."

She watched him, hurt beyond measure. "Why?" she whispered, agonized. "Why are you saying these things? Why are you leaving?"

"Cause it's time," he answered simply.

Becca felt her face flush. Suddenly she felt used. Giving him her back, she pulled at the ties of her light robe, tightened them around her waist until they pinched her skin.

The small pain helped her to gather dignity. She refused to beg. Dashing at her eyes, she said, "Hey, thanks for everything. Much appreciated and all that. Have a great life."

"Don't be mad, Becca. I told you. I'm bad."

She heard rather than saw his hand open the door.

Whirling, she said, "You know what I think? I think you use that word to describe yourself when you need emotional protection. It's a wall you build so *you* won't get hurt."

He shrugged, but she kept on. She had to. "I am mad at you right now, but mad doesn't even begin to describe this. I'm furious. And I *am* hurt. You're just going to walk out of here and out of my life like I don't matter to you?"

He remained silent.

"But I do, Rio," she said. The sadness had already started seeping in, pulling her down, down into a whirling vortex of agony. "I really, really do. Life won't leave you unscathed when you keep running from it. You *will* miss me. You're going to miss me something awful."

He just stared at her.

She could barely speak around the terrible lump in her throat, but she had to get out a final notion. "One last thing. You keep saying you're bad. You use it as a shield. I'm disappointed and angry. But there's a simple truth one day you'll have to face." She raised her chin. "You're wrongheaded and acting just plain stupid. And oh, and now insulting. But despite all that, you're not bad, Rio. You're good. You're a good man." Trembling now, she sent him all her pain and agony through her eyes. She pointed outside as though his leaving were all her idea. "Now go."

But it wasn't. It wasn't her idea at all.

Chapter Thirty-Eight

Two months later

Accepting her photo identification the uniformed desk clerk returned to her, as she had done on several prior trips to the county jail, Becca was led through a metal detector, down long hallways, through locked doors and into the visiting room.

She'd been advised to leave her purse and all valuables at home or in a locked car. She was told to dress conservatively. In the visiting room, other inmates sat at adjacent window talk boxes and shouted through the screen to be heard. Voices echoed loudly off the barren walls. In the gray room, it was loud, and there was absolutely no privacy.

Becca hid her distress. She hated coming here.

She took a chair and waited for her father to appear on the other side of the metal screen. He was led in and she saw that the baggy orange jumpsuit did his complexion no favors. His eyes were defeated, his face hangdog. The skin around his neck drooped and to Becca, her once-handsome father had never looked older. Ever since his arrest, he'd worn the beaten expression. It had become permanent.

She leaned toward the screen and raised her voice. "Hi, Dad. You okay?"

He gave a fatalistic shrug. "Good as can be expected. How are you and the boys?"

"Fine, we're back to work at the warehouse, doing what we've always done. The company is in shipshape."

"It's your company now, yours and the boys. I've signed everything over to you three. My attorney has all the paperwork." He glanced around at the drab gray walls. "It's not like I need a business any more. I'll be incarcerated, probably until I die."

"Maybe you won't be convicted, Dad." The moment the comment left her lips, she knew it to be a lie. His trial would take place in the coming months.

"I will, though. It's all right. I deserve it. So does Tim." He shook his head. "My mind got too filled with glory, and the prospect of political power. It was heady, and I was willing to do anything to achieve it." He glanced at the floor. "I lost my way."

She drew a deep breath. "The boys and I have set up a savings account. We'll deposit a salary every month. So, when you do get out, you'll have a nice nest egg. You won't be destitute. And if you want, you can come live with one of us, but you won't have to. You'll have means."

Abruptly, the older man's bloodshot eyes filled. "You don't have to do that."

"Of course we do, Dad. It was your company. We owe you that."

He smiled tremulously. "John visited me this week."

"I know. We're going to take turns. James will come next. Every couple of weeks, you can count on a visit from at least one of us."

He put his hand on the screen. "I'm sorry, Rebecca. I'm so sorry." He choked back a sob.

Becca fought tears. How far he'd fallen, from a wealthy, serious contender for a lofty senate seat, now to this woeful new low.

A jailer called his name and he jerked, then slowly faced his daughter again. "Thanks for coming by to see your old daddy." He shuffled out of the room.

Melancholy, she got up and followed a guard

guiding her through the locked and barred doors to outside the grim building, and to freedom. Although it was an eighty-degree day in San Antonio and the sun warmed her hair, she shivered. To be locked up, shackled, kept prisoner was something she'd experienced during her brief time as a captive of the Mexican cartel. She never wanted to relive that sort of thing again. Always law abiding, after these visits to see her father, she knew she'd never again even jaywalk.

In her car, she paid the parking attendant and pulled into traffic. On the seat beside her, there had been a bloodstain from Rio's injury. She'd had it professionally cleaned. When, the second morning, she'd woke to his scent on her pillow, she washed everything.

He'd left nothing behind, and she had nothing to remember him by, not a photo, nor article of clothing, nor the simplest talisman. At first she wanted it that way, wanted nothing around that would remind her of him. The agony was too sharp.

She had only her memories, and those she could not erase like the stain in her car or his smell from her pillow.

Each time they invaded her thoughts, her mood sunk to miserable, tear-inducing lows. At work, she struggled to concentrate, at home, she cried. A lot. Even feeding her frogs made her weep because she recalled how grateful she'd been when Rio had tended to her small pets. His thoughtfulness had touched her.

Like snapshots in her mind, memories of their times at the mountain cabin flashed by, of his warming her body when she was sick, and of her caring for him when he was injured. Finally, of their incredible lovemaking. Those times, she remembered most of all. And most of all … his tenderness.

Now, Rio was gone and there was nothing she

could do about it.

In the end he'd wounded her deeply. She'd been dumped. Hard. And he'd denigrated her work. It still bewildered her, why he'd felt the need to do that. If he'd wanted to be free of her, why not just walk away? Indeed, he'd been unnecessarily cruel.

The bruising of her feminine ego was the least of it. She missed him. Each day when she woke, her chest hurt and she wondered if that was the kind of pain that produced the term *heartbroken*. Of course the pain was only psychosomatic, not real. There was nothing wrong with the heart beating in her chest. She was healthy. But the pain persisted.

Her girlfriends called, but she refused their entreaties to go out. She didn't feel like company. Maria phoned from Mexico, from her father's mansion.

"You wouldn't believe how my father has strengthened security around here," Maria said. "He's so glad you were returned home safely, but he never wants anything like that to happen again."

"I'm just glad you two are safe," Becca returned. They chatted for a while and when they hung up, Becca thought of Rio rescuing her from her hostage takers, and again she burst into tears.

Now, even two months later, the ache was just as fresh as it had been the day he'd walked out.

She was afraid it would never end.

Chapter Thirty-Nine

Austin, Texas

Rio Lang, Ben Paxton, and two other ex-military operatives stacked up at the shoot house door in close quarters combat formation. Each was armed with his weapon of choice. Rio took up last position. Paxton took first.

The building, constructed by Paxton's security business, was two-story, held many rooms, and was equipped with easily moved targets. There were dummies of women holding babies, and cutouts of military-aged men, each designed to engage small combat units moving through.

Recently, Paxton had added holograms of both enemy fighters and innocent bystanders. The eerie images could be shone on walls and appeared quite real. So that the exercise was never the same, the building could be configured in hundreds of permutations. A man undergoing such training would learn when to dial up the violence and, just as important, when to dial it down. He'd hone his skills on high alert, thinking fast, fine-tuning muzzle control and target discrimination. He would take good kill shots, either to center mass or to the head.

For this kind of work, Rio liked the Navy's version of a MP5 Heckler & Koch submachine gun. His MP5 fired a 9mm Parabellum round in single shot, three-round bursts on full automatic. And it did that at an impressive eight-hundred rounds per minute. The weapon was small, light, and used by antiterrorist forces throughout the world. Extra magazines sat snug in Rio's canvas vest, just in case the men found any unpleasant surprises inside. No doubt they would. That was the point.

All four men wore combat fatigues, boots, and helmets. Although this was not battle, and the building stood safely on private American soil, Rio was already perspiring. The team-building exercise felt damn good and the anticipation stirred him. He sought eye contact with the two trainees waiting between Paxton and him. He said, "Remember our goals. Move, shoot, communicate." They both nodded.

How well he recalled the SEAL credo, *the more you sweat in training, the less you bleed in combat.* It's why they trained so much and so hard.

On point, Paxton gave the forward wave hand signal. As a coordinated unit, they moved inside. Paxton peeled off left and the next man went right, then the third took a knee, swept the area. Each covered his firing sector for threats. Close behind, Rio slipped in.

Sometime later when they came out the other side, most of their ammo was gone and not a single innocent had been '*killed.*' High fives and knuckle bumps were exchanged all around, and Ben Paxton faced Rio.

"Glad you decided to join our firm," he said. "We've really been needing a guy with your talents here at our training facilities."

"Never figured I'd grow up to be an instructor," Rio said dryly. "Thought I'd always need the excitement of operating in the field. Been thinking about it a lot. Found out, after all, I'm tired of getting shot at. I'm over it."

Paxton nodded. "Tough guy snake-eaters like you often stay in the game too long. I think your decision to come on board here is sound." Paxton met his gaze seriously. A *snake-eater* was slang for Special Forces operators.

"It suits me," Rio said, realizing he was finally right where he belonged. "I'm enjoying teaching the lads the skills you and I both came by in our SEAL training and in the field."

"Feels like you're giving back, eh?" Paxton looked at him shrewdly.

Rio cocked his head. "Yeah. Like that. Guess I don't need to get my ass shot off any more. Thought I'd still want the rush of action. But…" He gazed off into the distance, and grew pensive. He rubbed his jaw.

Paxton gave him a discerning glance. "What's going on with you?"

"Huh?"

"Don't shit me, Lang. Lately, you're always staring off into space. What's going on in your pea brain?"

Rio shrugged. "I dunno. Just thinking I should make a trip back up to Montana. See Big Jim and Sarah."

Paxton propped his hands on his hips. "For how long? Next month we've got a new cadre of recruits coming in. You're needed here."

"I'll be back to work soon. Just be gone two weeks or so."

"Okay, no problem, then," Paxton said, relieved. "We can do without you for that long. When you're up there in all that fresh air, maybe you can get your thick head cleared out."

"No worries," Rio said. "I'll get everything locked down. See you soon."

****

That very evening, Rio managed to catch a flight and by midnight was in Billings. Renting a truck, he drove to the ranch and let himself quietly into the house. Because he'd phoned his dad ahead, he didn't worry that

Big Jim or even Sarah would greet him in the dark from behind the business end of a pointed rifle. Any fool planning to rob that particular home would find himself very unhappily surprised. Recognizing his scent, the dogs stayed in their beds, their tails thumping. The house was still.

At last, Rio was able to lie down on his patchwork quilt and prop his hands beneath his head. His eyes now used to the dark, he stared at the open beam ceiling and wasn't quite sure why he'd felt it necessary to come home. He only knew that while he'd finally found a great job perfectly suited to him, in the past two months a great restlessness had gripped him. When he'd told Paxton he'd tired of the constant danger and various treacheries on both sides of the law, he'd meant it.

So, why this edginess? This disquiet?

It was difficult, but he had to admit a singular truth to himself: he missed Becca. On first acknowledgement of the unavoidable fact, he didn't like it. It felt like weakness.

After all, he was a loner by nature and preference, a lone wolf, footloose, free.

Somehow, Becca had ensnared him. But how? When he'd left her, she hadn't thrown a rope over his head. Instead she'd challenged him to look inside, to understand that all these years while he'd thought himself indifferent and untouched by anyone, she'd gotten past his barriers. *She'd* touched him.

Rolling onto his side, he closed his eyes. He recalled the brave way she'd followed him into the Rio Grande, and at the moment of their greatest danger, the deviltry in her eyes. Somehow that moment had become symbolic to him—of her courage, her pluck. He remembered how quickly they'd formed a team, working side-by-side to solve the gun-drug-and-girl smuggling mystery. He appreciated her bright mind, how she'd used something she found in her purse to help save them from certain death at Harrison's hand.

With no effort, he summoned her beautiful smile, her velvet brown eyes smiling into his. Upending his long-held belief that he was mostly unconnected to the human race, Becca had looked at him as though he was the best man in the world. She'd seen value in him. She'd wanted him. She'd made him feel good. It wasn't weakness she engendered in him, after all.

It was strength.

A long while later, he fell asleep, and in the morning when he woke, he reached across the bed for the warm body, the one that should be curled next to him. When he found only the old quilt, he groaned. Becca wasn't there. Each and every day since walking out of her life, he'd woken to reach for her.

And each and every day, the bed was empty.

****

At breakfast, it became immediately apparent that Sarah was furious with him. He took a seat at the kitchen table next to Big Jim, who was already eating from a filled plate. The dogs patrolled the floor, hoping for crumbs.

She set Rio's plate of bacon and eggs on the kitchen table and shoved it at him so hard that if he hadn't caught it at the edge of the table, one of the dogs would have been obliged to rescue it off the floor. Sarah went to the sink, and then threw a glare at him over her shoulder.

"Hey, what's your problem?" Rio spread his hands.

"I don't have a problem, Rio. But you sure seem to."

"Mind telling me what you're talking about?"

Tossing her long braid over her shoulder, she stomped to the stove and flipped four hot pancakes. When she refused to answer, Rio looked at the pancakes with longing. Nobody made them better than Sarah. "Can I have a couple?"

With a spatula, she lifted a thick pancake off the heat, waved it in the air to cool, and tossed it to a dog, who caught it deftly in mid-air. She turned her back on him.

Mystified, Rio sought his father's gaze. Jim was smirking. He said nothing, and continued to shovel in food. Rio guessed he wasn't getting any pancakes that day. He shrugged. *Women.*

Facing his dad, Rio asked, "Want to restring that stretch of broken barbed wire fence today? I'll get the posthole digger and sink some new posts."

"Gotta do that," Jim agreed, his mouth full, "and clear out a couple of water holes. Also, it's time to move the mother cows to the far meadow. Fresh graze there."

And so Rio's day began. When he was home, working the land with Jim, it felt right and good, and the outside world seemed far away.

Only the physical labor left him more time to brood about Becca. No woman had ever before burrowed her way into his mind like this. No woman had ever captured his imagination like she did, both in and out of bed. No woman had ever seemed as perfectly suited for him … as Rebecca De Monte.

Try as he might, he couldn't exorcise her pretty face and velvety brown eyes from his mind. Nothing stopped the flashbacks of her bright smile, or the gratification he'd felt when at last she'd begun to trust him. When they were midway through their treacherous Rio Grande swim, crossing into the States, how well he recalled the exhilarated look in her eyes. *She's like me,* he'd thought. No woman before had ever made him feel such simpatico. Beneath her ghillie hat, she'd audaciously winked back at him. He'd known she was frightened, but she'd pushed by those fears to join him in the adventure.

Nor could he forget the generous, wildly sexy way she made love to him. In bed, the woman was delightfully uninhibited, generous, and sensual as hell.

That last day, in the moment he'd walked out of her life, the thing he remembered most was the searing vulnerability in her eyes. She'd been blind-sided, caught unaware that he would be taking off and leaving her behind to return to his old life. He was determined to go, but more than anything, her expression of pain had given him pause.

So, he'd blasted her, torn down her understandable pride in her work and her family company. He'd belittled her hubcaps.

Deep down he knew why he'd done it.

The old green monster. How he envied her place in the world, her deep connection to others. She was the perfect center of her universe, both loved and appreciated by everyone she touched. Out of nowhere he remembered her office and its bulletin board proudly displaying the thank-you notes from her employees' children. In the vast sea of humanity, she had value.

And Rio? In the galaxy of his existence, he had pretty much spun through space alone. If not for his infrequent visits home to see Jim and Sarah, he was adrift, unimportant to anyone, valuable to no one.

Pausing a moment in the heavy labor of posthole digging, he drew a handkerchief from his pocket and wiped away sweat. Kneeling in the dirt at his feet, Big Jim used an old coffee can to scoop loose soil from the hole.

"Fuck is wrong with me?" Rio muttered beneath his breath.

Jim stopped scooping and screwed an eye up at him. "Why don't you ask Sarah that question?"

"Sarah?" Rio shoved the handkerchief into his pocket. He hadn't meant to say his comment out loud. "Why would I ask her?"

"She's a female. Women know these things."

Rio scoffed. He sure wouldn't be asking his sister any damn thing like that. With renewed energy, he began thrusting the digger back into the hard earth.

"Son," Big Jim said, still scooping loose dirt, "those jobs you've been taking have been pretty hard on you."

"I'm all right." He continued with the posthole digger. Thrust, lift and dig. Thrust.

"One day, a man should decide he's done enough saving the world, and let others who come after him take it up."

Rio paused in his digging. "Are you saying I'm getting old?"

"You're for sure no spring chicken. Not anymore."

Rio scoffed. "I'm only thirty-five."

"You've gone your own way, and I haven't tried to run your life or tell you what to do. And you've done well. Got a lot of money stashed away, right? I'm real proud of you, son."

"But?" Rio rested his gloved hands on his hips. May as well have Jim spit it out.

"But you can't be Jason Bourne forever."

"Are you saying I should slow down?"

"Not slow down, necessarily, just back out of the line of fire. You have a lot of skills. Use them. But stop sticking your neck out."

Rio was grateful he'd already come to the same conclusion. "Well, guess what? I've already changed things." He told his dad about taking the position at Ben Paxton's security firm, and how he'd likely stay there. He was done with the Black Eagle organizations of the world. When he was finished, Jim grunted in approval.

For so long, he'd lived an action-adventure fueled life unrivaled by any character in a movie, like the one Big Jim had named. His life had been more entertaining, more thrilling than any portrayed in film.

Yet, Jim was right. A time came for a man to evolve, to change, to grow.

How he admired Becca, who'd thrown herself into her family company, helped build their brand, made it better for them all. She'd made sure the parents on her staff were able to have their kids under the very same roof. She watched over them well. And the way she cared for her brothers and even her ne'er-do-well father.

He had to hold a mirror up to himself; her life had true meaning. Up until recent weeks, his … not so much.

At supper, Sarah again shoved his plate at him so hard he figured that at the very next meal, she'd probably throw it straight into his face. "All right," he said, giving up. "What's going on? Why are you such a hissing cat?"

She whirled, and her apron fluttered around her slender shape. "Where's Becca?" she demanded.

"Becca?" He was truly confused. "Well, she's in San Antonio. Where she lives."

"And you're living in Austin, right? What's that, about an hour's drive away from San Antonio?"

He scratched his chin. "Yeah, about that."

"So when was the last time you visited *San Antonio*?" she asked, with emphasis on the name of the city, like that was significant.

"Couple of months ago," he replied truthfully.

"Why?"

"Two months ago?" She spat the words as though they were epithets.

"Yeah."

Glowering at him, she shook her head. "I pity you. You are a damn fool." With that, she refused to speak to him any longer.

Beside him, Big Jim continued to smirk. "Told you," he said, further confusing Rio, "women know about these things."

Chapter Forty

San Antonio, Texas

Becca rested her chin on her hand and leaned her elbow on her desk. Coming from the back of the De Monte Wheel Solutions shop, she heard the familiar rumble and clang of forklifts moving crates of hubcaps. She heard the whine of a drill, heard shouting men. In the front offices, the secretaries were accepting phone calls, typing on laptops. The salesmen were taking orders—all familiar sounds of the workday.

On the desk, a full mug of coffee sat untouched. It cooled to room temperature and she ignored it. Before her face, the computer screen glowed, a work order up on the monitor. She tried to force herself to concentrate on the text. Instead, her mind wandered.

She smoothed a hand over her lap. The hot pink sleeveless sundress was a dramatic change from her usual attire. One day when Rio had been gone for a full month, she'd stood in front of her closet trying to decide what to wear. Everything there was a monochromatic black and white. It's what she'd always worn. It was her.

All at once, the lack of hue and pattern seemed boring and predictable. She didn't want to be just black and white any more. It was gloomy.

In a fit of energy, she purged at least half of her closet, delivering the clothing to a charity. Then, she'd taken herself to the mall and splurged.

In a way, despite her heartache, Rio had introduced color into her life. He'd brought excitement, wonder, and joy. Her drab clothing no longer felt right. At the mall, she'd chosen dresses in orange, hot lime, and butter yellow. She'd purchased pants in blue floral and stripes of salmon.

The change felt good.

He'd left her, and he'd denigrated the company she loved. She hated that. She was still angry and hurt to her core, but try as she might, she couldn't hate *him*. Despite her pain, she knew he'd been good for her. He'd shown her new things, new possibilities. Her world had expanded in different ways.

Yet despite the positive changes, she remained in abject misery. It still bewildered her, how profoundly his abandonment had affected her. It had been a wrecking ball, destroying her, breaking her apart. She was left crumbled.

Before Rio, she'd been fine. She'd enjoyed a reasonable family, good friends, a nice condo. Now, she defined her life as *Before Rio* and *After Rio*.

After Rio was dismal.

The short while he'd belonged to her hadn't been near long enough. He'd roared into her life like a speeding freight train, grabbed her up, and took her aboard for the wildest ride of her life.

On the other side of that ride, all was calm, peaceful. And lonely. He was *gone*. She was still having trouble adjusting to the agony that was *After Rio*.

Using the heels of her hands, she dug them into her eye sockets.

Now at her desk, she wondered where Rio was, what he was doing. Did he ever think of her? The usual pain in her chest clamped down, the endless aching, the hopelessness.

Her brother James stuck his head into her office. "Want some lunch? John and I are headed out for burgers. We can bring you back something."

"Naw." She hadn't realized it was already

lunchtime. Of late, her appetite was a thing long dead. "Thanks, but I've got a salad in the fridge."

"That salad is a week old, Becca," James said. "It's wilted lettuce and soggy tomatoes."

"Yeah, you barely eat any more." John appeared over his brother's shoulder. "C'mon, let us bring you back a juicy cheeseburger and fries."

"Or better yet, come with us. You've been moping around long enough." James gestured at her.

"I'm not moping—"

"Okay, okay. Just … smile once in a while, all right? It's hard on us all, with Dad in jail and probably ending up in a federal penitentiary. But he wants us to *live*, Becca. To have normal lives."

In truth, the fact that their father was going to be convicted made her sad, but it wasn't why she'd been *moping around*. She tried once again to focus on her work order.

"I'll buy her lunch." A deep voice came from behind the boys, and a taller man brushed by them.

Becca glanced up, shocked. Rio.

He wore jeans, tennis shoes, and a black t-shirt.

Her mouth fell open and she gasped. While she'd daydreamed about him constantly, obsessively, more than eight weeks ago he'd said a very definitive goodbye to her. She'd believed that when he said he was leaving, he meant it. Never did she think he'd come strolling into her office. Her heartbeat escalated to double time. It pounded so hard she felt lightheaded.

She had absolutely no idea what to say.

He walked to her and squatted beside her chair. Taking her hand in his, he held her gaze. His blue eyes were every bit as beautiful as she'd remembered. His thick, blond hair was still longish, growing nearly past his shirt collar, with strands rakishly falling over his forehead. He was tanned, lean, fit.

Freaking gorgeous.

Resisting the urge to look around for paparazzi cameras, Becca swallowed hard. Of course there were no cameras. He was not a movie star, and he was alone.

Stroking her fingers gently, he said, "I've missed you, Becca."

Still in the doorway, the boys elbowed each other and grinned.

Frozen to her chair, Becca returned his gaze. Woodenly, she said, "Told you ... you'd miss me."

"You said I'd miss you *something awful*. And I have. You were right. It's been awful."

"Ha!" she whispered. Withdrawing her hand, the memory of their last scene burst into her mind. The one where he'd walked out on her. The one where he'd disparaged her business. It was a sword plunged into her back, his casual betrayal, his dismissal. With dull eyes, she gazed at him. "Why are you here?"

"I'm here to tell you a few things, explain about some changes I've made. And to ask you something."

In the hallway, the boys glanced at each other. One identical face studied the other. "Looks like this is about to get personal."

"And private," the other said.

"Maybe we should go." In perfect agreement, the boys nodded to each other.

"You don't have to leave," Becca said. "You boys stay right there."

John's gaze went from Becca to an unsmiling Rio. He gave them both a hard glare. "Uh, yeah, we'll go." They disappeared.

Becca scowled at their retreating backs.

"I'm done with the black ops," Rio told her. "Took a job with a buddy of mine in Austin. A private security business. Remember Ben Paxton? Well, now, I'm an instructor. I go to work each day, come home early in the evenings. No more hazardous night missions. No more flying bullets."

Stiffly, she said, "I'm sure that's nice for you."

"Well, we do use live rounds at the training facility, but our safety protocols are stringent. The danger is minimal, nothing like my old life."

She took a difficult breath. Never had she imagined he'd want a life like that—a normal one. Like other men. Not that it mattered to her. They were nothing to each other. Nothing.

"Nice dress," he said. "Pretty color. It suits you."

She smoothed the bright fabric. "Thanks."

"Have you missed me?"

She glanced at her computer screen. In her chest, her heart continued to beat like a jungle drum. Collecting a sheaf of papers from her desk, she shuffled through them. "I've been busy. Really busy. Lots of work to do, you know. For my *damn hubcaps*." Now, why had she emphasized those words?

Rio lowered his eyes. "About that, about your business here." He hesitated, groped for words. "I'm sorry. Really sorry for those things I said." He gazed at her, a worried frown creasing his brow. "First, I have to tell you this: you saved us. That day when Harrison tried to force us into his hotel room. Your makeup-tossing trick. It worked. For once, I was the one needing rescue. You did it, Becca. You saved our lives. I didn't."

She shrugged awkwardly. "You're the one who shot him, not me."

"Maybe we worked as a team, then," he allowed. "You forced his attention away, and you gave me the Glock. You get the credit for keeping us alive." He looked around. "And now you have this company."

"Yes." She picked up her coffee and took a sip, forgetting it was cold. It tasted terrible and she wished she could spit it out. Instead, she swallowed the bitter brew. "My dad recently transferred ownership to the boys and me. I'm really proud of De Monte Wheel Solutions." She gave him a frosty glance.

"That's great." For the first time since she'd met him months ago, back when he'd tossed her out of the window of that Mexican cantina, he looked uncertain. He dropped his head, rubbed the back of his neck.

The idea of Rio being unsure about anything gave her pause. Imagine that, the arrogant Rio Lang feeling tentative. He put a hand out toward her, then let it drop.

Becca pursed her lips. Well, this had gone on long enough. She shoved to her feet and he rose with her. "If there's nothing else? I have work waiting." She walked to the door, stood beside it.

"Two minutes," he said on a low growl. "Just give me a little more time before you throw me out. I'm working up to something." He chuckled, but the sound was awkward, self-conscious.

She crossed her arms. "Sorry. I don't have time today. Send me an email."

"Becca." He whispered her name, ran a hand over his forehead. "I know now why I disparaged your hubcap business. I—I was jealous."

"Huh?" She frowned. What in the world?

"I envied your devotion to your father, to your uncle. The way you mother your brothers, in a good way, of course. How you care for everybody here at the company."

She waited, still lost.

"Even the kids write you notes." He gestured at her bulletin board filled with childish drawings. "You have purpose in your life," he went on. "I didn't.

Traveling around the globe for Uncle Sam, getting shot at, shooting back, what was that worth?"

She kept her arms folded over her chest, but she couldn't let that go. "But you rescued people. Hostages. You saved their lives." He'd saved hers, but she didn't say that aloud.

"I did. But it was just a job. I didn't care about any of them. I just got them away from captors. I was paid. I didn't have what you do—a reason to feel good about my life. So, I cut you down, tried to make you feel small. But it didn't work. I was the small one, not you."

She pushed off the wall and let her arms drop to her sides. At least the man had some humility. She could appreciate how difficult this apology must be for him.

Still, nothing had changed. He'd left her, trampled her feelings, abandoned her. "Quite a confession. Well, you said you've become an instructor now. I suppose that's gratifying for you."

"It is. Now I'm providing a service, a valuable one. The guys I train are taking their new skills elsewhere to protect others, or to fight for the homeland, or to rescue hostages, like I did. It's been good for me. I found a place for myself."

Becca didn't answer. Despite her deep anger and disappointment, she was pleased for him. Funny how the human heart worked.

"You—you changed me, Becca," Rio told her, his expression earnest.

Still, she said nothing. He'd changed her, too. Yet for the life of her she didn't know how to respond.

After a moment, he asked, "How are the frogs?"

"They're good." Moving to the bulletin board, she touched one note. It was a drawing of a frog. Her employees knew she loved them, even their children did, and that knowledge was expressed in many drawings of green amphibians. She kept her gaze carefully away from Rio. Suddenly, it was hard to breathe.

"I'd like to see the little guys."

She did glance at him then. Was he asking to come over? She narrowed her eyes. He'd hurt her, left her cold, crushed her tender heart.

The notion of inviting more pain into her life was daunting. She didn't answer him.

He approached her, but didn't come close. As though recognizing that right then she needed space between them, he stopped five feet away. "As I said when coming in here, if you're hungry, I'll buy you lunch. But I have a different idea, if you're game." The expression in his eyes was pleading … hopeful.

Despite her resolve, she found herself searching his features. His face was open, honest, humble. No, she wouldn't allow herself to be touched by that. She'd play it cool. "Oh? I'm pretty busy."

"How about we go to your place? I'll have a visit with the frogs, and you can pack a bag. The boys are capable of handling things here for a while. Everything's lined up, Becca, for a little trip. And when we get there, I have something important to ask you."

Her mouth dried up. Her heart stopped. The world tilted. "A little trip?"

"If you want to go." He waited.

"Where?" she asked, her voice hoarse. But she already knew.

Chapter Forty-One

When Rio took the wheel, driving a new pickup truck he'd recently purchased, Becca was deeply pleased to sit back and relax. The truck was a deep blue, with running lights, a navigation system, and satellite radio. On the bench seat, he held her hand the entire three-hour drive. At the border, for the first time, they crossed into Mexico legally, with passports and driver's licenses. Soon they met with Julio, the pilot. Boarding the battered Cessna, Rio set inside an overstuffed rucksack filled with groceries.

Becca was gratified to see that peeking from the top was a package of Arabica ground coffee. He'd certainly planned this. The idea felt gloriously sexy. The notion of being romantically kidnapped to a wild and remote location thrilled her. The closer they came to their final destination, the more the sensual anticipation blooming within her continued to unfurl. This kind of kidnapping, she could accept.

They were going to the cabin.

****

All day as they traveled, Rio had only dropped kisses into her hair, or on her temple, but he hadn't sought her lips. His eyes blazed often into hers. She'd reveled in his heated skin, in his whispered compliments.

"You're so beautiful," he'd told her in the car. "I have to have you." On the plane, he told her quietly, "I want your breasts on my chest, in my mouth." As she'd blushed, he caressed her fingers and when the plane landed, he whispered, "I'm dying to be inside you ... and to have you on top of me. In every way possible, I want you."

"Yes," she whispered, overwhelmed.

With every glance, his hot eyes burned in banked sensuality. Focused on her, he made her feel like the only woman on earth, madly desired, insanely attractive. She tried, and failed, to keep her own excitement to a low sizzle.

Impossible.

She wanted him with an ache only he could assuage.

By the time they arrived at the scooter, it was past nightfall. As before, riding behind him on the Vespa, Becca clung to his warm back. She laced her fingers together over his flat belly, loving touching him, loving being with him again.

She loved him. Whatever came of this trip, she would accept. For two long months she hadn't been able to take a deep breath, to get air. Her chest had hurt so much that breathing had become difficult.

Now, touching him, hugging his big body, she realized exactly why: Rio was her oxygen. Gladly, she drew him in. He felt like life.

During their long drive and flight, she'd seen iron-clad control in his locked jaw, in his tense and furrowed forehead. It was obvious he was holding himself in check. A magnificent male animal, his blood was up. In a primal instinct as old as time, her body recognized his silent need. She swore she could smell his pheromones, and her own responded in kind. The urgency was almost unbearable.

At last they arrived at the cabin door. Desire drenched her body, consumed her mind. Rio dropped his rucksack and she let her own bag, filled with her colorful new clothing, fall to the ground. He gathered her close and for the first time in months, he kissed her. His mouth ravaged hers, taking and giving. His tongue swept inside her mouth and she moaned. Stabbing her stomach, his hard-on demanded attention.

With his strong hands, he held her head. She felt his shaking fingers … and understood why. Without words, she knew that until they reached their destination, he hadn't been able to trust himself. She thrilled to the knowledge that he wanted her so much.

Lost in his kiss, Becca trembled, too.

"Buttercup," he whispered against her mouth, "I've missed you *something awful*."

"I know," she replied, and they both smiled.

He pulled her inside, lit the lantern and latched the door. Before he turned to her she yanked off her top and sweatshirt, and cast them aside. He paused, stared at her breasts.

"Oh, my," he said, his voice strangled.

His gaze on her nipples, he encircled her small waist, his thumbs just below her breasts' luscious weight.

Placing her palms on his chest, Becca lovingly traced his muscular pectorals. She cupped his shoulders, smoothed her palms down his biceps. Each contour of his masculine body, all hard angles and rigid muscle, was so different from her soft shape. He intrigued her.

"I'm so hard right now," he told her, "I could plow a field."

"Mmm. Maybe you could just plow *me*." She touched the top of her upper lip with her tongue, the same move she'd used months ago just before giving him oral sex.

His eyes lit, remembering. "If I don't get inside you soon I'm going to die," he said. "But I want to tell you one thing first."

She blinked, and held her breath.

"I love you, Becca," he said simply. "When we were apart, it felt as though a piece of my body was cut off. Like something vital was missing. It didn't feel good. I didn't like it. Being separated from you was wrong—all wrong." As though he were surprised at himself, a flash of wonder crossed his face. "Do you know what I mean?"

"Oh, yes," she breathed, and pulled his head down to hers.

Falling to the bed, they clawed at clothing, kissed every inch of newly revealed skin, re-learned each other in frenzied, sensual explorations.

Becca felt wild, frantic, needy. How she'd missed him, suffered the loss of his touch. She couldn't get enough of this man.

Because he was *Rio*.

He made her feel splendidly beautiful, his touch both tender and demanding, as if she were delectable, delicious, and he was desperate for her. The wanton female inside her knew joy and she gloried in her womanhood.

She had to have him. *Now.*

Lying beside him, she reached for his thick, straining cock and stroked him, marveled at his size and strength.

He groaned. "You better stop that or I'll come before I ever get inside you."

Without shame, she rolled to her back and bent her knees. In one deliberate movement, she opened them, drew them up so he could see her. With heavy-lidded eyes, she invited him to look, to touch. Her breath came out in little pants. "Then come inside me. I'm so wet for you."

"Oh, Becca." Sitting up, he stared at the apex of her thighs, and staring at her soft, pink folds, said her name like a reverent prayer. *"Becca."* He touched her sex and his chest heaved. He was panting, too.

She could tell he wanted to be gentle, to slow

down for her, but tonight she needed fast and she needed hard. In sensual demand, she pulled at him, urged him to cover her body with his own.

As he eased atop her, she guided his length to exactly where she craved him, and he obliged, pushing inside, her dampness easing the way. He filled her body and her mind with thoughts and sensations only he could engender in her. Only Rio.

She bit his neck, clutched at him, told him without words to take her hot and rough. Plunging in and out, he gave her what she needed, and like a wild mare she bucked beneath him. The bed creaked in a loud squeal of metal springs. Neither cared.

Together, they came in shattering, dual climaxes that left them only temporarily spent.

The second time, she climbed on top and rode him, deliberately grinding her sex against him in slow undulations. She arched her back, pushed out her chest, and he eagerly reached up. "I love your breasts," he told her, sucking in air.

She leaned down to him and licked his neck. "Call them boobs," she whispered in his ear, then bit the lobe. "Or better yet, call them tits. It's naughty, like flashing you. And with you, I feel like such a bad girl."

He grinned, raised a hand and gave her bottom a sharp slap. "That's for misbehaving," he said.

She yelped at the sting, yet the small punishment sent a thrill up her spine.

Gripping her hips, he commanded, "Now, naughty Becca, put your tits in my mouth. I want to suck on first one nipple, and then the other."

"Yes, sir." Easing up just enough to dangle her breasts over his face, she felt his lips surround her nipple and quickened her rocking on his body. Her excitement climbed, reaching fever pitch. Rio responded, flexing and thrusting his hips so his manhood speared her to the hilt. Sweat gathered on his chest. His breathing escalated.

His eagerness fed hers and she never wanted to stop. The friction on her body grew to delicious heights. His lips, tugging on her nipples, took her breath.

All at once she felt a tremendous climax crash over her. She shuddered, cried out, and then the next orgasm took over. When she rose again to the heights, Rio gave a final pump and lifted off the bed to pull her face to his.

As the final vibrations slammed through them, they kissed, and while they wound down, continued the kiss for a long time.

****

In the morning, they rose from tangled quilts to take water bottles to the clear stream and refill their reserves. At creek side in gentle sunlight, they sat on a bed of pine needles and soft loam. Giving her tiny kisses, Rio held Becca close to his side.

"I'm so in love with you," he told her. "It feels like you're part of me. Inside me." He laid one strong hand on his chest. "In here."

She looked at him, misty-eyed. "I'm glad."

Nestling her head on his shoulder, she felt happier than ever before. This man knew her, warts and all. He understood her. He'd seen into the depths of her heart and soul, and he loved her.

"I love you too." She whispered the words. Her throat felt raw.

Surprising her, he pulled a small box from his pocket. A telltale tremble shook his fingers.

Seeing the jewelry box shape, she gasped. "Really, Rio?"

"Yes, really." He set the unopened box in his lap. "When we first met I tried to remain detached. You were a job to me and I couldn't allow my thoughts to get twisted up. Not if I wanted to keep you safe."

"That's why you seemed so distant." Just as she suspected.

"I needed my head clear. Needed to stay focused. Over the years, it's been easier to be unemotional."

She didn't like the fact, but she accepted it.

He squeezed her waist. "You became so much more than a contract to me. More than just a job to complete."

Feeling her chin wobble in emotion, she smiled at him.

Opening his box, Rio sought her gaze. "Is it okay?"

A three-carat marquis-cut diamond ring set in a filigreed-platinum band sparkled in the sunlight. Becca gasped. "It's *huge*. So expensive! Are you sure—"

"I have money, Becca. All these years I've worked and haven't spent the paychecks. I don't have a lot of cars or property or clothing or anything. What I have is a fat bank account. A really big one." He named a high dollar figure and she gasped again.

"I want to share it with you," he said. "I'll buy us a house. Maybe halfway between your business and mine. We'll get a dog."

Lowering her eyes to the ring, she allowed him to slip it on. "I love it." She held up her hand, gazed in awe at the huge rock. "I want that house with you. And the dog."

"Good." He smiled and his dimple made an appearance. "I designed the ring myself, and the jeweler is prominent in his field. For you, only the best."

For a single moment, she hesitated. There was one matter left. "How do you feel about children?" She bit her lip, then before he could answer, she forced out the rest in an anxious rush, "Because I've fantasized about it, about bearing your son. Maybe even two."

A crease appeared between his eyes and deepened into a frown. Becca held her breath. If he didn't want children, her heart would crack in half. It would devastate her.

"We can't just have boys, Becca," he said. "I definitely want at least one daughter."

Relief washed through her. She threw her arms around his neck and they kissed. His frown disappeared.

Abruptly, her mood changed. She slanted him a mischievous glance. "Um, Rio? I'll be right back."

"Gotta pee? Okay, I'll wait."

She definitely didn't have to pee.

Getting to her feet, she left him sitting at creekside and made her way into the trees. Taking a circuitous route and keeping the undergrowth between them, she found the path to the ledge. Climbing up, she found the place where months ago, he'd run shouting to frighten away her stalking mountain lion, the spot where he'd tackled her and ended her escape attempt.

Then, it had been snow and ice covered. Now, beneath the trees, it was all fragrant soil and green foliage. Up on the ledge, she tore off all her clothing, and tossed it aside with joyful abandon. Resplendently nude, she felt cool air bathe her skin. She felt free and open and very turned on.

"*Rio*," she sang out.

Glimpsing him through the trees, she saw him emerge from behind the screen of leaves to find her. When he looked up, she shimmied her bare breasts so they swayed.

Spotting her, he gawked.

"Hey, baby," she teased, "want somma this?" Smiling in glee, she proudly thrust out her chest. Next, she turned to present her bare ass. Giving him an impudent grin over her shoulder, she patted her butt cheeks. "How about a little of *this*?"

Without taking his gaze from her, Rio put both his hands to his head. "You're flashing me? You little minx! Come down here."

"Come up and get me," she taunted.

Needing no further encouragement, he began to run along the base of the ledge to where it ended at the tree line choke point. As he ran, he never looked away from her. He wore a wolfish grin.

On a parallel path above him, Becca ran too, waving, blowing him teasing kisses. Her new ring glinted in the sunlight.

When finally they met, Rio swung her up into his arms.

Giddy, she laughed.

He bent his head to nuzzle her chest. "My little exhibitionist," he mumbled, then caught one pink nipple between his lips.

Becca gasped.

The remainder of the morning was lost in a haze of sensual exploration, delight, and fulfillment.

Becca had her man, she thought in wonder and appreciation.

And he was good.

The End

DORSEY ADAMS

EVERNIGHT PUBLISHING

www.evernightpublishing.com